No lights lit the front o........................staurant and fish store. I didn't even try the door. I hurried around to the alley and went in the back door.

Inside the kitchen, I called, "Tulia?"

She stuck her head out from a heavy stainless-steel door with a handle like those on refrigerated trucks. She waved me over and pushed open the door of the walk-in cooler. "Thank God you're here. It's awful, Mac. I didn't know what to do!"

"What's going on? Are you okay?" What in there could have made her wail and ask for help? Had she spilled her lobster bisque stock? Broken a five-gallon crock of homemade pickles and cut herself? I hurried across the kitchen to join her.

Tulia, shaking, pointed at the floor. She didn't shake only from the cold. On the cement lay Annette DiCicero, as still as a washed-up log of driftwood. . . .

Books by Maddie Day

Country Store Mysteries
FLIPPED FOR MURDER
GRILLED FOR MURDER
WHEN THE GRITS HIT THE FAN
BISCUITS AND SLASHED BROWNS
DEATH OVER EASY
STRANGLED EGGS AND HAM
NACHO AVERAGE MURDER
CANDY SLAIN MURDER
NO GRATER CRIME
CHRISTMAS COCOA MURDER
(with Carlene O'Connor and Alex Erickson)

Cozy Capers Book Group Mysteries
MURDER ON CAPE COD
MURDER AT THE TAFFY SHOP
MURDER AT THE LOBSTAH SHACK

And writing as Edith Maxwell

A TINE TO LIVE, A TINE TO DIE
'TIL DIRT DO US PART
FARMED AND DANGEROUS
MURDER MOST FOWL
MULCH ADO ABOUT MURDER

Published by Kensington Publishing Corp.

MURDER AT THE LOBSTAH SHACK

Maddie Day

KENSINGTON
PUBLISHING CORP.

www.kensingtonbooks.com

KENSINGTON BOOKS are published by

Kensington Publishing Corp.
119 West 40th Street
New York, NY 10018

All Kensington titles, imprints, and distributed lines are available at special quantity discounts for bulk purchases for sales promotion, premiums, fund-raising, educational, or institutional use.

Special book excerpts or customized printings can also be created to fit specific needs. For details, write or phone the office of the Kensington Sales Manager: Attn.: Sales Department. Kensington Publishing Corp., 119 West 40th Street, New York, NY 10018. Phone: 1-800-221-2647.

The K logo is a trademark of Kensington Publishing Corp.

First Printing: December 2021
ISBN: 978-1-4967-1510-4

33614082900480

ISBN: 978-1-4967-1511-1 (ebook)

10 9 8 7 6 5 4 3 2 1

Printed in the United States of America

For Our Neighbors' Table in Amesbury, Massachusetts, which feeds the hungry in twelve communities and allows its clients dignity and choice in the process.

ACKNOWLEDGMENTS

As always, I'm grateful to John Scognamiglio, my editor at Kensington Publishing, and the expert team of publicists (looking at you, Larissa Ackerman and Lauren Jernigan), artists, and salespeople there. Continued gratitude to agent John Talbot for making it all possible and smoothing the way.

Sherry Harris—friend, blogmate, author, and independent editor—gave this book a close read and saved Mac from several Too Stupid to Live episodes. Any remaining instances of TSTL in the book are all my fault.

Thanks to Cape Cod mystery author Barbara Struna, who provided information about red tide poisoning, and to my son Allan Hutchison-Maxwell for again helping with bike details.

I was delighted to be able to riff on my good friend and blogmate Barbara Ross's opening line in *Fogged Inn*: "Jul-YA! There's a dead guy in the walk-in." Thanks for setting the stage, Barb.

Thank you to volunteer Rose of the actual Our Neighbors' Table in my town of Amesbury, Massachusetts, who gave me the complete tour and rundown on operating procedures while the free food market was open. I've dedicated *Murder at the Lobstah Shack* to this very fine organization, located in the town where I live. The real-life Rose bears no resemblance to my fictional one except in her devotion to feeding the hungry.

Heidi Hunter, Financial Crimes Investigator, suggested several ways to skim money from a small partnership. Thanks, Heidi. I consulted with author—and retired Maine police detective—Bruce Robert Coffin on a few matters of police procedure. Amesbury Police Lieutenant Detective Kevin Donovan was very helpful with another scene. Leslie Budewitz, dear friend and author of *Books, Crooks and Counselors: How to Write Accurately about Criminal Law and Court Procedure* helped with yet another scene. Any remaining errors are of my own doing.

I spent some delightful time with YouTube videos of the taffy-pulling process. The Food Network visit to Salty Road in Brooklyn, New York, was one of my favorites: https://www.youtube.com/watch?v=H23AY8Kdx00

My apologies to the real past winners of the Miss Rhode Island and Miss New Bedford crowns for hijacking your titles for two of my characters. No aspersions on your talents or the actual judges are implied.

Always, thanks to the Wicked Authors for support, friendship, and inspiration. I love these women: Jessie Crockett, Sherry Harris, Julie Hennrikus, Liz Mugavero, and Barbara Ross. Please visit our blog and read their books under all their names. You won't be sorry.

My family is always in the background, cheering me on and congratulating my successes. Allan, Alison, John David, Barbara, Janet, Hugh: I love you all.

I put finishing touches on this manuscript while self-quarantining during the rise of the coronavirus pandemic. I hope reading cozy mysteries brought solace and escape to all of you during that painful time.

Finally, my daily gratitude to the late Ramona DeFelice Long and her seven AM Sprint Club on Facebook, where a bunch of us still gather virtually to check in, ignore the world, and write for an hour. It kicks off my creative day in the best of ways, even in Ramona's absence.

CHAPTER 1

The worst phone call I ever got came in on an early October morning.

"Mac!" Tulia Peters wailed. "You have to come help me. Quick!"

"What's wrong?"

"Just come."

I stared at my phone and the disconnected call. My no-nonsense friend didn't make a practice of wailing. At eight thirty, I'd already locked the door of my tiny house to walk the thousand yards to Mac's Bikes, my bicycle repair and rental shop. I steered myself instead to Tulia's Lobstah Shack next door to my store. Sunshine slanted through the reddening leaves of a Cape Cod fall.

No lights lit the front of the small seafood restaurant and fish store. I didn't even try the door. I hurried around to the alley and went in the back door.

Inside the kitchen, I called, "Tulia?"

She stuck her head out from a heavy stainless-steel door with a handle like those on refrigerated trucks. She waved me over and pushed open the door of the walk-in cooler. "Thank God you're here. It's awful, Mac. I didn't know what to do!"

"What's going on? Are you okay?" What in there could have made her wail and ask for help? Had she spilled her lobster bisque stock? Broken a five-gallon crock of home-made pickles and cut herself? I hurried across the kitchen to join her.

Tulia, shaking, pointed at the floor. She didn't shake only from the cold. On the cement lay Annette DiCicero, as still as a washed-up log of driftwood. Her skin, usually a warm Mediterranean tan, had become a yellowy porce-lain. A bright overhead bar of light illuminated the corpse. The light glinted off the chrome of an object em-bedded in her neck. Her eyes were wide, her brow fur-rowed, her open mouth drawn down.

Tulia's other hand covered her mouth. Her deep brown eyes brimmed with emotion. She stood between shelves laden with boxes of green peppers and see-through bags of sandwich buns, towered over by gallon jars of mayon-naise and sliced dills. The thing sticking out of Annette's neck, which was shaped like a lobster-claw, looked a lot like the handles on Tulia's custom lobster picks.

My breath rushed in with a rasp. I brought my own hand to my mouth. "This is terrible."

"It's exactly like in the book, Mac," Tulia whispered. "When Gus yells up to Julia, 'There's a dead guy in the walk-in.'"

"I know." My whisper rasped in the silence.

Except this was reality, not the first page of *Fogged Inn,* a cozy mystery set in Maine. Our Cozy Capers book group wasn't going to discuss Annette's death in a light-hearted banter about motive and suspects. In real life, right here, right now, there was definitely a dead person in Tulia's walk-in.

CHAPTER 2

I shook myself and stared at Tulia. "Did you call the police?"

Mute, she shook her head, her gaze still on Annette's corpse.

"Why not? You have to."

She waited a beat. "We'd argued, Annette and me. In public. About the . . ." Her voice trailed off.

Right. They'd argued right in front of Town Hall, too, and half the town saw them. "About changing the name of Columbus Day to Indigenous People's Day?"

"Yes," she whispered through chattering teeth.

I let out a breath. "Come on." I took Tulia's goosebumpy arm and nearly dragged her out of the cooler. I used my foot to shove the door shut, and it latched with a satisfying *ka-chunk*. I spied a heavy sweater hanging from a peg and wrapped it around her.

"We have to call this in." I pulled my phone out of my back pocket. I didn't feel totally steady, myself, but somebody had to take charge of the situation. Tulia clearly couldn't do it.

"Wait. What if they think I killed her?" Tulia's voice quavered.

"Tulia." I set my phone down on the counter and laid my hands on her shoulders. "Get a grip, my friend. You didn't kill her. They have to have evidence. They won't find any evidence you murdered her. Right?"

She nodded.

"Okay, then." I hit 9-1-1 and put the call on speaker. When the dispatcher picked up, I said, "This is Mackenzie Almeida. Tulia Peters, the owner of the Lobstah Shack on Main Street in Westham, has found a dead person in her walk-in cooler. She was frightened and called me because my shop is next door. We feel safe and no one else is here." I'd had to answer the routine questions before, unfortunately. But . . . I hadn't checked the front of the restaurant. Were we safe?

"Please stay on the line," the dispatcher said. "We'll have someone there shortly."

"Thanks. Tell them to come to the back door on the alley." I left the call open but set the phone down again. The kitchen had been cleaned. Like any place where good cooking went on, the air retained a hint of the delicious soups, fishcakes, and seafood salads and sandwiches my friend prepared.

Tulia hugged herself. When her gaze darted to the walk-in door, she shivered.

"Is this coffee?" I grabbed a lidded travel cup from the counter and handed it to her. "Is it still hot?"

She sipped and nodded.

"Good." I cocked my head. Sirens wailed to life in the not-so-far-away distance. The police station was a quarter mile down the street. I had maybe a minute to ask her a couple of things. "Was the door locked when you got here?"

She pursed her lips. "I think so. I mean, I didn't try it before I put my key in."

"Do you have an alarm system?"

"In Westham?" She brought her brows together. "No way. I've always felt safe here. But now . . ."

The *wah-wah* of the sirens grew deafening before they shut off abruptly. A loud knock on the back door preceded, "Tulia Peters? Westham police."

I hurried to the door, covering my hand with my sleeve, and pulled it open to a uniformed officer. With dark, Asian-looking eyes, she was maybe thirty, with hair the color of wildflower honey pulled back in a bun at the nape of her neck. Even with a wide, heavy duty belt that padded her waist, she looked as lean and wiry as I was. I'd seen her around but never met her.

"Officer Kimuri, ma'am."

"Come in. I'm Mackenzie Almeida." I moved back.

She stepped into the doorway. "Good morning, Tulia."

"Hi, Nikki," Tulia murmured. She kept her hands wrapped around her mug.

They obviously knew each other. Me, I'd been away from my hometown for years until I returned a year and a half ago. Outside, a bicycle officer rode up, having traded in his summer uniform shorts for long pants with the right leg in an ankle clip. August Jenkins, whom I'd met in the summer, leaned the bike against the wall. I gestured for him to come in.

He nodded to Kimuri, who said, "Jenkins, clear the front, please."

"Will do." He pushed through the swinging door to the dining room.

Good. One worry I could discard.

"Tulia," Kimuri said. "I need you to show me what you found."

Tulia stared at the floor. Her mug quivered in her hands.

"May I?" I asked. "She showed me when I came over a few minutes ago."

Kimuri blinked. "All right."

I reached for the handle of the walk-in.

"Wait. Let me." The officer pulled on purple latex gloves. "Did you touch the handle earlier, Ms. Almeida?"

I thought. "No."

"Good." She pulled open the heavy door. "Please stay out there."

"She's on the floor," I said over her shoulder. "You can't miss her." I didn't go in, but she didn't tell me I couldn't watch.

The officer squatted and laid two fingers on Annette's neck, leaving them there for a moment. She pulled her hand back and glanced around the body, touching nothing. Pulling out a flashlight the size of a stubby carrot, she shone it in Annette's eyes, on the object in her neck, and on the floor beneath. She flashed it in the darker corners of the cooler. When she stood, I backed away.

She clicked the walk-in door shut on poor Annette, who would never walk into anywhere again. An EMT bustled into the kitchen toting a red bag.

"She's deceased," Kimuri told him. "But do what you need to do."

The EMT pulled out paper booties and slipped them on before taking his bag into the cooler.

Jenkins pushed through the swinging door. It whapped behind him. "Clear in front."

Whew.

Tulia had perched on a stool at the counter. She gripped her cup as if it held salvation. The EMT had left the outside door open. My favorite state police detective, Lincoln Haskins, appeared. A big man, he filled the doorway.

"Mac Almeida and a dead body," he began. "Why am I not surprised?"

CHAPTER 3

Jenkins guarded the back door to the restaurant a few minutes later, or at least it looked like his job was to guard it. Lincoln had asked Tulia and me to wait in her car out back until he could come talk to us. He said the entire restaurant was a crime scene and we weren't allowed inside. Tulia and I sat in the back seat of her Honda with the doors open. She studied her hands in her lap while I tried to reach my bike mechanic on the phone. I'd asked Lincoln if I could zip next door and open my shop. He'd said he wanted me to wait. Orlean didn't enjoy running through my opening checklist, but she was going to have to. At least she had a key to Mac's Bikes.

She finally picked up my call. "Mac, shop's locked. Bunch of panda cars next door." Orlean was a woman of few words.

"That's why I called. There's been an emergency at the

Lobstah Shack. I came over to help Tulia. We're both fine, but the police want to talk to me before I can head over there. I apologize, but you're going to have to open up."

"No worries. What about sales?"

I groaned. She had a key but not the code to open the safe where I kept the starting cash. "Say it's credit only. Most people use plastic, anyway. I'll get to the shop as soon as I can. Derrick should be in by ten, too." Derrick was my older half-brother, who worked for me.

"Okay." Orlean disconnected.

"I'm sorry I dragged you into this mess, Mac," Tulia whispered.

I patted her hand. "Don't worry. That's what friends are for."

"How did Annette get into my cooler?" She finally looked up, her usual ruddy coloring a memory. "Who could have done that?"

"Do your employees have keys? You have a server and a dishwasher, right?"

"Yes, but they don't have keys, and I have a lot of turnover, you know, seasonally. It's safer if I'm the only one with access. And I have a spare at home." She started. "Mac, do you think I need a lawyer?"

Did she? "You probably will. Let's see what Lincoln says."

She nodded. She picked at a rough spot on her jeans.

I pictured the dining room of the restaurant. A counter at the side held napkins and cylinders of forks and knives. Next to them sat rectangular trays holding shell crackers and chrome lobster picks with a claw for the handle. Identical to the one currently in Annette's neck.

"Tulia, did you keep any of the lobster picks in the kitchen?" I asked in a quiet, casual voice.

The corners of her mouth turned down. "Probably. I mean, we wash them there and then bring them back out front. I don't know if there were any in there yesterday."

Lincoln stepped through the door. Jenkins moved aside but Lincoln beckoned to him. After some soft-spoken words I couldn't make out, Jenkins headed into the kitchen. Lincoln bent over to peer in at us.

"Can you both step out here, please?"

We obliged. Tulia stuck her hands in her pockets. I leaned against the car.

"So, ladies, what do you think?" Lincoln wore black-rimmed glasses. Dark hair curled over the collar of one of his signature Hawaiian shirts.

"What do you mean?" I asked, although I suspected I knew. Our book group had been eager to solve the last two murders in town, despite Lincoln's admonitions not to get involved. He probably figured we were already hot on the trail of this one. We weren't.

"I mean, how do you think the deceased ended up in your cooler, Ms. Peters?"

She cocked her head. "Lincoln, since when are you calling me Ms. Peters? We've known each other all our lives."

Hearing some spirit back in her voice made me glad. She must have known Lincoln forever. Tulia belonged to the Mashpee Wampanoag people, and Lincoln was half Wampanoag.

"It's a criminal investigation, Tulia," he said. "I need to be a bit more formal."

"That's nuts, but, whatever." She wagged her head. "I don't have the slightest idea how Annette got in there. Nobody but me has a key to the restaurant."

"What time did you arrive here this morning?" he asked her.

"Couple minutes past eight. I don't open until eleven thirty, but I have a lot of prep to do."

"As far as you know, the door was locked before you came in?" Lincoln stood with his hands clasped behind his back in a casual position, but his entire attention was focused on Tulia. "No one else was in the restaurant, that you knew of?"

"I think it was locked, but I didn't check. I put the key in and turned."

Her door had the same kind of simple, easily picked lock my shop had had until last August. In a town like this, people tend to feel safe—until they don't.

"And you didn't notice a body in the walk-in at the end of the day yesterday?"

"No," Tulia scoffed. "Of course not."

"What time did you leave?" he asked.

"At six, like always. The kitchen closes at four but sometimes people want to buy seafood salad or cod cakes or whatever. I stay open until six for that."

"Mac?" Lincoln turned toward me. "Any ideas?"

"I got nothing." Did his use of my first name mean Tulia was a person of interest but I wasn't? *Probably.* "Except that you must have noticed the lock isn't a very secure one, and there's no dead bolt."

He nodded.

Tulia stared at me. "I never thought . . ."

"I know," I said. "I didn't, either, before the summer." A murderer had tried to come after me a few months earlier. Thanks to my parrot Belle, it all ended well for her and me. Not so much for the killer.

Lincoln drew a lobster pick out of his pocket. "Is this a common design for a lobster pick handle?"

"No," she whispered to the pavement.

"I couldn't hear you," he said.

"No." She raised an anguished face. "I had them custom made."

"I understand you might have clashed with the victim about Columbus Day."

"Yes, we did." Her shoulders sagged. "But if you're saying I killed her because of the name of a holiday, I would never do that. Who would?" She lowered her forehead into her hand.

"I'm not saying anything at this time. We have to gather all possible information. Do either of you have additional information about Ms. DiCicero?" He'd used her name for the first time. "How old she was, where she lived?"

"She's in her thirties," Tulia said. "I don't know where she lives."

"Younger than me," I added. "I'd say early thirties. She brought her bike into my shop for repairs a couple of times. We chatted. I didn't socialize with her, so I don't— I mean, didn't—know her well."

Tulia dragged her gaze up. "She has a kid," she whispered. "Kendall. She's only five. The poor thing doesn't have a mother now."

CHAPTER 4

I walked into my shop—and near chaos—a little while later. Lincoln had said he wanted me to be finger-printed but told me I could go after I reminded him they already had my prints on file from a previous case. He also said that he needed to speak further with Tulia.

Orlean wore her blue latex work gloves as she jabbed the register. A line of people ten deep waited, some holding retail items, others outfitted with backpacks and biking outfits. My half-brother was nowhere in sight. I frowned. He had a habit of coming in late and today wasn't a good day for it. Sometimes he had a good reason for being delayed. I thought he sometimes relied on my good faith, which was running thin right about now.

Orlean spied me and scowled from under the Orleans Firebirds cap she wore every day. "Derrick's gonna be late." She bit off the words.

"How late?" I murmured to her.

"Eleven."

Ugh. That was an hour from now. "You can go back to your work," I told her. "Thanks for handling things. I got this." To the line of customers, I said, "I'll be right with you all, and I apologize for the wait. We had an unavoidable delay this morning." I hurried to my office, grabbed the cash tray out of the safe, and made it back to the counter in record time. I sold a tube, a pump, and a light to the first customer. The second bought matching his-and-her red cycling shirts. Everybody else wanted rentals. The busyness distracted me from dwelling on the mental image of Annette's corpse in the Lobstah Shack walk-in. It also distracted me from praying Derrick didn't have anything to do with Annette's murder. He'd been a suspect once before in a homicide.

The last person in line was a local named Doris Sandersen. She owned Paws and Claws, a pet supplies shop on the other side of the Lobstah Shack.

"What's going on at Tulia's, Mac?" she asked in her deep voice, her dyed-black hair stark against heavy pale makeup. "All those cop cars. I saw you leaving there. Is she okay?" A lover of both dogs and cats, Doris wore a yellow sweatshirt with an appliqued beagle on the front. Siamese cat earrings with eyes of tiny blue topaz stones adorned her earlobes. She smelled like she'd smoked a cigarette on the way over here.

"They asked me not to talk about it." I glanced around. I didn't know the shopkeeper well. What I did know was that she and Tulia had had an ongoing dispute about the smell of lobster shells in the alley. "I know Tulia is fine, though."

"I'm her neighbor." She lowered her chin to give me a

stern look, which revealed a line of white roots that divided long thick bangs from the rest of her hair. "I have a right to know what's going on. All that police presence is bad for business. How do I even know I'm safe?"

I gave her a little smile, even though she was clearly concerned for herself, not for Tulia. "There's no danger, as far as I know. I'm sure the authorities will release the information soon."

"I wouldn't put it past her type to have broken the law. It's criminal the way she stinks up the alley."

I gaped. "Doris, what in the world do you mean by 'her type'?" She couldn't mean Tulia's Wampanoag heritage. Could she? What century did she live in?

"Nothing, nothing." She batted away the thought.

"I've been in that alley plenty of times. I've never noticed a bad smell," I said. Actually, Doris's garbage smelled worse. One of her cats lived in the store, and Doris dumped its fragrant litter in the trash.

Her nostrils flared. "You don't have to try to operate a respectable business next to hers."

Did she think my shop wasn't respectable? *Deep breath in, deep breath out.* "Can I help you with anything else?"

"Mac, you know I don't ride a bike." Her voice dripped disdain. "I walk everywhere in town."

I kept my mouth shut. She turned and stalked out. *Sheesh.*

In a brief lull, I grabbed my sandwich—always ham and cheese—out of my bag, stashed it in the little fridge, and poured a mug of coffee from the carafe in the office. Orlean must have had time to make it before things got busy.

In the repair area, she tuned up a bike set on one of the two stands. "What went down over there?" She didn't look up.

I moved in to stand next to her. "Tulia found a body in her walk-in cooler." A shudder rippled through me. "The person was murdered, Orlean."

She lifted her face. "No sir!"

"It's true. Tulia called me before she called the police. I went over to help her out a little."

"Who died?"

"Annette DiCicero." Lincoln had said not to talk about it, but Orlean was far from a gossip. "Do you know her?"

"Pretty lady, right?" Orlean focused on her work again. "Heard she got the Miss New Bedford crown a few years back."

"I didn't know that. I can see how she would have been beauty queen material. The poor thing."

My mechanic nodded.

"Keep it under your hat, though, okay?" I trusted Orlean. "I don't want what happened to get out before the police release the name and the news."

"'Course. Lincoln on the case?"

"Yes."

"He'll figure it out. But three murders in Westham in five months. Kinda eerie, doncha think?"

"Exactly my thoughts." Had our beautiful little seaside town turned into Cabot Cove?

CHAPTER 5

Confidential: Tulia found Annette DiCicero murdered in her walk-in. Yes, like in FOGGED INN. Det. Haskins on the case. Meet tonight?

I sent the text to the Cozy Capers book group. I was frankly surprised the grapevine hadn't already kicked in, that one or more of the other book group members—all shopkeepers or town officials—hadn't dropped in to ask me about Tulia.

The wall clock showed ten thirty, and Mac's Bikes was temporarily empty except for Orlean and me. I filled the watering can and headed out front to water the window boxes. We hadn't had a frost yet, so the white and pink geraniums continued happy and healthy in their red boxes. We were still a week away from Columbus Day, and the first cold snap crept later every year.

Over at the Lobstah Shack, someone in uniform fixed

yellow police ribbon across the front door. Poor Tulia. She could lose a lot of money if they forced her to close for a few days. A police van rolled out of the alley and down Main Street with Annette's body in the back, I suspected.

A dark blue Westham PD cruiser followed it. *Oh, no.* Tulia emerged from the alley wearing a terrified expression. Officer Kimuri walked next to her, both headed toward the police station. At least Tulia hadn't been stuffed into the back seat of a cruiser like a criminal. Lincoln must want to be able to show she went in voluntarily.

Tulia hadn't asked Lincoln if she should get a lawyer, at least not in my hearing. Did I even know a criminal defense lawyer? None of my friends or family, fortunately, needed to have that kind of professional on speed dial. I wished I could talk to my boyfriend, Tim, about what had happened, but as a baker, mornings were his busy time. That conversation would have to wait.

My phone buzzed in my pocket. Zane King, proprietor of Cape King Distillery across the street, had responded to the group text.

Just saw Tulia walk toward police station with Nikki Kimuri. Arrested?

I tapped back.

Not while I was there. Probably want to talk to her more. Anybody know a good lawyer?

I picked up the watering can and gave all three boxes a good drink. A thin woman trudged along the sidewalk across the street, her dark hair scruffy under a watch cap, her pants and sweater equally as scruffy. She carried a tattered backpack and a plastic sack. My friend Gin and I both volunteered at the soup kitchen and free food market my father's Unitarian Universalist Church sponsored in the church basement several days a week. I'd served this woman, one of the Cape's homeless population. Her name was Nora or Nia, I thought.

Gin, who owned Salty Taffy's candy shop, and I had been talking about ways to really help the people who desperately needed food and housing rather than merely trying to alleviate the symptoms. Find people jobs? Provide mental health counseling? Make better lodging available than a shelter did? No one could easily fix the problem. And the contrast glared between the Our Neighbors' Table patrons and the well-off tourists and tidy shops and homes of Westham.

My phone buzzed again. Flo Wolanski, head librarian in Westham, had added to the thread.

I'll find her a counselor. Yes, let's meet tonight. Derrick's?

My brother and his daughter lived in a lighthouse as the caretakers, and the book group usually met there. I replied:

Not at the shop yet. Will ask him when he gets here. Zane chimed in.

Maybe Norland will know something.

Zane was talking about Norland Gifford, the retired Westham chief of police and now a member of the book group. In the past he'd sometimes been able to find out information the rest of us didn't have access to.

Two fit-looking older men paused on the sidewalk. One pointed at my Rentals sign. A young couple rode up on a tandem. A car with a bike sticking out of the trunk pulled into the lot. Time for me to get back to work. Before I could, I spied my little grandmother, my *abo*—otherwise known as Reba Almeida—who hurried toward me.

"*Querida*," she called. She lifted a knobby hand in a wave. Her signature rainbow-colored Rasta hat flopped with her exertions. Her late husband, my father's father, had been from Cape Verde. Reba had been born and raised in Boston, but she'd adopted a few Kriolu words like the rest of the family.

"Abo Ree, come on in. I'm just getting busy." I bent down to kiss her soft-as-new-flannel cheek.

"I heard some news about a body," she murmured. She followed me into the shop clad in her usual pink track suit.

"I'm not surprised. It was Annette DiCicero's. Can you hang around for a few? Derrick isn't here yet and—"

"And you have customers. I'll wait. Better yet, I'll handle sales." She set down her big bag behind the counter and hopped up onto the stool. She'd helped me out in a pinch before and knew how to operate the register. Despite having reached the ripe age of eighty, she had a still-sharp mind, and she stayed in good shape with aqua aerobics, lots of fast walks, and regular rides on her red adult tricycle up and down the Shining Sea Trail with my mom. "Hello, Orlean," Abe Reba called into the repair area.

My *abo*—Kriolu for both grandmother and grandfather—was a sunny treasure, and I adored her. She also happily acknowledged being a nosy old lady. She loved using the spyglass we'd given her as a gag gift to keep track of the goings on in town. She might have information about Annette and, with any luck, maybe she knew who would have wanted to murder her.

The two fit seniors had struck up a conversation with the young couple, who'd left their tandem outside. A few minutes later I'd rented the gentlemen a tandem for the

day. I filled out a repair ticket for the couple, as well as
for the flat tire on the bike that had arrived in the car.

"Thank you." Abo Reba beamed at a customer in tan
desert fatigues, who had bought a new helmet. "You
come on back any time."

"I certainly will, ma'am." The young man, probably
stationed at the nearby Otis Air National Guard base, had
a crisp military haircut and impeccable posture. He spoke
with a bit of a Southern accent. "I sure do love your pretty
little town. It's so peaceful."

Between murders, that is.

"I'll bet you never get a lick of crime here, am I
right?" he asked.

How had he missed the crime scene tape next door? I
opened my mouth, but my grandmother beat me to it.

"We're as all-American as anywhere." She beamed.
"Have a fun ride."

"Yes, ma'am, I will." He strode out, secure in his fan-
tasy.

"What?" Abo Reba said to me. "America has murder
everywhere you look. It's sad but true."

I glanced around to confirm we were again empty of
customers before I spoke. "Did you know Annette?"

"Not well. Her husband fixed up a chair of mine a few
years back. Nice man if you like that type."

"What type is that?" I leaned an elbow on the counter.

"He's not a person of tall stature, you see. Some short
men feel like they have to act like a bantam rooster, all
cocky and bluster. Phil's like that. But he does good work
restoring furniture."

"Do you know anything about his relationship with his
wife? A guy like that might not do too well in a marriage."

"No, honey, I don't know a thing about how the two got on. They have the cutest little daughter, though."

"Tulia mentioned that. How long has Phil had the business?"

"Long time. Has a business partner, a Quaker gentleman." She tilted her head. "Why all these questions about Phil?"

I took a deep breath. "Annette didn't simply die. Someone murdered her."

"I wondered about that. And you're hot on the case." She gazed at me. "The husband is always the first suspect, am I right?"

CHAPTER 6

By two o'clock I headed out with a fat bank envelope on my way to deposit the weekend till. I had my ever-present EpiPen in a bag I wore slung across my chest. I'm a person of many allergies, and bee stings were the worst of them. While I perambulated, I thought I'd stop in and have a chat with Gin, too.

Derrick had arrived at the shop at eleven, and our grandma had bustled off to the rest of her day. We'd had a busy few hours. When I'd asked Derrick why he was late, he'd said he had a meeting to attend. *AA*. I always encouraged him to keep up with his recovery, but it didn't usually make him that late.

"Try to find an earlier meeting, okay?" I'd asked.

Business had ebbed a little while ago. I carpe diemed the heck out of the lull by leaving the shop in his and Orlean's hands.

First I popped into Greta's Grains, Tim Brunelle's bakery, a three-minute walk from my shop. My boyfriend closed right about now. I went around to the back door and pulled open the screen door. Tim was wiping down the stainless counter. He paused to give me a big one-armed hug and a kiss worth a million times what I held in my bank bag. The place smelled of yeast and bread, but he was way more delicious than anything he baked, and that was saying something.

"How are you, Mackenzie Almeida, most gorgeous woman in Westham?"

I laughed. I had short curly hair matched by my lean, almost-boyish body, a product of an inherited high metabolism. Gorgeous I definitely wasn't, but if I fit the description in his eyes, it was all good.

"I'm all right. Did you hear the news?" I asked.

"That something bad went down at the Lobstah Shack?"

"Right."

"I heard a little, but no details. My assistant baker called in sick, and I've been flat out."

"Tulia called me this morning before I made it to the bike shop. When she sounded panicked, I went over. She found Annette DiCicero dead in her walk-in. And not merely dead."

His big baby blues went wider still. "Murdered?"

I stuck my hands in my jeans pockets and nodded.

"Are you okay, hon?" He laid his strong hand on the side of my face.

"I'm all right." I filled him in on the rest of the morning. "I have dozens of questions. I have no idea who would have killed Annette or how she got into the walk-in. Did you know her?"

"She used to come in with her little girl."

The now motherless daughter. "Have you ever had any contact with Phil DiCicero's business?"

"Furniture guy, right? I met him at some Chamber of Commerce mixer a couple years ago. Hicks, his partner, hired me to bake for an event his church held last year. The dude, name's Ogden, seemed a little odd, but I did it."

"Odd? How so?"

A bit nervous. Avoided eye contact. That kind of thing. Nothing big."

"What's Phil like?" I asked.

He made a little grimace. "He's got some attitude. Made a crack he tried to disguise as a joke about how tall I am. Kind of silly."

"Abo Reba said it's a short-male insecurity, that he's like a bantam rooster."

"That's a good description," Tim agreed. "Leave it to your grandma. But the daughter, now, she's a darling. Cokey's age, more or less."

My niece Cokey, Derrick's daughter—whom he was bringing up by himself—was in kindergarten.

"I always give little ones a ball of dough to play with if they want it. Kendall and I are buddies. She's a pistol." His smile slid off. "But now she doesn't have a mommy." He set down his rag and pulled me in for an embrace.

My man had an enormous kind heart, and he adored children. We were ever so gradually moving toward an agreement to have some of our own, with me being the one applying the brakes for reasons I strived to overcome.

I pulled away after a few moments of listening to the beat of his heart, inhaling his scent. "I have to keep moving, sweetheart." I held up the bank bag. "Book group is meeting on an emergency basis tonight to talk about the case, but do you want to grab a quick dinner before I go?"

He kissed my forehead. "I'd love to, but I promised the Dudes to go for a beer. Tomorrow for sure, yes?"

"Yes. Beer is actually an excuse to play chess, am I right?" The Dudes were a few guys, plus one Dudess, who loved nothing more than a few rounds of chess over brews.

"You know me too well, my dear."

I pulled open the screen door. "Love you, Tim."

"Love you, Mac."

CHAPTER 7

My banking done, I stepped into Salty Taffy's, the other most delicious shop on Main Street. The colorful bins of wrapped saltwater taffy were sirens of temptation, and the blocks of fudge behind a glass-fronted counter made me drool. Gin Malloy—book group member and my morning walking buddy—also stocked big striped lollipops, creamy chocolate truffles, and pretty much anything else sweet a person could want short of baked goods. I waved at the high-school girl at the register and popped my head into the kitchen.

"Hey, Mac, come on in," Gin called over the deafening machine noise of the taffy-pulling device. A big red contraption, it had kind of saved Gin's and my lives last August. "I'm almost done."

I pulled up a stool well out of her way and watched the

rotating arms work air into a river of stretchy golden candy.

"There." She hit the switch and slid off her headphones, then adjusted the hairnet covering her thick brownish-red hair. She was in her early forties, and some of her hair color was due to dye.

The quiet almost reverberated after the din. I pointed to the headphones. "Noise canceling?"

"Yep. Gotta do it, or I'd be deaf already." She handed me the end of a strand of taffy. "Sample? It's really soft when it's fresh." She set to work scraping the taffy off the arms with a plastic scraper a little larger than a playing card.

"Yum. Thanks." I chewed it and savored its silky texture. "What is it, sea salt caramel?"

"You got it. Let me guess, you're here to talk about Annette." Gin hefted the twenty-five pounds of taffy and carried it to an oiled stainless-steel table. "Was it completely awful to see her?"

I shuddered involuntarily again. I finished the taffy before I responded. "Not my favorite kind of morning, so, yeah. I'm glad we got our walk in before that. But Tulia had it a lot worse. She found the corpse."

"It's bizarre, isn't it? Do they have any idea how or why, not to mention who?"

"Not that I know of. Tulia says she always locks the back door, but she couldn't be sure if it was locked when she went in. It's a chintzy lock."

"That anybody can jimmy, right?" She removed her thin plastic gloves and tossed them in a trash bin. "I've been too busy today to respond to the thread, but I'll be at the meeting tonight."

"Good. Flo said we should meet at her house. Derrick

couldn't commit to hosting." We usually met at my brother's. He was caretaker for a historic lighthouse, where he and Cokey lived in exchange for leading tours on Sundays.

"I knew Annette from back home in New Bedford." She grabbed a rag and a brush and set to cleaning the puller.

My eyebrows went up. "You did? I forgot you were from there."

"I mean, not well, but our moms know each other. They were in a group together. Maybe a garden club. I'm older than Annette was, of course. I used to babysit her when I was in high school."

"What a coincidence. But you've lived in Westham for a while."

"About twenty years now." Gin worked in silence for a moment. "Mac, what disturbs me is that Annette would never be inside a shellfish kitchen. No way. She was deathly allergic to the stuff. I remember when she had a reaction once, to some soup her mom hadn't realized had lobster stock in it. Her mom whipped that EpiPen into Annette's leg faster than a sniper's bullet. Like you did to yourself that time the bee stung you down by the beach."

"I've had practice. I wonder how many people knew about Annette's allergy?"

"Certainly Phil would have." She tapped the counter. "They were having some marriage problems recently, I heard."

"You can bet Lincoln will ask about their relationship."

"He's sharp, I have to give him that," Gin said. She wrinkled her nose. "I certainly didn't enjoy being on the suspected end of his telescope in August."

"What if Phil killed Annette? If he's convicted, their daughter would be a virtual orphan."

"That would be wicked sad. I'm sure Kendall's grandma would take her, but still."

"Is it true Annette was Miss New Bedford?" I asked. "Orlean mentioned it."

"Absolutely." Her smile was a sad one. "She was a real beauty, with that dark Mediterranean look. I'd moved away by then, but Mom told me the contest had been close that year, between Annette and another girl. Annette won the crown, and she got a nice scholarship for college."

I watched Gin wipe the counter clean and then buff it with a dry dishcloth. Being a semi-obsessive neat freak, I approved. "Hey, remember this summer we talked about running a winter coat drive? It's going to get cold soon. We should get that started."

"Good plan. I can make up a poster."

Gin had awesome graphics-cred. Me, not so much.

"I'll let the Chamber of Commerce know," I offered.

"And we can distribute through Our Neighbors' Table, right?"

"Perfect. I'll tell Pa." My thoughts strayed back to the morning. "I wonder if Lincoln is done talking with Tulia yet." I checked my phone. "Nothing on the text thread."

"Do you think she'll come tonight?" Gin hung the dishcloth on a towel bar near the sink and smoothed it out.

"I hope so. I can imagine how she might not be up for it, though."

"Poor Tulia."

Poor Tulia, indeed. And worse, poor Annette.

CHAPTER 8

In my shop, Orlean adjusted the brakes on one of our blue rental bikes. Otherwise the quiet meant a lack of shoppers and renters. It would only become quieter as the season slid into weather not so friendly to cyclists. I should probably think about a fall promotion or some other way to make sure customers—and cash—flowed in. The business had thrived in the year and a half since I'd opened it, but that was never a guarantee it would stay that way.

I'd stopped by the Lobstah Shack on my way back here to see if Tulia had returned. The restaurant had been dark, locked, and still strung with the ominous yellow tape. I didn't know if she'd been released and gone home to Mashpee, or if they still questioned her at the station. I hoped it wasn't the latter.

My brother sat on the stool behind the Mac's Bikes retail counter and frowned at his phone. A big man, he stood over six-foot-two and tended to carry a bit of weight. I'd inherited my speedy metabolism from Abo Reba. Because Derrick and I were half-siblings, Reba wasn't his grandmother by blood, and his body took a much more relaxed approach to the food he consumed.

"Hey, Derrick. I'm back."

"Hi, sis." He glanced up and rubbed his light hair, which had begun to recede from his brow.

"What's the frown for?"

"It's this business with Annette. Her daughter Kendall is one of Cokey's friends at school. I feel bad for the kid, and I'm worried about what Cokey will think, how she'll react."

"Because her own mom disappeared from her life last year."

"Right. I think I'd better not go out to book group tonight. She's going to need me at home." He let out a breath.

"Did you know Annette or her husband?"

"I've met Phil around, and last summer I took Cokey to their house for Kendall's birthday party. They seemed like nice enough folks, although I thought Phil acted a bit nasty to his wife."

"Nasty? Like what?" I asked.

"You know. Putting her down. Making fun of her in a mean way. That kind of thing." His eyes flickered as he glanced at the door, where a group made its way in. "Here comes the afternoon rush."

Neither of us had time to talk about Annette's death again. Rentals, retail, and repairs took up the rest of the day. But I could tell my brother had concerns. I did, too. Cokey's mother had taken her to France to live as a new-born. She and Derrick had been a couple but hadn't married. He couldn't legally prevent her from moving abroad with the baby. When my niece turned three, her mother asked Derrick to come and get their daughter. After that, she basically dropped communications.

Our parents stepped in to help—Cokey stayed with Mom or Pa most afternoons—and the girl was a resilient little beam of sunshine nearly all the time. But sadness at not being with her *Maman* popped up from time to time. That my niece's friend lost her own mother would be tough to handle. And if Kendall's father was a mean-spirited man, he might not have the emotional resources to nurture his daughter through a hard time.

CHAPTER 9

"Hi, Mac," Belle said when I walked into my tiny house behind the shop at five that evening. "Belle's a good girl. Belle wants a snack. Hi, Mac."

"Hi, Belle." I greeted my nutso, slightly manic African gray parrot. "You're a very good girl." I set a few of her favorite frozen grapes and a couple of chunks of frozen carrot in her dish and set it on the floor. For my supper, I nuked the rest of the fish chowder I'd bought from Tulia Saturday and took it outside to the small patio. I left the door open for Belle, who joined me a minute later. The vet clipped her wings so she wouldn't hurt herself indoors, but she never tried to fly away when she joined me out here.

A warm, humid wind had picked up. The news had mentioned a storm coming up the coast. Whether it would hit us depended on how it tracked overnight. When I fin-

ished eating, I needed to secure my little wrought iron
table and two chairs, and my trash barrel, too. Cape Cod
often got slammed by storms, sticking out into the sea as
we did. As long as this one didn't turn into a hurricane, I
should be fine.

I was only two bites into my soup when my cell rang.
I greeted my mom, Astra, who sounded breathless.
"What's up?" I hit the speaker icon so I could set down
the phone.

"Mackenzie, Reba told us you found another body this
morning. Are you all right? What was it like? Do you
want to come over?"

I cringed at the word, "another." But she was right.
Annette's was the third dead body I'd encountered this
year, none of them having died from natural causes.

"What's up?" Belle mimicked. "What's up?"

"Do you have company, honey?" Mom asked.

"No, that's Belle." I loved my crazy pet, but she became crazy talkative when I came home after being at
work all day. I stroked her head. "Anyway, I'm fine,
Mom. And actually, Tulia found Annette. She called me
because it freaked her out. Finding a body would freak
out anyone. I went over to give her some support."

"I see."

"Did you know Annette?"

"No," she said. "I only met her once, when Cokey
wanted to have Kendall over to play after school. Annette
came to pick her up at the end of the afternoon and we
chatted a little."

"Poor Kendall. Does Cokey know her friend has lost
her mother?"

"I don't think so. I believe Derrick planned to tell her
at home tonight. When your grandmother stopped by

with the news a couple of hours ago, we made sure Cokey didn't hear."

"Huh." I fell silent. Had Phil called the police about his missing wife? Surely he would have noticed she hadn't come home last night. Lincoln hadn't indicated that a search for Annette had begun before I'd called in her corpse, though. Maybe she'd gone out for an early morning run and been abducted.

"Mac?" Mom asked. "Are you there?"

"Yes, sorry. My thoughts were elsewhere."

"I have always marveled at your brain and how you use it." She laughed. "It's because you have Jupiter in Scorpio."

I groaned, but I kept it silent. My mother, a professional astrologer, had an explanation from the stars and planets for everything.

"Anyway, do you want to come over? We have plenty of a taco chicken casserole your father made." My father was the minister at the Unitarian Universalist Church a block away. He and Mom lived in the UU parsonage next door to the church.

"Thanks, but no. I have chowder, and I'll be at a book group meeting in less than an hour."

"Oh, that's good, then. You'll be with friends. You know, your Pluto is transiting Mars right now. It's important for you not to spend too much time alone."

I rolled my eyes at Belle. "Gotcha."

"Gotcha!" Belle piped up. "Gotcha!" She gave one of her wolf whistles. "I'm fine, Mom. I'm fine."

"It's uncanny how much that bird sounds like you." In a fainter voice, Mom said, "What's that? All right, dear. Mac, Joseph said it's time to eat. You take care, sweetie."

"I will. Thanks for checking in with me."

"I'll see you tomorrow. My trike is feeling wobbly since I rode through that epic pothole." She and my grandmother had acquired the adult tricycles last summer.

"Bring it in any time." I shook my head and disconnected. I loved being back in my hometown. I liked my life, my work, and the proximity to my family. But once in a while it seemed almost too close.

"Take care, sweetie," Belle muttered. "Sweetie. Sweetie. Sweetie."

"I promise, Belle."

CHAPTER 10

Only four of us gathered in Flo Wolanski's living room at seven that night. We normally met on Thursdays, but needs must, as a Scottish friend liked to say. Librarian Flo had lined the room with bookcases that nearly overflowed with books. Gin and I sipped from glasses of pinot gris, while Flo and Norland each had beers. Flo, our group's organizer, also had a pad of paper on her lap and a pen at hand. She'd set out cheese, crackers, and grapes on a platter.

"Remember during that virus crisis?" Gin asked. "We had to talk about the books on a video call."

I nodded. "We couldn't leave our houses, and we sure couldn't share food."

"Or even shake hands." Flo said. "We were doing curbside pickup at the library."

"It's a relief that's over." Norland helped himself to a

slice of cheese and a few crackers. "We were lucky none of us or our loved ones died from it, either."

Zane hurried in last with a bottle of red wine in his hand. "Sorry I'm late. My evening clerk didn't show up, so I had to close the store."

"No worries." Flo pointed at the side table. "Glasses and opener are in the usual spot."

"Thanks." Zane glanced around. "No Tulia?"

Gin shook her head. "She told me she'd gotten home, but all of it had exhausted her."

"Good," I said. "I've been worried about her. She must not have been arrested or she'd still be at the station. Did she say anything about their line of questioning?"

"No," Gin said. "She didn't want to talk about it."

"The poor thing. I don't blame her." Zane opened the red, poured a glass, and sat. "Stephen couldn't make it, either. He had some powwow about Saturday's town meeting." Stephen Duke served as Westham's town clerk—and Zane's husband.

Norland leaned his elbows on his knees. "Tell us what you found this morning, Mac."

I wrinkled my nose. I recounted again the story of Tulia's phone call. "I went over. Annette DiCicero lay on the floor of the walk-in cooler. She had a lobster pick in her neck."

Gin grimaced. "One of the Lobstah Shack picks?"

"It looked like it," I said. "Chrome with a lobster claw for a handle."

"Those are hers," Zane said. "She had them specially made."

"Right." I went on. "Finding Annette like that really threw Tulia, as you might imagine."

"It's bizarre that we were just reading about Gus shouting up to Julia about the body." Zane shook his head.

"Mac," Norland chimed in. "Was there blood around?"

I squinted at him. I tried to remember. "That's a good question. It's weird, but I don't think I saw any."

Flo scribbled on her pad.

"Wouldn't there be blood?" Zane asked.

"Not if she'd already died when she was stabbed." Norland sat back in his chair.

Already died? I stared at him for a moment. "Gin, tell them what you said about Annette's allergy."

"I babysat her when she was younger," Gin said. "She had an extreme allergy to shellfish. I'm sure she never set foot in the Lobstah Shack."

"Not voluntarily, you mean." Flo ran her fingers through her spiky boy-short white hair. "Did any of the rest of you know Annette?"

"She had expensive tastes in wine," Zane offered. He would know. He owned the only liquor store in town. "Her husband's business must be successful."

"Did she work at a job, too?" Norland asked.

"She worked as an accountant," Flo volunteered. "I believe she kept the books for her husband's business."

"Which is?" Norland asked.

"He restores furniture." Flo wrote more on her pad then glanced up. "I saw Annette in the library last night. She told me she had a course to study for. Some kind of refresher for CPAs."

"I wonder if she worked for other people, too." I glanced around the group.

"She does my taxes," Zane said. "I mean, did. Shoot,

now I have to find someone else." He slapped his forehead. "I'm sorry. How insensitive can I be?"

"It's okay, Zane," Gin said. "Annette did my taxes,
too. She told me she liked the flexibility of being self-
employed, so she could spend more time with Kendall."

"That poor little girl," Zane murmured.

"I was wondering if Phil reported Annette missing the
night before or if she was attacked this morning," I said.

Flo pointed her index finger at me. "Good thought."
She bent over the pad of paper.

"I'll say." Gin nodded. "Maybe she habitually got up
early, and whoever killed her knew it. What time did
Tulia call you, Mac?"

"At eight thirty."

"If I might ask, what did Annette's skin look like?"
Norland gazed at me.

"Kind of yellow. Waxy, sort of. I think she'd been dead
a while."

Norland nodded. "Flo, when did the library close last
night?"

"At eight, as we always do on Mondays. Annette said
she planned to walk home. I looked up her address this
afternoon. The house is on Pebble Lane."

"That's not far from where Tim lives," I said. "I can
ask him if he saw her, or anyone else, near her place."

"Is Lincoln on the case?" Flo asked.

"He is," I said. "I'm sure he'll have a team of people
asking around in her neighborhood."

"And around Tulia's restaurant, too," Norland added.

"Speaking of that," I began. "Doris Sandersen came
into in my shop today. You all know her?"

"The Paws and Claws owner," Flo said.

"Yes. She tried to get me to talk about Annette's death."

"Maybe she killed her," Zane whispered dramatically. "Doris grouses to anybody who'll listen about how smelly the Lobstah Shack makes the alley."

"That's kind of an extreme solution, don't you think?" Gin asked.

Zane shrugged.

"And anyway, murdering Annette doesn't close down the Lobstah Shack," Norland said. "Not for long, anyway."

"Maybe Doris hoped Tulia would be blamed for the murder," I said. "Everybody knows Tulia and Annette had argued repeatedly about the name of the Columbus Day holiday."

"That's a good point," Flo said. "We need to figure out who would have wanted Annette dead."

Strictly speaking, *we* don't need to figure out anything." Norland stressed the plural pronoun.

"But you know we plan to try." Gin raised a single eyebrow.

"And you know Lincoln isn't going to want us to," I pointed out.

"That didn't stop us before," Flo said. "We just need to stay safe."

My detection efforts had landed me in danger twice before, once with Gin. Staying safe from a murderer took the top place on my list. Plus, I'd promised my mom I would take care. A vow to one's mother was not to be trifled with.

"I thought of one more thing," I said. "Derrick told me

he'd seen Phil be rude to Annette. Like putting her down and insulting her."

Norland's mouth drew down at the edges. "In public?"

"I guess."

"He shouldn't do that. No husband should." Norland had adored his wife, who had died the previous year.

"The spouse is always the first suspect," Gin chimed in.

In this case, maybe with good reason.

CHAPTER 11

I opened my eyes the next morning at six thirty to hear rain beat at the windows. The storm had arrived with a vengeance and strong winds. I grabbed my glasses and peered out to see marsh grasses bent sideways and precipitation flying crosswise, too. I wouldn't be swinging my arms with Gin this morning on our daily weekday walk at seven. It provided us an hour of aerobic exercise, as well as a way to catch up on news, talk about the week's cozy mystery, and otherwise solve the problems of the world.

Fifteen minutes later I sat on my little couch with a big mug of dark rich coffee, iPad on my lap, and a bird humming away on the arm next to me. I texted Gin to cancel, then found a local news site and a headline that screamed, "Local Woman's Death Ruled Homicide."

It went on to refer to Annette as a wife and mother—

but not an accountant—and said she was found dead in a popular local restaurant. Photos showed the outside of the Lobstah Shack, a picture of Annette that might have been from her Miss New Bedford days, and a shot of Lincoln and Westham police chief Victoria Laitinen—my former high school classmate—behind a podium. I clicked a link to the video of the press conference, dated last night.

The presentation stuck to the usual. Lincoln relayed the facts but omitted exactly where in the Lobstah Shack Annette was found. *Good.* It would be terrible for business if, once Tulia could reopen, people knew she'd discovered a corpse in the walk-in. He also didn't identify her as the person who had found Annette. Lincoln went on to say that for the moment, they did not have a suspect in custody, but they were pursuing several leads. I wished I knew what those leads were. He asked anyone with information to come forward.

Victoria said the WPD was cooperating fully with the state police. One of Westham's three select board members stepped forward to express sorrow for Phillip DiCicero and the couple's daughter. He said town officials had every confidence in the law enforcement efforts and that residents shouldn't be afraid, although exercising extra caution might be advisable at this time. *Extra caution?* Victoria finished by adding that she and the detective would take a few questions.

The camera panned to a room full of microphones and recording devices. A half dozen voices shouted out questions. Lincoln pointed at a woman.

"Do you suspect Tulia Peters, the owner of the restaurant?"

I groaned. So much for keeping her identity quiet.

"Ms. Peters is cooperating fully with our investigation," Lincoln said. "As yet we have no suspect in custody." He pointed to a man I recognized from one of the Boston news channels.

"What about Mr. DiCicero?" the reporter asked.

"Let me repeat. So far we have no suspect in custody."

"What was the cause of death?" another piped up.

"The autopsy is not complete." Lincoln held up his hands, palms out. "That will be all. Thank you." He and Victoria turned to go.

"Is it true she was stabbed with one of the restaurant's lobster picks?" the first woman shouted after them.

Lincoln's stride slowed, as if he might turn back to the pack of newspeople to answer the question. Apparently not. He kept going, instead.

I hadn't learned much from the back and forth other than Lincoln's mantra about not having a suspect in custody. *Yet.* Last night's discussion with the book group hadn't shed much light, either. We hadn't come up with action items for any of us. Flo must be slipping. She was usually on top of that kind of list.

Actually, what Norland had said last night had to be significant. If not much—or any—blood had been found on the floor under Annette's neck, then she'd already died when she was stabbed. Lincoln must know that, which would be why he hadn't answered about the lobster pick. I didn't know anything about autopsies except that people were cut open, which made me feel queasy even to think about it. The medical examiner or coroner or whoever carried out autopsies would figure out what actually caused Annette's death.

But what could I learn from the comfort of my cozy sitting room? My grandma had said Phil had a business partner. Had she said a Quaker?

I tapped "DiCicero furniture restoration" into the browser and found a website for the business. Scrolling down didn't yield much except the difference between the before and the after photographs of various pieces of furniture they'd restored, both wood and upholstery. Prices for the work didn't seem to be listed. I clicked the About tab to see pictures of Phillip and his partner, Ogden Hicks. Phil appeared to be in his forties, with his partner maybe a decade older. Too bad bios weren't included.

My gaze fell on the small drop-leaf table where I ate my meals. It had a been a hand-me-down and was a little worse for wear. I'd planned to refinish it myself but hadn't gotten around to it during the summer. Maybe I could solicit an estimate from DiCicero and Hicks. I wrinkled my nose. The only way I could fit the table into Miss M, my convertible Miata, would be with the top down. That wouldn't happen today, not with all this rain. I snapped a few pictures of the table and zoomed into a few of the worst spots. Photographs would have to do.

CHAPTER 12

The front of Tulia's shop was still dark when I hurried, hood up, through the rain to the back door of Mac's Bikes, although the yellow tape had disappeared. I'd sent her a text earlier and asked her to stop by when she could, but she hadn't responded. I was pretty sure today would be ultra-quiet in the bike shop. We certainly wouldn't get any new rentals. Maybe a few retail sales, and possibly a repair or two, although I wouldn't want to transport any decent cycle through the rain. Orlean could catch up on the repair backlog, though, and I always had paperwork to do.

Once inside, I squinted. The wind had blown something into my right contact lens. I removed it and rinsed both it and my eye before reinserting the lens. I'd switched to wearing contacts in middle school, and they had greatly improved my myopic vision.

I'd barely run through my opening check list, minus hanging out the Open sign and watering the window boxes, when Tulia pushed through the door. I hurried over to hug her. She looked terrible. Her normally ruddy cheeks were dimmed and the skin under her eyes looked bruised.

"I didn't know if you'd be around today," I said.

"They told me I could open, and I have to. But I've been over there scrubbing since dawn. I had to throw out all that food and reorder." She let out a long, shaky breath. "You know I always make my own bisque base. I had to order that in, too."

"I was thinking of that bisque. I'm sorry, Tulia."

"Thanks. Yesterday Lincoln hinted that the health inspector would require me to toss all the food. I would have done it, anyway."

"You could have asked us for help with the cooler." I straightened the display of sports lip gloss on the counter.

"It was too early. I couldn't sleep and drove over here at four in the morning. Anyway, I needed to get it all clean. For myself.

"Are you okay to be back at work?"

She cast her gaze around the shop as if in search of an answer. "Not really. But I have food to make and serve, my employee needs to work, and, well, I can't just sit home and worry."

"Do you want some coffee? I made a pot a few minutes ago."

She nodded mutely.

A minute later we each perched on a stool behind the counter with steaming mugs in front of us. Orlean still hadn't arrived and Derrick wasn't due until ten. In the absence of customers, I might as well have a good chat with my friend. "How did yesterday go?"

"Awful. Lincoln tried to be kind, but he asked me questions every which way, for a long time. Then Chief Laitinen asked me the same ones. I had to be fingerprinted."

"I'm sure it's just for elimination," I said. "They must have looked for prints on all kinds of things in your place yesterday." Like on the lobster pick.

"Right, that's what they said. I told them my prints will be on everything in the restaurant. I don't know what good it does them. And I had to sign a statement. But Mac, I don't know anything!" She sounded plaintive. "I found her. I don't know how she got there. That's it." She wrapped her hands around her mug.

"They didn't charge you with a crime?"

"Of course not. How could they?"

I was the one who had told her not to worry, that they wouldn't find evidence against her. But she must know she was at least a person of interest.

Two athletic-looking women wandered in, one with silver hair, the other with a lined face but reddish dyed locks. Visitors, not locals, as far as I could tell. After I greeted them, they headed over to browse the shirts and helmets on the far wall.

"People are already giving me the side eye," Tulia went on in a quiet voice. "And they named me at that press conference. Did you see it?"

"I caught it this morning online."

"I don't know if I'll have any business." She eyed the shoppers and lowered her voice to an even softer murmur. "Who wants to eat in a place where somebody was murdered?"

"It might be slow for a while." I should text the group to make sure everybody went to the Lobstah Shack to eat this week. That way Tulia would at least have some business and feel supported.

"Did you go to the meeting last night?" she asked.

"Yes, but we didn't exactly solve the case." Should I tell her that the lobster pick didn't kill Annette? If it were me, I'd want to know. "Norland asked if there was blood under Annette." I kept my tone quiet, too.

Tulia stared at me. "I didn't see any."

"Me, neither. He said that would mean she'd already died when she was stabbed."

The women approached, each holding a brightly colored shirt. "We'll take these."

Tulia sipped her coffee, and I rang them up.

"These are some of our most popular cycling tops." I handed one the credit card slip to sign.

"We're visiting from Santa Cruz in California, and we ride a lot," the shorter one said. "It'll be fun to wear a souvenir from Westham."

"We heard you had a murder here in town, in a restaurant." The other woman raised her eyebrows.

"Unfortunately, yes," I said.

"We're sure not going to eat there." The first woman pushed the signed slip across the counter.

Tulia stood abruptly. "Talk to you later, Mac. Thanks for the coffee." She hurried out.

"Here." I smiled politely as I handed the first one the bag. "The restaurant owner had nothing to do with the death, you know. You should try the seafood at the Lobstah Shack. It's the best in town."

The customer exchanged a glance with her friend. "Well, maybe. I think we'll stick to Jimmy's Harborside."

Poor Tulia.

The women had barely left when my mother hurried in with a rush of rain-scented air. I greeted her. She shed her rain jacket and shook it out.

"Mac, I wanted to see how you're holding up," she said without preamble.

"I'm all right. Tulia's not in very good shape, though."

She made a tsking noise. "Is your book group on the case?"

"We talked about the murder last night. I'm not sure 'on the case' really describes it." I drained my mug. Tulia had barely touched hers. "Coffee?"

"No, thanks. I had my one cup at home. Any more makes me wired, and you know I have a bit too much energy even without it."

True. "I thought you were going to bring in your trike?"

"It's too rainy. I'll bring it tomorrow." She fluffed the rain out of her curly flyaway hair, blond mixed now with white.

"Mom, do you know Phil DiCicero?"

She wrinkled her nose. "Not well. His partner, Ogden Hicks, is a bit of a weirdo."

"Oh? In what way?"

"Maybe weird isn't the right word, but I don't think he has a very high opinion of others, for one thing. Which is crazy, because he's a Quaker."

"Aren't they supposed to believe everyone is equal?" I asked.

"Exactly. I don't know, maybe he had a hard upbringing and acts badly for some deep-seated psychological reason. And I found out he's a Leo, so he would think the world revolves around him."

"That's no excuse for bad behavior. Has he been rude to you? Insulted you?"

She gazed at me with her light green eyes that were exactly like mine. "I saw him in action at a town meeting. He put down our only female select person, and once at the market he made fun of that boy who bags."

"The one with Down syndrome?"

"Yes."

"That's disgusting. Is Ogden married? Does he have a family?"

"I'm not sure." She glanced up at the wall clock. "Oh, my. I have an appointment with a client in ten minutes. I have to run." She kissed my cheek.

I said goodbye and watched her blow out the door to go consult with someone about their natal chart and to-day's configuration of the planets and stars. Ogden sounded like an unpleasant man, and his business partner Phil might be, too, based on what Abo Reba had told me. I still wanted to meet Phil for myself.

CHAPTER 13

The morning didn't end up as quiet as I'd expected. Rain or no rain, four different regulars brought in bikes for repairs or tune-ups. Orlean worked away in her area. We sold lights and tire patches and a pink bike with training wheels. A disappointed family of five returned their rentals, saying they'd hoped for one more day of riding. Busy was good for the bottom line. It only surprised me on such a stormy day.

At eleven we finally had a break on the retail side. I hit the ladies' room, then headed over to where Derrick was straightening a shelf.

"Derr, Mom said you were going to tell Cokey last night about Kendall's mom dying. How did she take it?"

"I thought she was going to be more upset. Instead my little girl showed a ton of empathy, Mac. I'm so proud of her. She drew a picture for Kendall, made me promise to deliver it today, and said we had to help take care of her friend."

"That's seriously sweet of her. I'm glad."

He pulled an envelope from under the counter and drew out a sheet of paper. "Check it out."

Cokey's picture showed two big smiling balloon heads with legs and hands sticking out from each. One head had yellow hair and the other brown, and the two girls were holding hands. Cokey had signed it with her beginner capital letters, including the E facing backwards.

"I love it. Are you going to drop it off?"

"I guess. I'm not sure I want to see Phil."

"Why not?"

"He's kind of a prickly guy." Lines deepened between his brows. He slid the drawing back into the envelope.

"Abo Reba told me he'd insulted Annette in public," I said.

"Yep." Derrick grimaced. "That said, I promised Cokey. I'll put it in their mailbox. I probably won't even see him."

"I need to run an errand if you think you can do without me here. Want me to drop off the envelope?"

His face lit up. "That'd be great. Thanks, sis."

"And tell you what. I'll bring back lunch for the three of us from the Lobstah Shack. I want to give Tulia the support."

"She's already open for business?"

"Yes. She stopped in this morning and said they told her she could open. And she seemed to want to."

"Lunch sounds great. Hey, how did book group go last night? Did anyone have any insights?"

I filled him in on what Norland had said. "And Gin told me Annette was violently allergic to shellfish."

"So what did she die from? Was she poisoned? Maybe she had a heart attack, and somebody wanted to make it look like Tulia killed her."

I stared at him. "I hadn't thought of her dying of natural causes. How awful. Or . . . what if shellfish poisoned her somehow?"

"I wonder if she had any other allergies."

"I don't know. Seafood and tree nuts are, like, the only allergies I don't have." Bee stings, pet dander, dust mites, mold, pollens, penicillin—all of them plagued me, some worse than others.

"Believe me, I know, Mackie. When we were young, you had to have all those pillow and mattress covers, and the cleaning people were extra attentive to your room."

"Plus, you never got that dog you wanted. Sorry, bro." I smiled up at him.

"I survived just fine." The door blew in a couple more customers. "Why don't you get going before we have a noon rush?"

"Perfect."

Derrick greeted the customers. "Let me know how I can help you."

"Orlean," I called in to her, "I'm bringing back lunch for all of us."

She raised a greasy, blue-gloved thumb in response. Too bad I couldn't give a thumbs up response to my investigative efforts on Tulia's behalf. Not yet, anyway.

CHAPTER 14

I dropped the envelope in the DiCicero mailbox at the Pebble Lane address Derrick had given me. The modest ranch house at number ten, part of a sixties-era subdivision not far from Tim's place, had no lights on. I didn't see a car in the driveway, although the garage door was shut. I supposed Phil and Kendall might be with relatives somewhere, or maybe the girl had gone to school and Phil to work. It seemed way too soon for that.

My GPS lady directed Miss M—with her top up and windows closed—and me to a small industrial park outside of town. A sign over one of the doors read, "DiCicero and Hicks Furniture Restoration." I parked in front of it next to a light-colored Prius. When I opened the door, a buzzer rang in the back.

Before and after photos similar to the ones on the website covered the walls of the front office. They depicted

dining tables, antique chairs, upholstered recliners, bu-
reaus, and more. Unmarred wood gleamed in the after
shots, and upholstery was unstained, untattered, and
stretched smooth. I knew they could do a lovely job on
my little table, but the price might be out of my range. A
small family portrait hung behind a couple of straight
chairs. I peered at a very much alive Annette seated in an
armchair. On her lap sat a little dark-haired girl with huge
brown eyes, with a thick-necked man standing next to
them. He also had dark hair, worn combed back from his
forehead, and he'd slung his arm around Annette's shoulders in a possessive stance.

A kid of no more than twenty in work pants and a canvas apron came through the door from the back. "Can I
help you, ma'am?"

"I wondered if I could talk with Phil?"

He narrowed his eyes. "Are you a reporter?"

"A reporter? No. I have an old table that needs restoring."

"Okay. It's only that . . ."

"They've been bugging you because of Annette's
death?"

"So you know."

"Yes. It's been on the news." I didn't need to tell him
I'd seen her corpse.

"It's, like, super sad. She was such a nice lady."

"Yes. About the table, can you give me an estimate?"

"That's literally beyond my pay grade, and Mr. DiCicero
isn't in. But Mr. Hicks can give you a price. Let me get
him."

"Thanks."

He pulled open the door to the back. Beyond I spied
furniture in all stages of repair. Giant rolls of padding and

fabric hung from rollers mounted on a wall, and scents of chemical strippers and furniture polish wafted into the front.

"Mr. Hicks," the kid called. "Lady needs an estimate on a table." To me he said, "He'll be right out. You can sit down if you want." He disappeared through the door.

A moment later a man pushed through. He looked a lot like the photo I'd seen on the website, except a bit worse for wear. "Ogden Hicks. Do you have the table in your car?" He stood a little taller than my five-foot-seven and wore the same black canvas apron as the kid had. He had a smudge of sawdust on his temple that matched thin hair the pale yellowy color of Cape Cod sand.

I'd rarely had a more brusque greeting. "I'm Mac Almeida. It's nice to meet you, Ogden." I held out my hand.

He shook his head. "My hands aren't clean, Ms. Almeida." He opened long-fingered hands colored with stain, hands that shook almost imperceptibly.

"No worries. No, I didn't bring the table because of the rain and my small car. But I have pictures." I pulled out my phone and scrolled to the shots I'd taken. "I really like the size and the drop-leaf, but it's old and isn't very pretty. Can you give me an estimate from the photos?"

I swiped through slowly so he could study them.

"Can you zoom in on the top?" he asked.

"Sure."

"The legs aren't turned."

"What does that mean?" I tilted my head.

"You know how some older tables have rounded sections on the legs, like knobs?" His voice had had a nervous edge to it. Now that he was talking about furniture it evened out. "Those are turned. These are Shaker style, smooth and tapered. That makes them a lot easier to strip and refinish. It's a nice piece. I'd say we could do it for three hundred dollars."

Gulp. Or I could wait until next summer and do it myself for the cost of the stripper and the finishing stuff. "I'll need to think about it a little."

He lifted an eyebrow. "Let us know." He fished a card out of a holder on the counter and handed it to me.

"Thanks. Hey, I'm sorry about your partner's wife. He must be devastated."

Ogden blinked. "We all are, naturally. The cops had better catch the guy responsible, and soon."

"The officer handling the case is good at what he does. I'm sure Detective Haskins will have someone in custody soon."

"You know the detective? Who are you?" His eyes blazed. "Undercover police? Some kind of private investigator? Sneaking in here like you want work done." He clenched his fists.

"No, not at all." I took a step back. "I simply asked about my table, and I happen to know the detective. Thank you for the estimate. I'm very sorry for your loss." I slid out the door as fast as I could.

He pulled it open and glared. I exhaled with relief once I'd put Miss M in gear and pointed her away from the shop. He'd shown one heck of a reaction. The guy didn't seem to like the police. But why not?

CHAPTER 15

After I entered the Lobstah Shack, I was surprised to see Sofia Burtseva working behind the counter. In August the tall young woman had been a server at Jimmy's Harborside, a larger seafood restaurant in town. I pushed back the hood of my rain jacket and approached the area where people placed takeout orders.

"Hi, Sofia. How long have you worked for Tulia?"

"I fill in shifts here when I can." She spoke with an accent from her native Russia, which went with her high, broad cheekbones and white-blond hair, but I could understand her English perfectly well. "I still work at Jimmy's, too. How are you, Mac?"

"I'm good. I'd like to order some takeout lunch." I studied the paper menu. "I'll take a crab cake sandwich, the large lobster roll, and an Asian seafood noodle salad."

Orlean was partial to crab cakes, Derrick loved lobster rolls, and the noodle salad was to die for. Tulia made it with chewy soba noodles, pieces of grilled shrimp and scallops, crunchy bits of celery and sweet pepper, all mixed with a slightly sweet sesame-soy dressing. "Oh, and three small chowders."

She looked up from the pad of paper. "Clam or fish?"

"Fish, thanks." I'd bill the food to the shop and mark it staff lunch. "Is Tulia here?"

"In the kitchen." She glanced at the swinging door. "But she keeps making mistakes in the orders."

That didn't surprise me. "Have you been busy?" The wall clock, with lobster claws for the hour and minute hands, read twelve thirty. Two diners sat reading the newspaper while they ate, and a table of older men talked and laughed. A woman swiping through her phone sat in one of the chairs where people waited for takeout.

"Not very. Usually lunchtime is a crazy rush." She leaned closer. "I think people are freaked out by the, you know, dead lady." She shuddered.

I nodded. "I can understand that."

"Let me give Tulia your order."

"Will you tell her I'm here?"

"Sure. Please have a seat." She disappeared through the swinging door.

Before I could sit, the front door opened, and Flo hurried in, furling an umbrella.

"Hey, Mac. You had a great idea, for us to support our friend." She raised her eyebrows and pointed her head toward the back. "I ordered online."

"And I ordered lunch for my staff." I beckoned her closer and spoke softly. "I left the DiCicero shop a few minutes ago."

She folded her arms. "And you're the one who has always told us to do what Haskins says and not to go nosing around."

True. Nosing around was exactly what had gotten me in trouble before. "Hey, I have a table that needs to be refinished. What can I say?"

Flo snorted.

"Anyway," I went on, "Phil hadn't come in, but I spoke with his partner."

"Hicks?"

"Yes. The man must have had a bad experience with the police in the past. He accused me of snooping and got furious."

Flo gave a low whistle. "Think he's our villain?"

"I doubt it. Why would he murder anyone? And her in particular."

"I don't know, but we have to keep digging, Mac. When I get back to the library, I'll run a search on him."

Sofia reappeared and set down three paper bags stapled at the top. "Here you go, Mac. Hello, Ms. Wolanski. I have your order ready, too." She stepped closer. "Tulia does not want to talk to anybody. We just got big takeout order. She is flat out back there. I am sorry." She handed a bag to the woman who had been waiting, too, who thanked Sofia and hurried out.

"No worries," I said. I checked the amount and handed her more than enough cash.

"She said to tell you both she appreciates the business.

I am getting your change." Sofia moved toward the register.

"Throw it in the tips jar."

"Thank you." Sofia pulled a check out of her pocket and headed to the table of men.

"I'd better get back to work," Flo said.

"Don't you have to pay?" I asked her.

"Mac? Get with the program. If you order online, you pay on the spot, with the option for including a tip. Tulia has PayPal set up, and it's easy. I basically don't use cash for anything anymore."

"Fine." I sighed. Flo was two decades older than me, and she did way more in the digital world than I did. "Except if I pay cash, it saves Tulia money, so that's what I do."

Flo only rolled her eyes. We both headed for the door. Flo reached to push it open, but it swung in on its own. Or rather, Lincoln Haskins pushed it open and stepped inside.

"Ladies." He bobbed his head and narrowed his eyes behind his glasses.

I held up my bag. "Just here for some takeout. Glad you let Tulia reopen." I knew he suspected we were up to no good being here.

"I'm here for lunch, too," he said.

"See you, Mac, Detective." Flo sidled past him and out the door.

"Lincoln, can I talk with you for a second?"

He cast a glance toward the door to the kitchen. "Just for a moment. I have a couple more questions for Ms. Peters, and I also have to get my lunch and be back at the station for a meeting. Let's step over here."

I followed him to the corner farthest from anyone. "Did Phil DiCicero report his wife as AWOL?" When he opened his mouth to object that I was sleuthing, I rushed on. "Yesterday you didn't seem to have known she'd gone missing. It seems odd to me, that's all."

"We asked him. So far he says," Lincoln said, with stress on the last word, "he took their daughter to have dinner in Pocasset with his mother and the two spent the night. We're attempting to verify that now."

I blinked. "I guess that makes sense. Flo said Annette studied at the library until they closed at eight."

"She did, did she?" He frowned at the door Flo had left through. "And do you know why Ms. Wolanski hasn't reported this to the authorities?"

"She didn't?" I swallowed. "No, I have no idea why not." Silly Flo. She should have. Had I mentioned that to her last night? Probably not.

Lincoln pulled out his phone and tapped in a text. "Someone will interview her without delay."

Should I tell him about Ogden's reaction to my knowing Lincoln? Nah. He'd never buy my story about wanting an estimate on my table.

"Have you 'learned' anything else, Mac?" He put "learned" in finger quotes.

"My grandmother said she's seen Phil insult Annette in public. And my brother confirmed it."

"Derrick knows DiCicero?"

"Yes. Their daughters are both in kindergarten, and they've become friends. You know, play dates and such."

A shadow seemed to pass over his eyes. I knew he'd had some tragedy with his own child in the past, but I didn't know what had happened.

Lincoln blew out a breath. "Thank you for that. Is that all? Because I do have to get going."

"No, that's it." I didn't need to ask about the lack of blood. That was the business of professionals, not rank amateurs like me. "And, yes, I'll let you know ASAP if I happen to accidentally come across other information."

He had the grace to smile at the word "accidentally." We both knew that the tidbits I learned usually didn't happen by accident.

CHAPTER 16

At a quarter past four, I set down the box of peppers I'd brought out from the free food market's cooler in the UU church basement and opened the top. On Wednesdays I left closing Mac's Bikes to Derrick and Orlean and headed over to the market for my volunteer shift. The market opened at four thirty and we had to get the shelves fully stocked by then. The organizers, in the space Pa and the church board had donated, had set up what looked like a regular, albeit tiny, grocery store. Brightly lit refrigerated and freezer cases lined two walls. Shelves of nonperishables were organized by type, a row held bins full of vegetables and fruit, and a bread area nearly overflowed. Some of it had been donated by Tim that very day, whatever hadn't sold by the time he closed at two. Our clients pushed around small shopping carriages and took what they needed, or at least what they wanted, with only a few limits set on items in short supply.

The process enabled our clients to shop for themselves instead of being handed a charity bag someone else had filled, which could contain food or products the shopper didn't like. Our Neighbors' Table had originally been labeled a food pantry, but to call it a market was more accurate and afforded dignity to the shoppers.

I lined up the green and red peppers in neat, pretty rows, next to bags of carrots and a pile of onions, all donated by a Mashpee farmer. Behind me Gin unloaded a case of spaghetti and lasagna noodles, and a petite, dark-haired volunteer named Rose added jars of peanut butter to another shelf. My father worked in the cheese case, setting out half-pound bricks of cheddar and American. He had Cokey for the afternoon and had given her the task of stocking juice boxes on a low shelf. Her blond angel curls were in two tiny braids today, with wavy wisps that popped out everywhere.

"The children are going to be happy with juice boxes for their lunches, aren't they, Titi Mac?" Cokey lisped.

"You bet." I reached down and held up my hand for a high five. "Nice job stocking, Cokester."

She slapped it with her little hand. "Nice job with the peppers." She scrunched up her nose. "But the kids won't like them."

"They might," Gin chimed in. "Red peppers are sweet. My daughter loved them at your age."

"Well, I don't." My niece pushed out her lips. Her face brightened. "But Kendall does. She loves peppers."

Gin and I exchanged a glance. "I'm sorry about your

friend's mommy," I said. "Daddy showed me the picture you drew. That was really nice."

"He taked it to her mailbox," Cokey said with a solemn look. "It'll make her feel better."

"I actually drove it over there for him this morning." I knelt in front of her.

The little girl gave a firm nod. She knew family would come through for her.

I took her hand. "Did it make you sad to hear Kendall's mother had died?"

"Yeah. Abo said she went to heaven. But Kendall can't talk to her, because they don't even have cell phones in heaven."

Gin smothered a laugh.

"No, they sure don't," I said. "As far as we know."

"Abo Joe, can I have my snack now?" Cokey lisped to my father.

"Of course, *querida*. It's in the office."

Cokey skipped out to the room next door we called the office, but it really served as the catchall space for paperwork, extra nonperishables—and snacking. Better she wasn't underfoot when the shoppers flooded in, anyway. The operation had another whole section for intake. We weighed everything that came in and stored full boxes of food until we could transfer it to the market itself. The church had gotten a big grant to set it all up, and the congregation had approved transforming nearly all the basement into the charity.

Pa surveyed the market. "Are we done? People are already in line."

I glanced at the casement window to see pairs of legs lined up. The need was great among those who struggled to get by, of which Westham had a not-insignificant number.

"Sure." I moved toward the door. "I'll take check-in." First-time shoppers had to fill out a registration form with us, but they didn't have to prove income—or lack of it. The form asked for it, but the number only served a statistical purpose.

"I'll do checkout," Gin offered.

Because we weighed all food donations, at checkout we also weighed all the food that went out.

"And I'll float," Pa said.

"I'll keep stocking," Rose added.

A steady stream of people flowed through. People could fall on hard times for a zillion reasons. That those of us in more comfortable circumstances could do a little to make their lives easier—and less hungry—made me glad. But it wasn't enough.

A thin, scruffy-looking woman stepped up to my table, the one I'd seen pass by my shop recently.

"Good afternoon. Your name, please?"

"Nia." She gazed at me with large hazel eyes and full, dark lashes. She must have a been a real beauty before she fell on hard times. Now her skin looked weathered and dry from living in the elements and not having enough to eat.

"Welcome, Nia. And your last name?"

Frown lines appeared at the edge of her dark watch cap. "I don't get why you need that. I want to pick up food. Who cares what my name is?"

"I'm sorry. We're required to take it down."

She gazed hungrily at the shelves of food, but finally grunted, "Rodrigues."

"Thank you." I found her name on the list and didn't have to ask her to register. "Do you need bags?"

Nia nodded. I handed her three sturdy papers bags with handles. We'd gotten a grant from an environmental organization to buy them, so we didn't proliferate single-use plastic bags.

"Is dinner offered tonight?" she mumbled.

"No, that's on Tuesdays and Thursdays."

She nodded and shuffled toward the bread and peanut butter section. Boxes of pasta didn't do much good if you didn't have a kitchen.

CHAPTER 17

Tim had invited me for dinner at six thirty. After the food market closed, I'd had time to zip home and clean up. I also fed Belle and got her into her cage, which I covered for the night. Now I hurried along Main Street, my head down against the windy rain. An umbrella was useless in this kind of weather, but I had a good raincoat. My feet would be wet by the time I reached Tim's, exactly why I kept a spare pair of slippers at his house.

Approaching the Friends Meetinghouse at the far end of the main drag, I paused. The lights in the tall windows of the simple building broadcast a welcome comfort in the stormy dusk. They must be having an evening event. I'd never been inside, and on a whim I peeked in the open front door.

An entryway ran the width of the building, with open

doors on the left and right that led into the main part. A snowy-haired man in a blue shirt and suspenders stepped out of the door on the right. His white beard grew so long it hid his neck.

"Good evening," he said. "The lecture doesn't start until seven, but you're welcome to come in now."

I stepped in, pushing back my hood. "Thank you. I'm actually just passing by and have never been inside. May I take a peek?"

"Be my guest. This side is our fellowship room, and the other side is for worship." He stepped back to give me room to enter. Tables and chairs and bookcases filled the room, with a small sink at the near end. Another door stood open at the far end on the left. A plate of cookies and one of brownies on a table looked homemade—and delicious. "I'm readying the refreshments."

"When was the meetinghouse built?"

"In 1855." He pointed to the wall on the left. "This divider actually raises to make the two rooms into one. In the nineteenth century, Quakerism flourished, and they would fill both sides on First Day.

"Is that Sunday?"

"Yes. You can go into the worship room if you'd like." He pointed to the opening.

I made my way there and stood at the entrance to a simple room with pews arranged in a rectangle. Wood paneling ran up the walls to about six feet, and an old clock ticked peacefully. The windows had to be eight or ten feet tall. I turned back to the man, who now measured coffee into a filter.

"It's lovely," I said. "How big is your congregation now?"

"Thirty at most, often more like ten or fifteen. We don't believe in evangelizing, which is to our own detriment, some say."

"My father is the UU minister."

"I know Joseph. A fine man."

I smiled. "He is. But his congregation has been shrinking, too."

"Alas, young families aren't making worship a priority these days. Pretty soon we'll all have hair the color of mine, and that will be that."

"I met a member of your church today, an Ogden Hicks," I said.

My host turned to the coffee maker, poured water in, and switched it on before he faced me again. "Yes, he is a long-time member. Friend Ogden has not had an easy way of it."

"Oh?"

"He lost his wife, and his only son experienced a traumatic brain injury when he was twenty. Ogden is devoted to his care, which is quite costly."

The poor man. "That must be very difficult."

"Indeed."

My phone dinged with the half hour. "Shoot, I have to go. Thank you so much for letting me look around, sir." I held out my hand.

He shook it. "We worship every First Day morning at ten. You are always welcome. I'm Silas Carter, by the way."

"I'm Mac Almeida. It's good to meet you, Silas."

Silas tilted his head. "You own Mac's Bikes."

"I do. We open every day at nine. You are always welcome."

He smiled at my twist, then sobered. "And you are a kind of private investigator, am I correct?"

"No, not at all." I shook my head. "Although I'm afraid I came a little too close to a couple of homicides this year, and I guess I did help the police solve them." And hopefully I could help solve this one soon, too.

CHAPTER 18

Nestled into Tim's arm on his couch, I sipped from the apple cidertini he'd made me. "Man, this is good. Did you invent it?" I savored the sweet cider mixed with vodka and another liquor. An apple slice garnished the edge of the glass, and he'd added a cinnamon stick for stirring, not that it needed it.

"I did, indeed. Zane sold me an apple brandy that was the perfect complement." He sampled his own.

I sniffed the air. "What smells so good?"

"It's only a lobster quiche."

"Only?" How lucky was I? Who went around making lobster quiche on a Wednesday night? Tim, apparently. "It must be National Seafood Day. I had Tulia's seafood noodle salad for lunch today. Also to die for." I wrinkled my nose. "Not the best description for this week, is it?"

"No, but don't worry about it. Is the Westham Sleuthing Club making any progress on Annette's homicide?"

I elbowed him. "Hey. We're a cozy mystery book group."

"The members of which like to get involved in solving local mysteries. I bet they don't seem as cozy when they happen in your own back yard."

"They sure don't." I thought about my day. "Cokey did the sweetest thing for Kendall. She drew a picture of the two of them and signed her name. The kind of picture where it's all head with arms and legs sticking straight out."

"Who needs a torso or a neck, anyway?" He squeezed my shoulder.

"She insisted Derrick take it to their house. I was going out and dropped it off."

"Where do the DiCiceros live?"

"Down the road from here, on Pebble Lane. It didn't look like anyone was home, though."

"What's the number?" he asked.

"Ten. Why?"

Tim grew quiet.

"What?" I twisted to face him.

"I saw someone lurking around there on Monday night. I went to that talk in Falmouth on coastal preservation, remember? I drove home about nine, and I saw this homeless woman I know hurrying away from the house. I know it was number ten because they have extra large numbers on the mailbox, and they're reflective."

"I saw those numbers, too." I thought quickly. According to Flo, Annette had left the library at eight. If she'd gone straight home, she would have been there by eight thirty. On the other hand, she could have run an errand or gone to see friends. I thought a little more. "Wait. Did you say a homeless woman you know?"

He nodded at the same time the timer dinged from the kitchen. "To be continued." He stood.

In the kitchen, I sat at the small table. When he invited guests besides me over, he used the dining table in the next room, but I'd assured him long ago the kitchen table was fine for the two of us. Still, two candles were lit, and a cloth napkin lay under the forks. While the quiche was settling on a cooling rack, Tim threw together a mixed greens salad topped with late gold cherry tomatoes, small chunks of apple—which he said were all from the farmers' market—and toasted walnuts. I finished my drink and admired the grace with which he moved his muscular body. I also admired his rear end. Mostly I wondered if the woman he'd seen was Nia. I'd started to ask, but he was a single-focus guy and had requested I wait.

After he dished up two plates of quiche and brought over the salad, he poured a chilled Chardonnay into stemmed glasses and sat.

"Here's to you, darling Mac."

I clinked my glass. "And to you." We gazed at each other for a moment before sipping.

As we ate, we chatted about his bakery, about Belle's latest new words—including "gotcha" and "sweetie"—and about the food market. Which brought me back to Nia.

"Will you tell me about the homeless woman you know?" I asked.

"Right. I was about to when the timer went off. I've passed the word around that on days when the free food market isn't open, hungry people can come by the back door at two. I give out whatever baked goods didn't sell during the day."

I set my chin on my elbow and gazed at him. "Have I ever told you I love you?"

"Not in the last hour, you haven't." He leaned over and kissed me lightly.

"How come I didn't know about your bread give-away?"

"Come on, Mac, you know me. Do I like to toot my own horn?"

I shook my head. "You do not." I savored a bite of the rich, smooth quiche, the dill a perfect seasoning, the mushrooms silky. "So, this woman you saw on Pebble Lane is a leftover bread regular?"

"She is. Her name is Nia."

Bingo.

"I like to get to know the people who stop by," he said. "You know, to try to understand how their lives went south, at least financially."

"Do you know why Nia's did?"

"No." Tim frowned. "She keeps her history locked up inside, and I don't pry. I feel bad for all of them, but especially for her, for some reason."

"When you peer past the grime and scruff, she's a natural beauty."

He nodded. He'd noticed, too.

"Her last name is Rodrigues," I went on. "She shops at Our Neighbors' Table, and she came in today. But even though she'd already registered, she only reluctantly gave me her last name at check-in." I ate my last bite of quiche. "This is superlative, you know. Really delicious."

"Thanks, sweetheart." He studied me. "I bet you wonder why Nia lurked around the DiCicero house on the night of Annette's murder."

"Well, duh. Don't you?"

"Only casually. I'm not as keen on being an amateur detective as you are. I know you find this hard to believe. And you know what I'd rather be doing." He gave me an odd smile.

Was it a wistful one or a wicked leer? I opted for the latter. "I brought my overnight kit." I waggled my eyebrows.

He reached for my hand. "You know I'm glad."

Ah. I'd guessed wrong.

"But you know how eager I am to start a family, Mac." He gazed at my face with so much intensity I had to sit back. "Don't you want to raise little ones together? We'd be good at it. I know we would."

We'd discussed this many times and had almost split up over it. I was the reluctant member of our duo. I liked my neat, orderly life, disrupted only by the occasional murder. I knew how much living with Tim and having babies would disrupt that. It would be messy and scary and a challenge. But I'd turned thirty-seven in September and was older than him by four years, at least until he hit his next Capricorn birthday. And family meant the world to me. I didn't want to lose this man or the chance to be a parent, to create a family with him. The wind pattered rain at the windows with an irregular beat. I took a deep breath and let it out.

"Shouldn't we get married first?" I cocked my head and gave him a tentative smile.

Tim stared. His gorgeous face softened. He stood and

scooped me off my chair into his arms. He hugged me so tight I couldn't breathe. He pulled back, his hands on my shoulders, and looked at me with those big blue eyes full of water.

"Yes, Mackenzie Almeida. We should get married first."

We never did get to the salad.

CHAPTER 19

By the next morning, the rain and clouds had blown through. Tim always left way before dawn to do the morning baking. His usually quick goodbye kiss as I slumbered had lingered longer than usual, and I knew I'd made my man happy with my proposal last night. Right now I was a little surprised at my own rosy, full heart. I hoped my decision wouldn't come back to bite me.

The temperature had dropped, and I'd donned gloves and a windbreaker for my morning walk with Gin. She and I swung our arms at a few minutes past seven, our habit while we speed-walked along the Shining Sea Trail, the former railroad line that ran all the way to Woods Hole. Detritus of leaves and broken branches from the storm lay everywhere, and an onshore breeze made the air smell of salt and sea. As we walked, Gin told me about her daughter's acceptance to graduate school at Brown

University an hour's drive away, and that Lucy had gotten engaged to her longtime boyfriend, as well. I smiled to myself.

"Hey, Cheshire Cat." Gin stared at me. She pulled at my arm to stop, facing me. "What's going on?"

"I took the plunge." I pulled off my left glove to show her the engagement ring Tim had slid onto my ring finger last night. He'd had it ready, just in case. The slender gold band featured a Victorian knot with a small diamond embedded in the middle.

"Girlfriend!" Gin screeched. "Oh, my gosh. I'm so happy for you." She gave me a fierce hug. "Do you have a date for the big event?"

"Are you kidding? I only proposed to him last night."

She shook her head. "I should have known you would switch roles. That guy's a big teddy bear if I ever saw one."

"It didn't bother him a bit. On the contrary. Anyway, we'll probably have a quick UU ceremony followed by a cookout in my parents' backyard. I can't imagine either of us wanting some fancy traditional wedding. Although . . ." I gazed at her. "You'll be my best woman, or whatever they call it, right?"

"Does an osprey catch fish?" She grinned. "I wouldn't miss it for anything."

"Don't tell anybody yet. I need to let my family know first."

"You got it."

"Hey, can we get walking again? I still have a shop to open, and so do you."

Gin laughed but resumed her stride. "So you got over your, shall we say, obsession with mess avoidance?"

"Apparently." Then I frowned. "But I'm totally going

to need you if the pregnancy thing happens. I can't even imagine how I'll deal with that."

"*If?* You're a healthy woman well under forty."

"A bit under forty, and you never know. To Tim's credit, he didn't suggest we wait to see if I conceive and then get married. I mean, I knew a couple who did that, crazy as it sounds. But really, if my eggs are too old or whatever, we can always adopt children. It's not like there aren't lots of kids out there who need stable, loving families." And I'd realized when I'd spoken of marriage last night that I truly wanted to spend my life with Tim. No matter what shape our family took.

We strode along in silence for a few minutes. I imagined what my future would look like. Now that I'd taken the plunge, it didn't look nearly as scary as I'd thought it would.

"Did you see Flo's latest message?" Gin asked.

I fell off my happy cloud. *Right.* We still had an unsolved homicide in town. "What? No. What did it say?"

"She looked into Ogden Hicks."

"I forgot to tell you—or text the group—I went by the furniture place yesterday and talked to him."

"And?"

I told her about his reaction to my saying I knew Lincoln. "On my way to Tim's last night, I stopped into the Quaker Meetinghouse. The lights were on and I'd never been inside. I mentioned meeting Ogden to the man setting up. He said Ogden had had a rough life, not an easy path, or words to that effect. The guy told me Ogden's wife died, and he's responsible for an adult son who had a brain injury."

"Flo wrote about the injury, but said it came about through a run-in with the police."

"I must have missed that text from her." I turned my head to look at her, but nearly tripped on a root that had pushed up pavement. "That could explain the way he reacted." I walked and thought some more.

Gin continued. "She said the son lives in a nursing home in Bourne, the Seaview Manor Care Center."

"Interesting. I also learned a tidbit from Tim about Nia Rodrigues."

"The woman who shopped at the market yesterday?" Gin asked.

"Exactly. Tim knows her because he gives away unsold bread from his back door after he closes. He saw her lurking around the DiCicero home the night before Tulia found Annette's body."

Gin's breath rushed in. "Do you think she killed Annette? But why?"

"I don't have an answer for either question. It's suspicious, for sure. But there might be some reasonable explanation."

"You need to let the group know."

"I know. More importantly, I need to tell Lincoln." I blushed. "I was a little bit occupied last night."

She elbowed me. "I can only imagine."

The path opened up to the causeway over a salt pool. An osprey circled above. I watched it plummet like the fish hawk it was, talons extended, and rise back up. The osprey clutched a struggling fish whose life had come to its end. Had Annette's killer similarly pounced to end her life?

CHAPTER 20

I called my father after I got home from my walk. "I'll
stop by at eight thirty. I need to talk to you and Mom
for a minute."

"Are you all right, Mac?" He sounded worried.

"Yes, I'm fine. Everything's fine." I didn't want to tell
them about my engagement over the phone. I knew how
happy they would be, and I really wanted to see their
faces and receive their blessing. "I'll see you then." I disconnected in a hurry before he asked me any more questions.

"Everything's fine," Belle chimed in from her perch.
"Treats?"

"You bet, but let me make my coffee first."

"Belle's a good girl. Coffee first. Coffee first. Treats?"

"You're hopeless, Belle." I gave her some frozen
grapes to shut her up and then ground my coffee and lis-

tened to it happily drip away. I took a quick shower and put in my contacts. I poured granola in a bowl, cut a banana into it, and added whole milk. My fast metabolism demanded a good-sized breakfast. I ate, sipped the dark, rich java, and admired the new adornment on my left hand. Tim knew exactly the simple kind of ring I would like and must have gotten my ring size from Mom. *Wait.* That would mean . . . my parents already knew of his plans? I laughed. It didn't matter. I planned to pretend they didn't.

"Hey, Belle, we're going to live with Tim sometime soon."

She gave the wolf whistle she always produced when she saw him or heard his name.

"I agree. He's a total hunk."

"Hey, handsome." Belle's uncanny imitation of my voice always amazed me.

"Exactly," I said. I sounded like I'd agreed with myself. "And a total sweetheart, too."

She muttered "sweetheart" over and over. I gazed around my beloved and well-designed tiny house, where everything had its place. In its efficiency, my living quarters resembled a boat that had been built to be lived on. The place featured built-in storage nooks and cupboards tucked into every available space. I hadn't moved it since the builder had finished it, but the house had always been a trailer on four wheels. Tim had a spacious backyard. After we married, we could park the house there to be used for a guest room, a retreat, or whatever. Maybe even an Airbnb property. My 400-square-foot home had a composting toilet and a propane tank and only needed hookups to water and electricity. Belle would live in the main house with us. I knew I'd miss my own space, over which I had control. Giving up some of that precious commodity felt worth it for a life with Tim.

My happy cloud once again darkened. I remembered I hadn't texted Lincoln what I'd learned about Nia Rodrigues and Ogden Hicks. I might be a blissful fiancée, but that didn't mean an unsolved homicide had magically gone away—or been solved overnight. Unless it had.

I tapped out a text to Lincoln.

Learned Ogden Hicks has disabled adult son, result of head injury in police encounter. Tim Brunelle (Greta's Grains Bakery) saw Nia Rodrigues (homeless woman) lurking at DiCicero home nine thirtyish the night before Annette's body found.

Was that it? Probably. I copied the text before I sent it, then pasted it into our book group thread and sent that. I scrolled back through the thread but didn't find any new information. I didn't know where Nia lived but I thought of one more bit for Lincoln.

Nia is Our Neighbors' Table patron. She will likely be at soup kitchen tonight at 5.

As soon as I sent the message, one came in from Norland on the group thread.

Possible Nia R knew victim in New Bedford. Digging deeper.

Interesting. If Nia had known Annette, she might have asked her for money. Or . . . I wrinkled my nose. What if they'd had some kind of history, some conflict, and Nia had tried to get back at Annette? Would she go as far as murder? Would she have crossed that line almost nobody did? But to what benefit? Regardless, a past friendship could explain Nia's presence at the DiCicero home.

I glanced at the clock. *Oops.* It read eight twenty-five already. I hurriedly gave Belle her breakfast, promised to clean her cage when I got home this afternoon, and headed out. I locked the door carefully before I left. Belle and her digital buddy Alexa had rescued me—and Belle, herself—from a homicidal attacker in the summer. I wanted to be sure another one trying to enter my house in my absence didn't have a chance.

CHAPTER 21

When I approached the parsonage on this breezy, still-brisk morning, my grandma had pulled open the door. "Abo Ree," I called.

She whirled. "Goodness, Mac, you startled me." One hand on her chest and the other on the door, she waited for me.

I kissed her cheek when I got there. "Why are you here?"

"Me?" Her rheumy eyes went wide. "Why, I'm, uh, just, well . . ." She raised her eyebrows with a vaguely panicked look, as if she searched for an answer. "Your father invited me to breakfast. Yes, that's why I'm here."

As if.

"And you?" she asked in a fake-innocent tone.

"I need to talk to him and Mom. I'm glad you're here." I held the door open. "Shall we?" We went into the somewhat worn but warm and comfortably furnished home that the church provided. My father had been the minister here since before I'd been born. This was the only home I'd known until I went away to Harvard.

Inside I followed voices to the big kitchen, the center of our family's life over the years. The pine farm table seated ten and had been dinged with dents, burns, paint, and oil. It reflected the love of a couple who had always encouraged family dining, doing art and science projects in the kitchen, and encouraging children to cook before they were quite tall enough to manage. I only prayed I could be an equally relaxed and loving mother when the time came, but I had my doubts.

Now a bottle of orange juice and four jelly jars sat on the tabletop. An aproned Pa turned with a beam toward me from the stove, where he tended a pan of cheesy scrambled eggs. "Good morning, *querida*."

Mom hurried toward me from the counter where the toaster oven sat. "Mackenzie, good morning." She threw her arms around me and hugged tight. She pulled back. "Thanks for coming, Reba."

"Hi, Mom, Pa." Tucker, the Portuguese water dog they'd adopted in the summer, mostly as a pet for Cokey, trotted up to greet me. "Hey, Tuck." I scratched his silky black head. They'd found a hypo-allergenic rescue puppy in a nod to my allergies. At five months old, he didn't come up to my waist yet, but he would after he reached his full growth. "You've gotten so big." He yipped his agreement and gave my hand a big sloppy lick.

I rubbed it off on the back of my pants and headed over to kiss Pa's cheek. "I can't stay long. I have to get to the store to open."

"You said you had news for us?" His voice had the low and resonant timbre of a news announcer or voice-over artist. It worked for a minister, too. He turned off the burner.

Seized with nerves, I took a deep breath and let it out. I extended my left hand to all three of them. "Tim and I are engaged to be married." My throat thickened, and I could barely finish.

As her eyes filled, Reba grabbed my hand with both of hers. "I knew I had a reason to live a long time." She squeezed and let go.

My parents each slung an arm around me and around Abo Reba. We held each other in a four-way embrace.

"I have the feeling you guys knew," I murmured. "This ring fits me perfectly, for example."

Mom dropped her arm. "Funny about that." Her eyes sparkled.

Pa swiped at the corner of his eyes. "Your young man came to me a while ago asking for my permission. Such an archaic practice, but I gladly gave him my blessing. He was waiting only for you to give your own permission."

Mom drew out a bottle of Cava from the fridge. "We need to celebrate." She busied herself removing the foil.

"Mom, it's not even nine o'clock!"

"A little mimosa never hurt anyone," she replied without looking at me. "Anyway, Derrick will open the shop for you."

I gaped. "You DID know."

"Tim phoned me this morning, sweetheart," Mom said. "I've never heard the man happier."

I gazed around at my joy-filled elders. I couldn't blame them. They'd waited a heck of a long time for me to settle down. I sat and accepted a jelly jar full of OJ and bubbly. I accepted their toasts. I even accepted a plate of eggs and one of Tim's cranberry scones, despite having already eaten. My family knew me as pretty much a bottomless pit when it came to breakfast.

"To Mr. and Ms. Brunelle-Almeida," Reba said.

"Or will it be Almeida-Brunelle?" Mom asked.

"I have no idea," I replied. "I truthfully haven't thought about it, nor discussed it with Tim." I clinked my glass with theirs and took a tiny sip. Breakfast drinking wasn't my idea of the optimal start to a productive day. I switched to a scone and savored its tart, sweet, perfect crumb. I glanced up. All three looked expectantly at me. "And we don't have a date yet, either. Maybe in a few weeks? November?"

"You want to move right along," Mom observed.

"Why not?" I asked. "I mean, why drag it out?"

Reba raised her eyebrows but kept her silence. I knew nothing of wedding planning. I wasn't getting any younger, and I figured becoming pregnant had to be the first priority. Mom and Reba commenced to talking of relatives they might want to invite and good places to shop for a wedding dress. I was so not into organizing this affair. If they wanted to, I had no problem with it.

I turned to my father on my right side. "Pa," I said in a soft voice. "What do you know about Nia Rodrigues?"

He set down his own jelly jar. "I might know a bit. Does this have to do with this week's events?"

"It might."

He glanced at the women. "I'll need to tell you later. All right?"

I gave a single nod. "Later today?"

"Yes."

What did he know? If he could shed light on Nia's relationship with Annette, that could be golden. At least for Lincoln.

CHAPTER 22

I didn't linger too long at the parsonage. I was back in the brisk fresh air aimed for my shop by nine thirty only slightly tipsy. Mom had suggested sending along a mimosa in a travel mug for Orlean and plain OJ for Derrick, but I told her not to. Derrick was a recovering alcoholic, and I didn't want that temptation anywhere near my shop, no matter how well he was doing. I also doubted sips of bubbly would help Orlean's fine-motor control, an important factor in working on bicycle parts.

Across Main Street from the church sat a town park. It didn't resemble the scenic green in front of the library and the town hall closer to the center of town. The town didn't maintain this rather seedier natural space very well. The various sleeping bags and ragtag tents scattered under scrubby cypress trees made the park even less visually attractive—to some. Pa always said the encampment of the homeless transformed the park into a godlier place, not something to be scorned. Certain people in town didn't agree with him. The local paper had published letters that maintained the campers should be cleared out entirely. That the park had become an eyesore and drove away tourists.

Pretty soon the temperature would make it too cold to sleep outdoors, and even now the tents and bags were drenched from the storm. Gin and I needed to get that coat drive underway, and soon. Another friend had organized a collection of socks and toiletries to give out, and I knew Zane bought a bunch of rotisserie chickens a couple of times a month and dropped them off to each temporary resident. All these were only Band-Aids on a much wider problem. But we did what we could.

I stood rooted to the sidewalk. Nia Rodrigues very likely lived in that cluster of makeshift homes. I wanted to talk with her. I also expected if I poked around in the campers' privacy, such as it was, I would be entirely unwelcome. I'd have to wait to run into her somewhere. Or . . . she would probably be at the free dinner at the end of today. I hadn't signed up to work, but I knew they rarely turned away an extra pair of experienced hands from helping out at the meals.

I moved on. When I walked into the shop, Derrick had already begun helping rental customers. He gave me a thumbs up and turned back to them. I poked my head into the repair area.

"'Morning, Orlean."

My mechanic set down her wrench and stripped the blue glove off her right hand. "Hear you have good news. Congratulations." Orlean, normally as undemonstrative as they come, extended her meaty, weathered hand.

Wow. Mom must have called Derrick and he'd shared the news. I smiled and shook her hand. "Thanks. I'm very happy."

"Brunelle's a good man. Hang onto him." She pulled the glove on again and returned to her work.

"I'll do my best." Clearly dismissed, I turned away.

"I mean it, Mac," she muttered. Orlean had been married to a man who had ended up incarcerated. The brother of my backup mechanic, Orlean's husband had been released and had come back to apologize to her, but they hadn't been able to work things out.

"So do I." I knew I had a steep learning curve in front of me. I would need to figure out how to live with Tim, how to be a mom, the works. But what was life if not a series of new things to learn?

The return of the sunshine, no matter how brisk the temperature, brought a flood of customers who sought all three Rs: repair, retail, and rental. During a momentary break Derrick hurried over and enveloped me in a massive hug. "I'm happy for you, Mackie." He pulled back, his eyes glistening.

"You're such a teddy bear, Derr. And thanks. See my pretty ring?" I showed him my left hand.

"Very nice. Tasteful and simple. That Brunelle knows what he's doing."

I agreed completely.

I stood at the register handling sales. My thoughts moved away from my future and back to the day Tulia found Annette's body. Doris had stood in this line—and not to shop. She'd made a jab at Tulia's ethnicity and complained about the discarded lobster shells. Sure, once in a while it smelled a little when Tulia's seafood compost guy hadn't picked up the barrel promptly. That rarely happened, in my experience.

As we'd discussed in the group, if Doris had known Annette, she could have thought staging her death in Tulia's walk-in would put the Lobstah Shack out of business. It was a long shot. But stranger things had happened. Maybe I'd stop by Doris's later and see what she stocked for parrot food. I usually bought Belle's food from the hardware store. The man who owned it offered a good price and often tucked in a treat for Belle, too. And I could—

The man who faced me across the counter cleared his throat. "Could I have my slip, please?"

Oops. I held the credit card receipt for his tube, patch kit, and chain lube in my hand. No more musing on murder while customers waited. "Thanks for your business, sir."

My bottom line would rejoice today. We sold three new bikes, a pre-owned children's tricycle, and a steady stream of socks, pumps, helmets, and lights.

The shop had started to empty at eleven when Mom and Abo Reba strolled in.

"I left my trike outside," Mom said. "Can Orlean fix it while we wait?"

I glanced at the repair area. "I have no idea but go ahead and ask her." I rang up the last remaining customer.

"We want to get a ride in today. The weather is glorious." My grandmother beamed and sidled up next to me. "Astra and I were thinking you should have a New Year's Eve wedding. Just imagine, your husband would never forget the date." She winked.

"But that's almost three months away." Now that I'd

taken the plunge, I wanted to jump into marriage with both feet. Some switch had turned in my brain—and my heart, to be honest—and I didn't care to delay. "Why wait so long?"

"You know you have aunties, uncles, and cousins on both sides of the family scattered everywhere. I'm sure your betrothed does, too, not to mention his mother, living on a Caribbean island the way she does. And his father in California. They're all going to want to be here. Plus, you can't rent a place with only a week's notice. Why, there's the caterer and the florist and the invitations. And what about your dress?"

I set my elbow on the counter and sank my forehead into my hand. What happened to my vision of a simple ceremony and a backyard barbecue? We sure wouldn't be able to hold an outdoor cookout on December thirty-first.

I straightened. "First things first, okay, Abo Ree? Tim and I haven't even discussed what shape our wedding should have, or when. Can you and Mom please hold off until then?"

"Hold off on what?" my mother asked, hurrying up.

"Planning my wedding without consulting Tim and me." Even though I'd thought that would be an excellent plan a couple of hours ago.

"But the planets will be in a perfect place for a union on the last day of the year." Mom's eyes sparkled. "And think of the significance!"

I set both hands on her shoulders. "Mom, I love you. I love your passion for astrology. But this is my special day, mine and Tim's. Let me talk to him and I'll get back to both of you. Soon, I promise."

"Sure, honey." Nothing dampened Astra's spirit. No

wonder she and her mother-in-law were close. "We're headed next door for lunch."

"To Tulia's?" I asked.

She nodded. "Can we bring you a sandwich? Some chowder?"

"No, thanks. I bought lunch there yesterday. Tell her I'll stop by later, will you?"

Mom agreed. I gave her and Abo Reba each a kiss on the cheek and watched them bustle out. Together—and separately—they were a force of nature. Darn, I'd wanted to ask them if they had any dirt on Doris, or even on Nia. Well, not dirt as much as information of any kind. Never mind. I'd see them later, together or apart. And I really didn't care if the stars were aligned for solving a murder this week, although I supposed it couldn't hurt. The sooner Lincoln cleared Tulia's name, the better.

CHAPTER 23

A dog dish filled with water sat outside the front door of Paws and Claws, Doris's shop, when I finally got there around two. A sign on the door advertised a doggie groom and nail-clip event on Saturday morning. Inside, Doris was busy at the register with a customer. While I waited, I poked around the shelves holding leashes, cat toys, rawhide chew bones, canned treats, and bags of food and cat litter until I came to the bird area.

Doris stocked the treats Belle liked—a dried fruit mix especially for parrots—but not her organic pelleted food, which the hardware store was happy to order for me. I gulped at the price on the treat, but I grabbed a bag and took it to the counter in the back. I couldn't believe too many locals shopped for pet food here. Maybe affluent summer people picked up their pet's food at Doris's so they didn't have to drive to the box store in Hyannis.

Tourists would want to pick up a souvenir to take back to their fur baby at home. And, obviously, all of us Main Street merchants wanted people to shop locally.

Next to the register sat a donation can from the People for Cats shelter, with a photograph of an adorable yellow kitten taped such that it stuck up behind the slot in the top of the can. Good tactic. The beast was so cute it made me want to stuff money in there, and I couldn't even be around cats.

The customer finished up and turned to go. An out-of-uniform Nikki Kimuri was the purchaser.

"Good afternoon, Officer Kimuri," I said.

She gazed at me for a moment. "Mackenzie Almeida. Hello." She grasped a green cloth bag that looked like it held lots of small cans.

"Please call me Mac."

Kimuri's gaze flicked toward Doris and then back to me. At least, I think it did. Was she telegraphing a message to me about Doris, or one to Doris about me?

"And I'm Nikki, at least when I'm out of uniform," she murmured.

Doris gazed back and forth between us. "In a town this size, you two don't know each other?" A gray and white cat leaped up onto the counter and purred. Doris stroked its long-haired coat and murmured to it.

I sneezed. "Hi, Doris. No, we only met the other day." When I showed the officer Annette's body, but Doris didn't need to know that. Nikki Kimuri wore civvies. Had she come here to shop on an undercover mission? Did the police know about Doris's movements the night or morning Annette was killed? More likely, my imagination had shifted into nutso mode, and the officer had a cat at home she needed canned food for.

"I'll see you ladies around." Nikki headed for the door. "Have a good day."

"You, too," I called in return. I laid my purchase on the counter and sneezed again, into my elbow. We'd all gotten that drummed into us during the pandemic a while ago.

"Have they . . ." Doris tilted her head toward the door. "I mean, the police, made any progress on the killing? I've heard you assist them with these things."

"Where did you hear that?" I handed her my credit card.

"I don't remember. Here and there." She busied herself with the iPad that served as her cash register.

"On the contrary." I shook my head. "They specifically asked me not to get involved. Anyway, I don't think they have anyone in custody. Have you heard about an arrest?"

"No." She turned the tablet toward me so I could scrawl an indecipherable signature with my finger.

"Did you know Tulia before you opened your shop?" The Lobstah Shack had been there for years, first opened by Tulia's mother, but I couldn't remember Doris's shop from before I left town.

"I only moved to the Cape three years ago and opened Paws and Claws shortly after that. That's when I met Tulia. I wish I had a different location, but I couldn't find any other vacant storefronts at the time."

"Do you own a house here in town?"

Doris pulled a face. "Are you kidding? Who can afford to buy in Westham?"

Ouch. A number of us could, Tim and me included, and Gin, too. But what about rentals? Were apartments really that expensive? Maybe Doris's shop didn't do very well, or perhaps she had a mountain of preexisting debt. I decided not to press her on where she lived. A half dozen framed pictures adorned the wall behind the counter. Five were of cats or dogs or both, but one showed a young, dark-haired woman in gown, sash, and tiara. I peered at it. You couldn't miss a resemblance to Doris.

"It looks like your daughter won a beauty pageant." I pointed to the photograph.

Doris's nostrils flared for a second. "I don't have a daughter, Mac."

"I'm sorry."

She mustered a smile, turning to glance at the picture. "That's me in my younger days. I won the Miss Rhode Island crown."

Wow. The years hadn't been kind to her. Could I rescue myself? "I picked up the resemblance to you right away. I'm not surprised you won."

"I sang an aria from *Bolero* for the talent portion." She set a hand on her thick waist and smoothed back her hair in a ghostly gesture from her past. "And I coached other girls for years after that."

"Did you coach Annette DiCicero?"

Doris didn't answer for a moment. "As a matter of fact, I did. She became one of my biggest successes. She wasn't DiCicero then. Her maiden name was Andrade."

A Portuguese moniker, a common heritage in this seacoast region with its history of fishing and whaling.

Three high school girls pushed through the door and started to squeal about how wicked cute the dog collars, vests, and toys were.

"I'd better run." I picked up the parrot treat. "Nice to chat with you."

She blinked "Anytime, Mac." In a murmur, her gaze

on the girls, she added, "The tall one was Miss Junior
Barnstable County last year." To the students, she called
out, "Can I help you, girls?"

I slid past the girls. The former Miss Whatever, in a
pale pink sweater that brought out her peaches-and-
cream complexion, exclaimed to her friends, "Wouldn't
my Jojo be totes adorbs in this pink collar?"

Maybe Jojo would be a complete darling in pink, as
her owner already was. The world of beauty contests was
completely foreign to me and seemed completely archaic,
too. But apparently women and girls still competed for
beauty crowns. And I—or rather, Lincoln Haskins—might
need to delve more deeply into that world. Doris had had
a close connection to Annette in the past, on a competi-
tive and possibly cutthroat circuit. Had they had a connection in the present, too? Had Annette threatened to
reveal a fact about Doris, some bit of past wrongdoing, a
threat that led to Doris terminating Annette's life?

CHAPTER 24

Wearing a frown, I walked with slow steps the few yards toward the Lobstah Shack. Had I indulged in flights of fancy about Doris, or did her pageant past—and possible conflict with Annette—merit further investigation? That world had to be a complicated one. Combine ambition and aspiration with women's self-image and the culture's ideal of beauty. The possibility of backstabbing, sabotage, revenge, or worse had to be in the mix. And had I imagined that Nikki Kimuri had sent me an unspoken message about Doris? If so, I hadn't understood it.

My hand rested on the Lobstah Shack front door when my phone rang with the Beach Boys ringtone I'd programmed in for Tim. I stepped away from the door, looking forward to a bright light to erase my frown.

"Hi, handsome." I could hear the happy in my voice.

A white-haired gentleman ambling by turned in surprise. A little sheepish, I waved and pointed to my phone. He smiled and nodded before he strolled on.

"How's my beautiful fiancée?" Tim sounded breathless. "Sorry, I just finished my run."

"It's a good day for one." I held out my left hand to admire the ring. "I'm well. And happy. And standing outside the Lobstah Shack, where I'm pretty sure I can obtain dinner to go if you'd like to join me in a few hours."

"Don't you have book club tonight?"

Oh. "It's Thursday, isn't it? Nobody has mentioned actually talking about the book." Come to think of it, I hadn't checked my texts in a while. "Even if we're meeting, I'll still need to eat. Come by at five thirty? I want to see you."

"I'll be there, with bells on." He gave a growl.

"Ha! I want to see that." We ended in several gooey endearments before I disconnected. I still beamed when I walked into the restaurant, but my smile quickly slid away.

Tulia, fists on hips, scowled at Victoria Laitinen. The diminutive chief, my high school nemesis, glared right back. Her arms, elbows out, hung at her sides in that stance I'd only seen officers of the law use.

"I don't know why you want that," Tulia spat out.

Sofia watched from behind the counter but busied herself with her work. Last summer she'd been wary of any police officer. She'd said her work visa was in order, but she'd seen the kinds of raids the authorities had been making. I didn't blame her for a desire to stay far from the scrutiny of someone like Victoria.

Victoria kept her voice calm. "The detective needs to see any email correspondence with Annette DiCicero. It's about the proposed Columbus Day change and is part of the warrant he obtained Tuesday afternoon."

"I'm supposed to turn over the password to my personal email? So Lincoln can read everything I've ever written or received?" Tulia whipped her head to look at me. "Mac, can they do that?"

I gave a little finger wave. "Hi, Victoria."

The chief rolled her eyes. "Why am I not surprised you're involved in this?"

"Hey, Tulia is my friend, and I came in to buy takeout for dinner." I fixed my gaze on Tulia. "About the email, I'm pretty sure they can. Did they take your laptop? Did Flo give you the name of a lawyer the other day?"

"I don't have the bucks for a lawyer, Mac. After Lincoln got that warrant, I had to let them take the laptop, but I use Gmail. My email is in the cloud, not on my computer."

"Does Lincoln need a separate search warrant for email?" I asked Victoria. I had no idea if he did or not, but I might as well try to find out.

She tucked a strand of her white-blond hair behind her ear, an out-of-character gesture for Victoria. I hadn't seen her with her hair out of a stern bun since we'd graduated from Westham High almost twenty years ago, but now she'd gotten it cropped into an ear-length do.

"Ms. Peters, our guy can get into your email. It's easier if you turn over the password. Detective Haskins has the permission to search based on the initial warrant."

"All right." Tulia stalked to the counter and scribbled on an order form. "This make you happy?" She thrust the slip of paper at the chief.

"Thank you. We'll be in touch." The bell on the door jangled when Victoria left.

Tulia plopped into a chair. She propped her elbow on the table and sank her chin onto her hand. "Am I completely screwed, Mac?"

"What?" I perched opposite. "You are not."

She glanced at Sofia and lowered her voice. "I didn't kill Annette. How can I make them understand that?"

"Just stick to the truth. And know the group is on this. I dropped in next door before I came here, and I have a few thoughts about Doris."

"You do?" She gaped at me.

"Have you ever looked at the photographs behind the counter?"

"Mac. You know I don't have any pets. And if I did, I wouldn't shop at that rip-off store."

"Doris was Miss Rhode Island back in the day."

Tulia studied my face like I'd transformed into an alien. "What do you mean?"

"She was a beauty queen. And then she coached other women. Actually, girls was how she put it." I waited as Tulia put it together.

"Including Annette?"

"Including Annette."

CHAPTER 25

By three I'd arrived back in my shop. I stashed Tulia's shrimp chowder and Irish shepherd's pie in the mini fridge. The place was quiet enough to check my texts. A flurry of messages over the last hour among the book group members had resulted in an agreement to meet at Derrick's tonight to talk about *Fogged Inn*. I glanced around the bike shop, but I didn't see my brother.

"Orlean, where's Derrick?" I called.

"Had to pick up the girls."

"Girls, plural?"

"He said Cokey's bringing a friend. He'll be right back."

Sure enough, five minutes later Derrick hurried in carrying two miniature pink backpacks. Cokey followed, holding hands with a dark-haired little girl in a purple dress with green striped leggings. This had to be Kendall DiCicero.

"Titi Mac, look who I bringed!"

I squatted down to hug Cokey. "Is this Kendall?" I smiled at the girl.

She nodded without speaking or smiling, her chocolate-brown eyes enormous in a heart-shaped face.

I held out my hand. "I'm pleased to meet you, Kendall. I'm Mac, and this is my bike shop."

She nodded again, extending her hand. I shook it gently. With an adult, I would have expressed my sympathies. I decided against it with Kendall. I didn't know if that was the right thing to do, but I didn't want to upset her. I thought it better to let her have fun with her friend, to simply be a little kid.

Cokey whispered to me in a loud lisp, "She's shy." She pulled her friend toward the children's bicycle area. "Come on. I'll show you the bikes and then we can draw, okay?"

"I have your snacks when you're ready, girls," Derrick called after them. "Sorry, Mac. Pa had a meeting and Cokey insisted she wanted to play with Kendall. Phil will pick her up by four."

"You know that's not a problem." *Huh.* That reminded me. Pa said he'd get back to me today to talk about Nia. He must have gotten too busy. "You know this is a family-friendly shop, and I'm interested in meeting Phil. He must be pretty broken up."

"Haven't seen him yet. We texted about the arrangement."

"So book group plans to meet tonight at the lighthouse?" I asked.

"Right. You hadn't responded, and everybody seemed to want to gather. Have you finished the book?"

"Not at all. You?"

"Nope. You know we'll probably end up in a discussion about . . ." His voice trailed off. He glanced at the girls, who now sat on the floor in a corner with paper and crayons.

"I imagine so."

Business picked up again, but the girls stayed out of the way. Derrick gave them their string cheese, little bags of Cheez-Its, and juice boxes. They sat on the floor in the corner and played with the small toys I kept in a basket behind the counter for Cokey. Then, with intent, focused expressions, they resumed drawing with the crayons and paper I kept on a low shelf.

Cokey ran up to me at one point. "Titi Mac, why do both our names begin with the 'kuh' sound, but Kendall writes hers with a K and mine starts with a C?" She wore the expression of a serious researcher perplexed about the inconsistencies of orthography.

"English is funny that way, *querida*." I stroked her head. "Both ways are fine to spell that sound." English had way more confusing ways to spell than that.

She ran back and whispered to Kendall. The art efforts resumed.

Phil DiCicero appeared a few minutes after four. Derrick was busy with rental customers, and Kendall didn't appear to notice her father. I approached with my hand out.

"Phil? I'm Mac Almeida, Derrick's sister."

His thick hand matched his neck. "Phil DiCicero."

"I'm very sorry for your loss," I murmured.

"That's what everyone says." He dropped my hand and ran his over his big square head and his thick, nearly black hair that hung over his collar. "Did you know my wife?"

"She'd been in a few times and we'd had the kind of chat one does with customers. So no, not really."

"I hope my daughter hasn't been a bother." He gazed at the giggling girls, and his expression softened.

"Not a bit." I straightened a pair of cycling shorts on a display. "I met your partner yesterday."

He whipped his face back toward me. "Ogden?" He stiffened.

"Yes. I have a small table that needs to be refinished and I stopped by your shop."

Phil's stance relaxed. "Ah. That's what we do. I hope he helped you."

"He gave me a quote, but I'm not sure it's in my budget right now. You guys do fabulous work. The before and after pictures you have in the office are impressive."

"Thank you. Needless to say, I haven't been in this week. I have a lot to arrange. And the police, well . . ."

The police, who were likely spending a good deal of time questioning him about the death, about Annette's habits and movements in the days leading up to her murder, about his own whereabouts.

Phil pressed his lips into a line. "They won't even let me have Annette's body yet. How can I arrange a funeral without a body?" He shook his head in disgust.

"Daddy!" Kendall ran toward her father and threw her arms around his legs.

"Hi, princess. Ready to go home?" He tousled her hair.

Cokey joined us. "Hi, Mr. DiCicero."

"Thanks for playing with my girl, Cokey."

"We're going to have a sleepover on Saturday, right, Kendall?"

Kendall glanced up at Phil. "Can I, Daddy? Cokey lives in a lighthouse. Please?"

"We'll see, honey." To me, he said, "Thanks for having her, Mac. Is Derrick here?"

"He's probably outside with rental customers." I pointed to the side door. "Oh, and here's Kendall's backpack."

Phil grabbed the pack and headed out.

Cokey gave Kendall a big hug. "See you tomorrow."

"See you." Kendall looked up at me. "Thank you, Titi Mac."

"You're welcome here any time." I watched the girls skip out, hand in hand. Kendall had been quiet around me but not weepy, and she'd certainly relaxed playing with Cokey. Her father also hadn't been weepy, man-style. Did he grieve about his wife's death, other than for his daughter losing her mommy? I couldn't tell. He'd gotten his back up when I said I'd met Ogden at the shop. But why?

CHAPTER 26

Customers dwindled to zero at the shop, and we didn't have any rentals due in. I sent Derrick and Orlean home at five and closed up. Bag of takeout dinner in hand, I turned toward my house.

Wait. I'd wanted to see if I could talk with Nia Rodrigues at the soup kitchen. Tim had texted me that he wouldn't be over until closer to six. They would have started dinner service in the church basement a few minutes ago. And I needed to stop calling it a soup kitchen. Similarly to the free food market not being labeled a food pantry, the soup kitchen organizers called the twice-weekly Our Neighbor's Table event their Free Dinner. They rarely served soup, anyway, and always sent diners home with an extra serving of the meal to enjoy later.

Five minutes later I'd aproned up and had been assigned to table tidying, meaning when a diner left, I wiped the table and finished clearing if they hadn't taken their plate and utensils to the window. I couldn't have asked for a more perfect job for a neat freak like me.

The organization regularly served a hundred or more people at these dinners. I waved to Norland on the line of servers. He dished out portions of a steaming mac and cheese to diners before they moved on. Also on the menu tonight were a colorful coleslaw, slices of ham, and dishes of apple crisp. My empty stomach grumbled to see—and smell—the array.

A family of four cleared their places and left. I headed to their table with my damp rag, a clean dishtowel slung over my shoulder. I'd wiped the table dry when Nia shuffled up. I hadn't seen her go through the line, but she held a tray with a brimming plate, a dish of dessert, and a plastic cup of milk.

"That looks good." I smiled at her. "Nia, right?"

She squinted at me as she sat. "How do you know who I am?"

"I checked you in at the free food market yesterday, remember? I'm Mac Almeida."

"Right. You do-gooders get around." She forked in a big bite of mac and cheese.

Ouch. But correct. I was fortunate that I'd never been food deprived. I'd never had to go without a meal or weigh the relative merits of groceries against rent or medicine. And I wanted to give back, to pay some of my good fortune forward.

"I heard you were friends with Annette DiCicero," I murmured, even though the clink of forks on dishes and the buzz of conversation would make it hard for anyone but her to hear what I said.

Nia froze.

"I'm sorry for your loss," I went on.

She set down her fork. "Who did you hear that from?"

"Somebody I know. It doesn't matter."

"Annette and I used to be friends. Long time ago. I didn't get a chance to talk to her again before she died."

Was murdered, more precisely. "Where did you know her from, if you don't mind my asking?"

"It doesn't matter." She echoed my phrasing.

"Annette came from New Bedford. Were you friends there?" I pushed my luck here, but I had to try.

"Lady, it doesn't matter. She's dead." She dug into the coleslaw and didn't look up.

A thin man with shaggy hair and duct tape covering the elbows of his jacket brought a full tray to the table. Nia glanced at him and nodded.

"Good evening, ma'am. May I have the pleasure of dining with you?" He gave a little bow to Nia.

"Please, Witter. Sit down." To me she rolled her eyes a little at his formality.

"My name is Witter, ma'am." He inclined his head to me. "Will you be joining us?"

"Nice to meet you, Witter. I'm Mac, and no, thank you. I'm supposed to be working."

"Very well." He sat and unfolded his paper napkin with a flourish onto his lap.

Three people vacated a table and a line of others holding full trays waited to sit.

"Good to chat with you both," I said. "Enjoy your meal."

Nia didn't acknowledge me. I got busy clearing and wiping. Some diners hurried through their meals, but every time I glanced over, Nia still sat alone with her friend. I'd set down a stack of dirty plates when I heard a familiar voice nearby.

"Elenia?" Doris, holding her own tray of food, stood in front of Nia. "Elenia Rodrigues?"

Elenia? From here Nia looked taken aback.

And . . . shopkeeper Doris needed a free dinner? She must be harder up than she'd let on. The table next to Nia's had conveniently emptied. Off I went with my rag.

After she plopped onto the seat across from Nia—or Elenia—Doris caught sight of me. She lifted her chin as if she was feeling defensive about taking a free meal. "Hello, Mac."

It surprised me she'd come for a free dinner, but I didn't care one way or the other. "Hi, Doris. I see you know Nia."

"I know *Elenia*, or used to." She stressed the name and gave her tablemate a steely look. "I coached her for competitions, didn't I?"

Elenia sank her forehead onto her hand. I'd been right about the beauty under her veneer of hardship.

"Elenia is such a pretty name," I said gently. These two had some history, and I should probably bow out before I got labeled a total Susie Snoop.

"It is a beautiful name befitting a beautiful lady." Witter's smile lacked half its teeth but that didn't dim its wattage for Elenia. He beamed next at Doris. "As are you, ma'am. My name is Witter and I am delighted to make your acquaintance."

Doris ignored him. Out of the corner of my eye I spied Norland looking intently at Witter. The retired chief saw me and nodded. He made a little pointing gesture, but I couldn't figure out who he'd signaled for me to watch.

Elenia pushed up to her feet. She grabbed both sides of

her tray and leaned forward over it. She glared at Doris. "Some coach you were," she snapped. "You coached me right into second place. I needed that prize money way more than Annette did. My family had nothing, and you knew it. My beauty was supposed to be the ticket out of poverty for all of us."

Doris opened her hands, palms up. "I acted as a coach, not a judge."

"You could have fixed it."

Whoa.

"You told me you would." Elenia's shoulders slumped, the fire drained out of her.

"I never would have said that." Doris gave a nervous laugh.

"And look at me now. I'm a bum." Elenia picked up the tray and trudged away.

"As are many of us, for many reasons," Witter observed sagely.

Doris shot me a glance. "She's obviously lying about the pageant."

Somebody had lied, for sure. But maybe not Elenia.

CHAPTER 27

I clinked my glass of white wine with Tim a few minutes
past six. "Cheers." We sat inside at my not-refinished
table. The temperature at sunset made it too chilly to dine
on the patio.

He returned the sentiment and took a sip. "How did
your first day as an engaged woman go?"

"Happy." A blush crept up my cheeks. "And full.
Yours?"

"Same, except I wasn't a woman." He nudged my foot
with his.

"Very funny." I savored my first spoonful of shrimp
chowder. The combination of corn, cut-up shrimp, and
heavy cream with stock—even if the base was commer-
cially produced—made a delicious soup worthy of a gold
medal. Better Tulia than me. I'd never gotten into cooking. Between takeout, and Tim's and my parents' meals, I

didn't suffer a bit. I could nuke a frozen entree with the best of them, and I found nothing wrong with a peanut butter sandwich for dinner in a pinch.

"Speaking of being engaged, we need to talk about the actual event," I said. "Mom and Reba are already full-steam ahead with plans for our wedding."

"Why does that not surprise me?" A fond smile played around his lips. "What have they dreamed up for us?"

"I told them to hold off, that we hadn't even discussed it yet. Do you have thoughts about how you'd like us to get married?"

"Other than soon?" Tim took a bite of chowder. "Keeping it simple, I think. You know, not a big fancy event. Joseph doing the honors, if he will, followed by a nice party with our friends and family. Right?"

"That's exactly what I had imagined. However . . ." I finished my soup and buttered a hunk of the baguette Tim had brought and warmed.

"However?"

"What about your mom? She'll need to make travel plans." I wrinkled my nose. "Abo Reba talked about aunties and cousins who'll want to come. And you'll invite your sister, right? I know you're not close, but—"

"I'll want my whole family with us." He frowned at his empty bowl. "Mom would hop on a plane tomorrow. Dad would, too, but Jamie might have to make some arrangements." His sister in Seattle, a single mom of three, had issues he'd only hinted at to me.

"Then Astra and Reba started talking about flowers and food. A venue. A dress. Abo Reba suggested New Year's Eve for the date, which is months away." I blew an exasperated raspberry. "Ugh. Why does it have to be so complicated?"

Tim reached for my hand. "We'll figure it out, sweet-heart. Right now I want to try Tulia's Irish shepherd's pie, and you have book group to get to."

"Right."

Tim dished up a portion of the fish pie topped with mashed potatoes. The base looked creamy, studded with still-green peas, and full of a flaky white fish with bits of smoked salmon scattered throughout. Tulia had added a sharp cheddar to the topping, from the taste of it.

"Wow," I said after I sampled it. "Tulia outdid her-self."

He swallowed his own forkful. "She absolutely did. Around here I always think of seafood with Cape Ver-dean and Portuguese influences. But we all know Ireland is surrounded by ocean, too, only a more northern one."

Elenia Rodrigues had Portuguese heritage. Annette did, too. "I learned Nia Rodrigues's real name today."

"Oh?"

"Yes. It's Elenia. She'd been a beauty pageant finalist in her younger years. We were right about her good looks underneath."

Tim cocked his head. "How odd. Why use a name like Nia when she has such a musical one?"

"I know one reason people change their names."

"To hide their identities?"

"Exactly. Except she gave out her real last name at the free food market yesterday." I blinked, thinking.

"One can always claim a nickname for their first name. I suppose changing a last name would involve a fake ID and such." He held up his hand. "Not that I have any direct knowledge of that."

Funny. I believed him, naturally. But in the last year, I'd become aware of how many people harbor secrets.

Some harmless, a few not that harmless. Tim would know about false identification from books and movies and TV shows, same way I did. At least I hoped that was the way he'd learned about it. Did he have secrets I didn't know about? He would be my husband soon. We hadn't talked much about what he'd done other than surfing before he landed in Westham. We needed to do so. I fingered my ring. I loved this man, and I trusted him. I'd never seen a thing to cause me not to. And hoped I never would.

CHAPTER 28

I trudged up the circular staircase to the second floor of Derrick's lighthouse with my brain also going around and around. Tim and I hadn't come up with any concrete wedding plans, while the questions about Annette's murder were also a swirl. And Pa hadn't gotten back to me about Elenia. I'd called him as I walked over here, but he hadn't answered.

In the cozy living room, a purple-pajamaed Cokey was demanding to be allowed to stay up. Derrick said no. He frantically tidied magazines and toys, and Flo stood in intense conversation with Norland, wine glass already in hand.

"Come on, Cokester." I held out my hand to her. "Let's go read a book in bed."

"Will you tell me a story about Princess Seashell instead, Titi Mac?"

"Your wish is my command, my sweet." Cokey's real name was Coquille, which meant seashell in French. I shut the door to her room behind us and switched on the seashell night light. I tucked her into bed and lay down beside her.

"Once upon a time there was a brave and strong young princess named Seashell." I figured part of my job as an auntie was to counter all the comments girls typically got about their looks. I led with "brave and strong" to describe the princess every time.

"She was pretty, too," Cokey added. She always did. She held a small pink blanket to her cheek and rubbed her thumb on the satin ribbon edging it. It had been her comfort object ever since Derrick had brought her back to Westham to live. "And she had a pet unicorn."

"She was very pretty. She had a pet unicorn, who had traveled to visit his sister in the next land, and the princess was on her own. One day in the fall Seashell left the castle and walked down to the market in the town. She saw the man who sewed clothes for the local children arguing with the old woman cobbler."

"Abo Astra made me a berry cobbler in the summertime," she lisped. "We ate it with ice cream."

I pictured a little round blue shoemaker. "Berry cobbler is yummy. But a cobbler is also someone who makes and fixes shoes. Anyway, Seashell was good at listening. She asked the two what was the matter."

"Titi Mac, Kendall's a good listener, too. She told me her daddy and mommy were fighting. It was the last time she saw her mommy."

Uh-oh. Fighting right before Annette was killed? I gazed at my niece. "That's too bad. Did she say what they were fighting about?"

"She didn't know. Her mommy went off to work and her daddy made some soup."

Was this a kindergartner's non sequitur? "Does Kendall like soup?" Phil didn't seem like the domestic type, but what did I know?

"I don't think so. They took some to her grandma, but her daddy left a bowl for her mommy."

My eyes went wide. *Soup?* What if Phil added seafood to his wife's soup? He could have killed her with it. My breath rushed in, but I tried to cover it with a cough so I wouldn't alarm Cokey.

"He writed a note, too." Her face brightened. "I'm learning to write in school, Titi Mac."

"I know." What had the note said? Had it been a garden-variety couple's squabble or a more serious conflict? I assumed Lincoln and company would have found the note—if Phil hadn't destroyed it. Maybe he was trying to cover his tracks or lead the police in the wrong direction. "You showed me your writing last week."

"I'm gonna write a book about Princess Seashell. Finish the story, Titi."

I put poisoned soup out of my mind. "The princess listened carefully to both the man and the woman. She asked them some questions, and they realized they weren't really mad at each other. Her unicorn flew home." I knew I had to end the story with the unicorn back with the princess and with the two sharing a meal. "The princess ate lunch with him, and they all lived happily ever after."

Cokey's eyes had drifted shut. If I didn't get out of here soon, mine would, too. I kissed her forehead. "Good night, sweetie. Sleep with the angels."

"'Night, Titi."

Back in the living room, the crew had assembled. Zane

sat next to Gin with Tulia on the other side, and Derrick had set out cheese and crackers, plus a bowl of popcorn and a plate of Thin Mint cookies courtesy of our local Girl Scouts.

"Barbara Ross must really like to cook," Derrick said. "All the recipes in *Fogged Inn* are for complicated entrees. I didn't try to make any of them."

We liked to make one of the foods mentioned in the cozy mystery we read, whether the book included recipes or not. That plan didn't always work out for an evening meeting.

"I believe it's the author's husband who comes up with the recipes," Tulia offered. "On a blog somewhere she wrote that she doesn't cook at all except for baking Christmas cookies."

"Speaking of husbands," Gin said. "Before we start, let's have a toast to soon-to-be-married Mac and Tim. Show them, Mac."

My cheeks warmed, but I extended my left hand.

"Ooh, girlfriend, that's a wicked nice ring," Zane gushed.

Derrick lifted his can of flavored seltzer. "To Mac and Tim."

I clinked my glass with his drink, and with everyone's. Even though my brother was in recovery, he'd said he was fine with us bringing wine to book group. I was proud of his progress.

"How did I miss that ring this afternoon?" Tulia shook her head.

"Thanks, everybody," I said. "Tulia, we had other things to talk about."

"When is the happy occasion?" Norland gave me his avuncular beam.

"We don't have a date yet, but you're all invited. And you might want to reserve New Year's Eve, just in case." Had I resigned myself to waiting that long? Apparently.

"I like that idea," Flo said.

"Tulia, how are you, hon?" Gin asked. "I'm glad you came."

"I've been better. I want to thank you all for supporting me, buying lunches and takeout and so on." She sniffed and gazed around the circle. "It means a lot. Detective Haskins making an arrest so people around town will stop giving me the stink eye? That would mean a lot, too."

"Let's hope he's getting close," I said.

Derrick held up a hand. "Wait. Mac, is Cokey asleep?"

"She went right out after she got the obligatory Princess Seashell story."

"Thank you, as always, for that." Derrick pointed at me. "You're a pro with her."

I guess I was. Cokey made it easy, though. She was such a burst of sweetness and energy. "I love telling her stories." I frowned. "Do the rest of you know Cokey is friends with Annette and Phil's daughter, Kendall?"

All except Derrick shook their heads. I continued. "Cokey told me something that might be significant." I sipped the wine Gin had handed me when I sat. "Kendall told her that her parents were fighting the day before Annette's murder. She said Annette went to work and Phil made soup."

"By 'work' she must have meant Annette going to the library," Flo said.

"I'd agree," I said. "Then they took the soup to Kendall's grandma but left a bowl for Annette, with a note.

What if Phil purposely added shellfish to the soup to kill Annette?"

"That's exactly what I was thinking, Mac." Gin gave me a keen gaze.

"And took their daughter to his mother's for the night because he didn't want Kendall to witness the death." Flo said.

Zane swore. "That's too awful to even think about."

Norland pointed at Zane. "Somebody killed the poor woman."

"And somebody left her in my walk-in," Tulia added.

"What if it's two people?" I asked. "One poisoned her, and one broke into the Lobstah Shack, dumped her body, and stabbed her."

"Way to confuse the issue, Mackie," Derrick said. "Just kidding, but whoever did it must have known she was already dead."

"I know," I said. "Norland, at the free dinner earlier, did you send me a silent message about one of the people at that table?"

"I've heard a little buzz about that man."

"His name is Witter," I added.

"Yes," Norland said. "He lives at the homeless encampment and has a record of multiple incarcerations. The authorities are looking into whether he had a connection with the murder."

"That's too bad. He seemed gracious," I murmured.

"Gracious doesn't exempt him from criminal activity," Norland said.

No, it wouldn't.

"Now, about *Fogged Inn*," Flo began.

Gin sipped her wine. "I, for one, didn't come close to finishing it. Anybody?"

"I sure didn't," Zane agreed. "I wanted to, but it's been that kind of a week."

Nobody else had read the whole book, either.

"It's a great read," I said. "I didn't want to put it down, but with Annette's death and her body at Tulia's, I couldn't concentrate."

By the reactions in the room, everyone agreed.

"We can extend the discussion to next week," Flo pointed out. "It's not like anyone but us cares if we read a book a week or not." She pulled out her signature yellow legal pad and tapped it. "What have we learned about the case?"

"I've uncovered a couple more puzzle pieces, even though I don't know where they go," I said. "Doris used to coach beauty pageant contestants. She coached Annette. A woman who is a patron of Our Neighbor's Table competed with Annette when they were younger."

"Nia Rodrigues?" Norland asked.

"Yes, but her real name is Elenia. Doris coached her, too. They talked about it at the dinner a couple hours ago. Elenia told me she'd tried to see Annette but hadn't succeeded before she died. Tim knows Elenia, because he gives out free bread when he closes the bakery. He said he saw her lurking around Annette's house the night she died."

"Elenia was runner-up the year Annette won Miss New Bedford," Norland said. "I've been digging."

"She must have been the other girl," Gin mused.

I bobbed my head. "Elenia said Doris told her she would fix the contest so Elenia would win. She claimed Doris had ruined her life, more or less."

The group digested all that for a moment.

"So this Elenia is lying, and she killed Annette," Flo mused.

"How did she get her into my cooler?" Tulia asked.

I shook my head. "I'm sure she doesn't have a car."

"Would Doris have any reason to hold a grudge against Annette?" Gin asked.

"She sure holds one against me." Tulia pulled a wry face.

Flo glanced down at her scribblings, then back up. "All I can say is, what a mess. We'd better hope Haskins is doing a better job than we are."

Hope and pray and keep our fingers crossed, too.

CHAPTER 29

I woke up to a text from Gin at six thirty the next morning. She wrote that she didn't feel well enough to
walk. I decided to take the day off, too. I turned over and
hoped to snooze for another half hour, but I'm a total fail
at sleeping in. My brain starts going, and more rest be-
comes a lost cause. And when my thoughts were laser focused on the entirely confusing facts and hints of a
murder case? Forget about it.

I slid out of bed and reconsidered the idea of a solo fast
walk. The outdoor thermometer read sixty-two, and the
forecast was for a perfect fall day in the high seventies,
which meant it would be busy at the shop. Despite how
good brisk exercise would be for my overall wellness, I
thought a quiet hour around the house might be even better. Maybe I could do a little research too.

"Good morning, Belle." I lifted the cover to her cage and opened the door.

"Good morning. Hi, handsome. How ya doin'? Sleep well? Okay, take care, talk to ya soon. Alexa, take a shopping list. Grapes. Peanuts. What's up, Mom? Sure, no problem. Snacks, Mac?" Belle often ran through an entire repertoire first thing in the morning, like an actor warming up her vocal folds.

Even though what she did was more like warming up her vocalization engine. Birds used a completely different physical mechanism to speak than humans did. I'd read up on how a parrot talked. Sounds were produced from an organ called a syrinx at the base of the trachea. Also, I now made sure I powered down the Alexa until I needed to use it. After Belle had learned to talk to Alexa—who talked back—my parrot had started ordering her own groceries. I'd gotten a very odd delivery last summer heavily slanted toward Belle's favorite foods. Now she could talk to Alexa all she wanted. Her digital buddy just wouldn't be listening. After I'd bought the device, Alexa—and her swoopy yellow overlords—listening to whatever went on in my life became way too creepy.

After I started my dark roast brewing, I nuked Belle's breakfast, a quinoa and pinto bean mix she loved. I made sure it wasn't too hot before I set it on her blue and green tropical place mat on the floor. I settled in at the table with my coffee, a pad of paper, and a gel pen. One way to quiet my brain was to write down what I knew and didn't know. Once again last night we'd come away without assigned action items. Flo had definitely lost her edge, but none of the rest of us had thought of it, either. I figured if

I could come up with a list, I'd assign research tasks to the group myself.

Across the top of the first sheet I wrote "Suspects, Motive, Alibi, Questions." Under Suspects I began a list:

Phil
Doris
Elenia
Ogden?
Witter?

I scowled at the headings Motives and Alibi and tapped pen on paper. I didn't have a clear idea of why any of them would want Annette dead. And I didn't have a clue to all those folks' whereabouts during the period of time Annette must have died.

I focused on a possible motive for Phil. Maybe he had a lover stashed somewhere he'd rather be with. Or had taken out a big insurance policy on his wife. It should be possible to check either of those. Or perhaps he'd gotten so soured on Annette that his well-known temper flared up. In the Questions column I jotted, "Lover? Insurance policy?"

I couldn't think of a single reason Doris would have killed Annette except to discredit Tulia. On the other hand, the younger former beauty queen—Annette—might have had her own dark side. Maybe she knew dirt about Doris and had blackmailed her, which would explain Doris's financial straits. Next to Doris's name, I wrote, "Why poor? Being blackmailed?" in the last column.

And then we had Elenia, former competitor of Annette's. Would she have asked Annette for money, been refused, and lashed out? She'd appeared wistful that she hadn't had a chance to talk with Annette before she died. Elenia had seemed most angry with Doris. The pet shop owner might want to watch her back. "Annette refused to give her money?" and "Why homeless?" were the only questions I could think of for the homeless woman.

I'd placed a question mark next to Ogden. I didn't have an actual reason to include him on the Suspects list, but he was Phil's business partner. And . . . Annette did the books for the furniture restoration company. What if she'd discovered some financial discrepancies in trans-actions Ogden had carried out and confronted him? That idea earned him a "Cheating the business?" entry.

Witter was a complete unknown. I'd loved his flowery speech and gracious manners, but I knew nothing else of him. And, as Norland had pointed out, gracious didn't mean he hadn't acted badly.

Which circled me back to Phil. Maybe he'd been the one who had cooked the books. Annette had accused him. He'd killed her. To the Questions column across from his name, I added, "Cooking the books? Did Phil do it?"

"Did Phil do it?" Belle asked.

Ugh. I must have been talking aloud.

"Did Phil do it?" Belle cocked her head. "Did Phil do it?"

"I don't know, Belle. Do you?"

"I don't know. Snacks, Mac?"

When I caught sight of the clock I swore, but silently. I didn't want to teach the bird any worse words than she al-ready knew. The clock read eight fifteen and I'd neither eaten nor showered. I took two more minutes to tap out a group text. I listed my suspects and the questions for each and ended it with a plea.

Sign up for action items!

Everybody in the group had different strengths, contacts, and research tools at their disposal. We'd figure this out even if Lincoln didn't. I added one more line.

But stay safe doing it. Online or behind the scenes only.

Now all I had to do was follow my own advice.

CHAPTER 30

I almost didn't make it, but by nine I had the shop open and ready for business. A good thing I did, because a man walking a bike approached on the sidewalk. A customer? I hung out the Open flag and took a second look.

"Good morning, Mr. Carter." I greeted the Quaker I'd met the other evening.

"Please call me Silas." Wearing a flat-brimmed hat—not a helmet—he wheeled an ancient red single-speed bike. "I am confronted with a flat tire, Ms. Almeida. Would you possibly have a moment to repair it for me? I formerly did my own repairs, but these arthritic hands simply aren't up to the task anymore." He gazed at his knobby knuckles. "'Tis the way of the old."

Orlean didn't come in until ten on Fridays, and he was the first customer. This morning, I didn't have "a lot of people asking for my time," as Joni Mitchell had put it. I had plenty of time to change a tire.

"I'd be happy to, but please call me Mac. Wheel her on in." I gestured to the door and showed him the way to the repair area. I was a fully competent bike mechanic—which had given me the idea to open the shop—and had subbed in for Orlean many a time. It helped organize my thoughts, too, when I was intent on keeping the parts of a derailleur or a wheel assembly in order.

I hoisted the bike on the repair stand and spun the wheel. "How old is this machine, anyway?"

Wearing the suspenders he'd sported the first time we met, he leaned against the door jamb. "We Friends believe in simplicity, and for me that includes not purchasing a new version when the old one will do. I've had this bicycle since I attended Earlham College as an undergraduate. And believe thee me, that was a long time ago." He stroked his long snowy beard, his eyes bright in a nearly unlined face.

He looked to be over seventy. Which made the bike, well, old. "You know, single-speed bikes are making a comeback." The bike had an ancient quick release lever, but I managed to free the wheel and set it on a wheel stand to work the tire off the rim.

"With coaster brakes?"

The kind of brakes where all the rider does is peddle backward to stop the bike. When I was little, Abo Reba had had a children's bike with coaster brakes that I'd learned to ride on. She'd had a stick-shift VW bug, too, but I hadn't done as well as a beginning driver with that.

"No, fixies don't have coaster brakes, and you have to have a lot of leg strength to control the fixed gear."

"They're not for me, then."

"Do you want a new seat?" I ran my hand over the saddle. The wide curved triangle of leather was cracked and stiff. "We have some very nice cushioned ones. It would make for a much more comfortable ride." I glanced at him.

"I will concede that a new seat would be a welcome change for this aging Quaker. Please."

I held up the cracked tire. "And a new tire would be in your best interests, too."

"Very well." His blue-eyed gaze was intense.

Wait. He'd obviously come here for more than one reason. "Silas, with all due respect, why do I get the feeling you'd like to talk about more than your bicycle?"

"Thee is a perceptive person." He clasped his hands. "I am in possession of a small tidbit of information. I believe it might relevant to the investigation of Annette Di-Cicero's murder, but I hesitate to divulge it."

My heart rate quickened. "You should take it directly to the detective in charge of the case, Lincoln Haskins." *But tell me first.*

"I am acquainted with Lincoln. He is a good man."

I selected a new comfort saddle from the shelf and unwrapped its plastic covering. "How does this look?" I extended it to Silas.

He blinked, looking startled to be back in the world of bicycle repair. He stroked the leather. "That will be a grand improvement."

With some difficulty, I convinced the old seat to come loose and attached the new saddle to the seat rails. I made sure the bolt was tight enough not to swivel.

Silas gazed at his hands. "About the information. I, ah,

am not certain my tidbit would rise to the level of Lincoln's interest. Perhaps you could help me evaluate that."

"Sure. If I can." I was curious about this tidbit. I selected a new tire of the right size and fitted a tube into it, then worked it onto the rim after I aligned the valve stem with the label on the tire. I held up my hand. "Wait one second before you go on. This will be noisy." I inflated the tube inside the tire bit by bit until the tube seated properly, then I went up to the specified pounds per square inch. "Please go on." I slid the wheel back into the fork and tightened the bolt, then gave the pedal mechanism a squirt of lubricant.

He removed his wire-rim glasses and rubbed the bridge of his nose. "You see, several years ago, Ogden—"

The door burst open. In clacked the cleats of bike shoes on a dozen cyclists outfitted in bright-colored Lycra. Behind them Doris hurried in.

Rats. "Welcome, everyone," I called out. "I'll be right with you."

Silas frowned at the sight. I followed his gaze, which he'd aimed at Doris. Did he know her?

"You have customers," Silas murmured. "What I want to tell you is rather complicated. It will have to wait until later."

"Please tell me sometime soon. I'm interested in what you know." I lifted his bike off the rack "Here you go. Good as new."

"What do I owe you?"

"Come with me." Out at the counter I wrote up his slip and accepted his cash. Three of the newcomers already waited in line to make their purchases. Doris stood near the door with arms folded, her back to me, as if studying the public notice board I kept there. I handed Silas my card and said, "You could email or text me, if you'd like."

"I don't indulge in such practices. I shall find you in person before too long." He touched the brim of his hat. "Good day, Mac."

I watched him wheel his bike out the side door, politely excusing himself to the wearers of hi-tech fabric. Silas, in his cotton clothes and suspenders, didn't text or use email. I'd have to wait for some good old-fashioned in-person communication to find out what he knew about Ogden. I shook off my disappointment and beckoned to the first customer.

"I'll ring those up for you." I still had a business to run, murder or no murder.

CHAPTER 31

Twenty minutes elapsed before I completed the tour group's purchases. The leader, last in line, introduced herself.

"Can you fit us all in for quick safety checks tomorrow?" Her skin was nut brown, likely from riding outdoors.

"Twelve bikes tomorrow? It's Saturday. My mechanic isn't in until ten today, and I'll have to make sure she's okay with a big workload on a weekend." The wall clock read nine forty-five. "I would help her, but I can't. Tomorrow is town meeting, and it's forecast to be a long one." Westham had decided to move the annual town meeting from its usual Tuesday night—which always needed to be extended to an additional evening or two—to a Saturday, in hopes of the daytime slot would lure more citizens to participate. I'd committed to my civic duty, but Orlean didn't live in town. She'd be here on the job.

"We're from Oregon," the woman said. "What's a town meeting?"

"Instead of a mayor and a city council, most smaller New England towns have three elected select board members. They govern together, but the whole town gathers to vote on the business of the town and on expenditures over a certain amount."

The leader looked at me like I was nuts. "Doesn't that get kind of cumbersome?"

"It definitely can, and it can also have the feel of the-atrical comedy. Anyway, I have a backup mechanic, but I'm not sure he's free." I handed her a Mac's Bikes card. "My cell is listed. Please text me your contact info and I'll get back to you as soon as I can." I was ninety-nine percent sure she, unlike Silas, wasn't about to tell me she didn't text.

"Will do, thanks."

Bingo.

"You have a great shop, and our group loves West-ham."

"I appreciate that. We all do our best."

She leaned in. "But didn't a woman get murdered here a few days ago?"

"Yes, and we have an excellent police force, both lo-cally and on the state level. You have nothing to worry about." At least, I hoped she didn't. Below the counter, I crossed my fingers.

She narrowed her eyes as if she didn't believe what I'd said, but she thanked me. She said she'd be in touch, then clacked out. Doris turned toward me. From the back I'd thought she had her arms crossed in a defiant stance. Instead it looked like she was hugging herself, with her mouth drawn down at the edges.

"Doris, is something wrong?" I made my way toward her.

"Mac, have you seen Beanie?"

"Your store cat? No. Did you lose her?"

"Beanie's a male, Mac."

"Sorry." I stayed as far away from cats as I could. On the other hand, they were irresistibly drawn to me and all other allergic people. Gin had a tiger cat. When book group met at her house, she always shut the kitty in a back bedroom and did a thorough vacuuming. Despite that, I still had to take an antihistamine before I went, or I'd spend the evening sneezing and rubbing my eyes.

"And yes, he's missing." Doris's voice rose. "I couldn't find him in the store this morning. I can't understand it."

"You must be worried. He never goes outside?"

"No, of course not." Her tone of panic switched to disdain. "It's dangerous for cats to go out."

I served as guardian to a mostly indoor bird, myself. I'd recently learned that I should have a harness on her when she came out onto my deck with me. I was lucky she hadn't flown away before.

"So how could he have escaped?" I asked.

"I think Annette's murderer has turned his attention to cats. The same person who broke into Tulia's place." She glanced around as if we were being overheard. "The same guy probably broke into my store last night and absconded with my furry buddy," she whispered.

"Wait a sec, Doris. Why would someone kidnap your cat? Is it a special breed?"

"Not a bit, but he doesn't play well with other cats. You know I have five more at home."

"No, I actually didn't know that." Five seemed like a lot, but if they'd been rescue cats, then good for her.

"I let the little guy have the run of the store, instead." She stared at me. "Can you contact that cop friend of yours? They need to start looking for Beanie."

"You mean Victoria?"

"No, the other one. The detective."

I doubted Lincoln would start hunting for an AWOL cat. "You want the animal control officer, not a state police detective. I'm sure the number is on the town website."

Now she glared. "You don't care."

Ouch. I would be similarly desperate if Belle disappeared, and I hadn't shown much commiseration for Doris's worry about her kitty. I opened my mouth to offer some when she blustered on.

"You don't think I matter, because I got a free dinner. They're for anybody, Mackenzie Almeida. Simply because you don't need free food, you go all elitist on me."

What? How did she get there? I'd been inwardly judging her, too, though. "That's not true at all, Doris. I only meant that—"

"Just see if I help you when you need it." She whirled and stalked out.

It was like a tornado had swirled through. I'd be willing to bet this Beanie had found some new nook to snooze in. I knew one thing about cats. Most of them were going to respond to a summons when they were darn good and ready to and not a New York minute sooner.

Her accusation about me being elitist hurt. Did I come across as condescending? A do-gooder, as Elenia had put it? I tried to pay my blessings forward. Maybe I should stay behind the scenes, stocking shelves while the free food market was closed instead of interacting with patrons. Prepare the free dinner in the kitchen instead of serving and busing tables. I'd thought I had decent people skills. Maybe I didn't.

I pressed my eyes closed, but my brain saw only the image of a masked villain scooping a tabby cat into a burlap bag. Maybe Doris's crazy idea wasn't that crazy. But why? Why abduct a kitty from the store of someone . . . I frowned at the door Doris had left through. She'd had history with Annette. Could she be the next victim, and the cat was a warning?

CHAPTER 32

By later in the morning I had a fully staffed shop—
which I needed, as it turned out—and I had to put
Doris's concerns on the back burner. I hoped she'd find
her cat safe and sound in the store and that its disappear-
ance had zip to do with Annette's murder.

Orlean, as usual, worked away in the repair area, this
time focused on a complete tune-up on a Trek Madone, a
high-end bike. With the sunny breezy weather ahead of
the three-day weekend, Derrick rented bikes right and
left. I sold inventory and made a tally of what I needed to
order in. My sales software would do it, too, but you
couldn't beat a handwritten list.

I called my backup mechanic and confirmed he could
work tomorrow and would help tend the shop if necessary. Derrick and I would both need to be at town meet-

ing. But what about Cokey? My parents and Abo Reba were responsible town citizens. They would be down at Town Hall, too.

"Derrick, do you have a babysitter for Cokey tomorrow so you can attend town meeting?" I asked when we'd both finished with customers.

"I do. The high school band, honor society, and drama club students are providing babysitting at the school for anyone who needs it. They're only asking ten dollars, which will go toward their club expenses. They're going to play games, make music, have face painting, serve hot dogs, the works. It's a great service for parents."

"That's fabulous." I wondered if Phil would be at Town Hall for the meeting. No, that would be too soon for a new widower. "Is Cokey okay if you leave her at the high school?"

"Are you kidding? She can't wait. And she wants Kendall to go with her."

So maybe Phil would be there. A new rush of customers descended on us. I didn't have a free brain cell to spare to think about the homicide-related lists I'd made at home. And I hadn't had a chance to check my phone and see if anybody in the group had volunteered for research jobs based on my thoughts.

By twelve thirty my stomach growled, but my employees came first. I poked my head into the repair area. "Go ahead and take your lunch, Orlean."

She gave me a silent blue-gloved thumbs up.

Derrick ushered the last group of renters out the door. "Have a great ride," he told them.

Pa replaced the tourists in the doorway. With customers at the register, I gave him a wave. I crossed my fingers on my other hand that he'd come here to tell me what he knew of Elenia. He raised his hand in return, but he didn't smile. Instead he spoke with Derrick in a low tone, an intent look on his face.

Uh-oh. I had a bad feeling about this. Someone I loved was in trouble. I felt it in my gut. Derrick glanced over at me. I couldn't read his look. Or maybe my imagination ran wild. Neither of them appeared overcome with worry, as they would if Cokey were ill, or Abo Reba had had a heart attack, or Mom had been in an accident.

I returned a woman's card and handed her the paper bag holding a new neon green biking jacket, the back cut longer to cover the cyclist's bent-over torso. I rang up a few bike maintenance items: a compact toolkit with an under-saddle pouch to carry it in, a patch kit, a bottle of Pedro's Syn Lube, and another of Pig Juice, a degreaser and cleaner whose name always gave me a giggle. I still had a line of three customers in front of me, but I kept my eye on my father and brother until I had to look down at the credit card reader.

Glancing up, I spied Pa leaving the way he came. *What?* He didn't have time to even come over and greet me, or more importantly, tell me what he knew? I swore silently. Because Pa didn't text, I didn't have that option. I'd also wanted to ask his opinion about my people skills. I apparently had to postpone the whole agenda.

Orlean returned through the back door, where she'd taken her sandwich to eat at the picnic table I kept out there. Shade from the huge old swamp oak fell in a wide swath. In nice weather, the table offered a pleasant place to get away for a few moments. I'd had more than one conversation with Lincoln Haskins there, too. Speaking of him, it surprised me he hadn't stopped by more—or at all—this week. Maybe because our group hadn't come up with much information for him? I'd texted him about Ogden, when, yesterday morning? Even as I greeted and rang up purchases, I mentally scolded myself that I hadn't passed along what I'd learned about the connection between Elenia and Doris yesterday.

The last customer finally left. With no new ones, I hurried over to the rental counter, where Derrick went through the slips.

"What's up with Pa?" My questions tumbled out. "Is everybody okay?"

"Everybody's fine, Mac. A pipe burst in the church and he has to deal with it. Mom has clients lined up all afternoon and Reba is off visiting a friend for the day. I'll need to leave to get Cokey from school this afternoon and bring her here again."

Whew. "That's no problem. I'm glad it's a relatively minor issue. From the way you two looked, my brain went straight to a lot worse thoughts than a broken pipe."

"Sorry about that. He's worried, no surprise, and hopes to get everything squared away before Sunday services."

"Sure. Hey, Orlean is back. Take your lunch if you want."

"That's okay. I had a big breakfast. I'll grab a bite when I leave to get Cokey. You should go ahead, while it's quiet."

I thanked him and headed for a restroom break first. A few minutes later, lunch bag in hand, I'd aimed myself for the picnic table when Lincoln walked in. Apparently I could tell him about Elenia and Doris in person.

"You're exactly the person I wanted to talk with. I was about to text you." I hadn't been, but I'd thought about it. "Come on out back."

He blew out a breath but followed me. After we sat, he folded his hands on the table. "You were about to text me?"

"Yes. Yesterday I volunteered at the free dinner."

"Our Neighbors' Table?"

"Right. Elenia Rodrigues came to eat."

He narrowed his eyes at the name but didn't speak.

I filled him in on what I'd learned about Nia, Annette, and Doris. "You know Doris used to coach beauty pageant contestants, and had been one herself at a younger age?"

Lincoln blinked. "Go on."

All righty, then, as my grandmother said. He obviously could choose not to tell me what he knew—or didn't know. I went on about the coaching and Elenia losing the crown to Annette.

"Interesting." He drew out a notebook and scribbled in it. "Do you know where Ms. Rodrigues lives?"

"Not for sure. Maybe the tent encampment in the park?"

He bobbed his head once.

"I haven't gone to look for her, just so you know." In case he thought I exhibited overzealous tendencies. "A guy named Witter ate dinner with her. He probably also lives there. He seemed nice enough, but I heard he has a criminal record. Do you think he might have been involved?"

"Anything else, Mac?"

Stonewalled again. "Did I send you a message about Annette's seafood allergy?" Had I?

"I don't believe you did."

I scrunched up my nose. "Gin told me Annette was deathly allergic to seafood. Annette's daughter, Kendall, is friends with my niece, Cokey."

"Derrick's daughter."

"Yes. Kendall told Cokey that the day before Annette died her parents fought and her father—Phil—"

"I know who Annette's husband is, Mac," Lincoln broke in with an impatient tone.

I stared at him. "Do you want to know what Kendall said?" In the sky, a flock of ducks silhouetted in black honked by in a messy vee, headed north. Wrong way, birdies. I watched the leader at the point steer its followers into a massive U-turn. I wished I were also headed for Florida or Mexico or whatever warmer locale they chose as their overwintering grounds.

Lincoln looked away for a moment, then back at me. "Sorry. I'm short on leads in the case. Nobody's happy with that, me least of all, and that makes me short tempered. Please continue."

"Kendall said her parents fought. Her mother went to work—which probably means studying at the library, as reported by Flo—and her father made soup, leaving a bowl for Annette and a note. What if he poisoned her with seafood in the soup stock? Did your evidence people find the soup bowl? The note?"

"Thank you," he stonewalled. "Do you have anything else?"

I thought about Silas Carter. He had something to tell me but said he wasn't sure if it was anything the police would be interested in. I'd wait until I learned what he knew before bothering Lincoln with it.

Lincoln fixed his dark gaze on my face. "Is there a reason you haven't been as forthcoming with your messages this time around?"

Ugh. Did I have a reason? Should I tell him about Silas? I scrambled. "I've been busy." My gaze fell on my newly adorned ring finger. Maybe that would get me off the hook. I held up my hand. "And I'm planning a wedding."

He gave another single nod. "Congratulations. I'm sure you and Brunelle will be very happy." He pushed up to his feet. "I'll get out of your hair. Please, if you can find the time, let me know what else you happen to learn."

"I will. Good luck, Lincoln."

He pulled a wry face. "Thank you. I'll need it."

CHAPTER 33

I did get a moment mid-afternoon to text the group. I said I'd talked to Lincoln and that he wanted to be kept up to date on our discoveries. I didn't include what Silas had hinted at, since he hadn't told me anything of substance.

Tulia responded first.

Doris is acting frantic. Saying somebody murdered her cat. Implying I had something to do with it.

I tapped out a response.

She came in here earlier with the same complaint. Ignore her if you can.

Flo chimed in.

Doing research. Will stop by the bike shop in a bit.

I replied.

I'm here 'til 5:00.

What kind of research? She clearly didn't want to in-

clude whatever she was digging up in the thread. I'd have
to wait.

"Mac, I'm heading out to pick up Cokey," Derrick
said, clipping on his bike helmet. "Back in a flash."

"No problem." I loved that he used the seat on the
back of his bike to transport his daughter around town
whenever he could. She loved her pink helmet, my brother
got more exercise that way—which he needed—and you
couldn't beat the cost.

Another text pinged in, this time from Zane.

**DiCicero stocked up on the hard stuff today. Single
malt, Hendrick's gin, and my own ZS rum.**

I wrote back.

Pricey purchases.

Zane confirmed.

No kidding.

Tulia added a comment.

Party time, now he's single? Definition of poor taste.

Flo contributed.

Or drinking away his sins?

Maybe Phil had already been a heavy drinker, and his
supplies had run out. With a wife around to be the responsible one, he might have developed some bad habits.
As a single dad, though, that was going to have to change.
Or had Flo been right, and Phil wanted to avoid thinking
about what he'd done? I read over the thread. All of us in
the group were veering close to being judgmental. I added
a note to that effect.

**Too judgy. We shd ease up a bit on Phil. He did just
lose his wife.**

Norland responded.

Agree. Not our job to convict.

Several customers wandered in, and my phone went

back into my pocket. Derrick returned with Cokey, who ran over to hug me.

"Titi Mac, I learned a new song today," she bubbled.

I smiled my apology at the gray-haired customer I was assisting and leaned down. "Cokey, I'm helping this nice man. You sing it for me later, okay?"

"Okay." She skipped off to where she'd dropped her backpack.

"Sorry about that. She's my niece."

"No worries, ma'am. She's a cutie." He handed me his credit card. "I have three granddaughters, myself. They keep me young."

I rang up his pink handlebar streamers and a kiddie-sized helmet. "I guess these aren't for your own bike?"

"Indeed not." He chuckled and signed the slip. "I live in Sandwich, but you have the best bike shop around."

"Thank you so much."

"It's worth the trip. You know," he lowered his voice. "I heard there's a . . ." He glanced at Cokey. "An investigation in progress here in Westham. I hope you won't lose business because of it."

"Unfortunately, you heard correctly. My business doesn't seem to be suffering, thank goodness, and we have excellent law enforcement officials on the case. May I recommend picking up some delicious seafood to take home to Sandwich? The Lobstah Shack next door has takeout chowder, cod cakes, and seafood salad that you and your family will love."

"That's the kind of recommendation I like. Thank you." He picked up his bag. "I'll be back."

I returned his thanks, feeling all rosy inside. A customer who drives cross-Cape to buy a few things for his grandkid's bike? My favorite kind. I hoped Tulia's takeout would hook him in the same way, because her business had suffered from the murder of the week more than mine.

Next I explained the difference between a road bike, a hybrid, and a mountain bike to a mother shopping with her adult daughter. I showed another customer where we kept the patch kits and a third our array of shirts. I'd finished ringing up the hefty purchase of our highest-end hybrid to the mother-daughter duo when Flo hurried in. Did Flo ever not hurry? She always seemed to zip around.

"Mac, you gotta hear this." The words tumbled out of Flo.

I held up my hand. To the bike buyers I said, "Bring it back after your first couple of rides and we'll make sure it's all working properly." I thanked them, then turned to Flo. "Just keep your voice down, okay? The little one with the big ears is here." I tilted my head toward Cokey, who busily drew at the rental counter. My niece had remarkably acute hearing, and she always paid attention. All of us grownups had learned to be careful about what we said when she was in the room, even if it looked like she was immersed in her own activity. My grandfather customer clearly knew to not use words like "murder" near a child even though he didn't know Cokey from anybody.

"Turns out Doris is living with Ogden Hicks," Flo began, her eyes bright.

Interesting. "Like, living with in a relationship or does she rent a room from him?"

"I don't know. The town voter roll has her at the same address as his."

"Curious. Or maybe not. I mean, he's a widower. She's unattached, as far as I know."

"Right." Flo frowned. "I tried to dig into her personal past and didn't get far."

"Beyond being Miss Rhode Island way back when?"

"Exactly."

"A few days ago," I began, "I asked Doris if she owned a house in Westham. She scoffed and basically said she couldn't afford to buy. Maybe Ogden gives her a room on the cheap to help him with his mortgage payment."

"Because he supports his disabled son. That could be, Mac."

"Don't take this wrong, but Doris's address is all you found out?"

"Afraid so. I might be on the track of more, but it's too early to share it." She glanced at her smart watch. "I have to get back to the library for a meeting."

Too early to share. That reminded me of what Silas almost told me. "The Quaker man who knows Ogden also knows something about him, but I don't know what it is.

"Wait. What Quaker?" Flo stared at me.

Right. I hadn't told the group about Silas. "Never mind. He's a guy I met."

"Fill us in when you can. Listen, I really have to go."

"Okay. I promise to tell the group. See you at Town Hall tomorrow?"

"I wouldn't miss it for my mother's funeral."

I gaped.

"Just kidding, Mac. Mama died twenty years ago, and we don't do funerals in my family. Give me a good old-fashioned Polish wake any day." She bustled out, nearly clipping an incoming customer.

Cokey materialized at my side. "Titi Mac, what's a fewnrill?"

I tousled her angel hair. "It's where people say good-bye to . . ." I gazed down at her. "It's a goodbye party, honey."

"Will Kendall and her daddy have one for her mommy?"

Out of the mouth of babes. "I expect they will, Coke-ster." When and what shape it would take was above my pay grade, for which my gratitude knew no bounds.

CHAPTER 34

At Greta's Grains, I perched on my usual Friday night stool at the counter at a little after eight. Tim's pop-up bar, Breads and Brews, was in full swing. Every week he transformed the bakery into a pub, a dance floor, and a gathering place. It utilized the space in a great way and brought in a hip crowd. You couldn't beat the markup on alcohol, either, he'd told me.

He opened at five for the after-work folks and didn't close until eleven. He tried to switch out different local bands, too. This week three women were producing truly rocking Celtic music. One fiddled and clogged at the same time. Another beat a flat drum in an irresistible rhythm, and the third played penny whistle, guitar, and squeeze box. You couldn't help tapping your toes to the music, and I suspected I might have to get up and dance at some point.

I sipped my glass of ale. I'd opted tonight for an Outermost IPA from Hog Island, although Tim also served wine, hard cider, and locally made root beer and fruit-flavored tonics. Soft drinks, that is, or soda pop, depending on where you came from. Abo Reba, a true Bostonian, always called any non-alcoholic carbonated drink a tonic, and I loved using that term, one used less and less.

"Hey, darlin'." Tim leaned over the counter to kiss my cheek. "You look like you could use a piece of Tim's Tasty Tomato Torta."

"Mmm. How did you know?"

He circled his palm over his face in a dramatic gesture. "I can read minds, lovely lady." His delivery, in a bad Eastern European accent, was also dramatic. With a flourish, he handed me a small plate of the pie. I'd had it before, and the torta was, in fact, terribly tasty.

I spied Elenia huddled around a small table in the far corner with a man and another woman, who both looked like they might also live on the rough.

Tim leaned toward me. "I've let them know they can come on Friday nights to eat at no charge, and have a drink, if they'd like." He lifted a shoulder and dropped it. "It doesn't cost me that much."

"I love you." I gazed at this big-hearted, generous man of mine. "Do you know that?"

He laid his hand on my cheek. "I kind of got the idea."

Isaac, Tim's assistant, pushed a tray of tortas and mini pizzas into the passthrough window. A newcomer to the bar waved her hand. Two men vacated their stools, leaving empty glasses, plates, and tips on the counter.

"Work calls, hon."

"Go," I said. I took a bite of the hand-sized torta. In a miniature pastry crust nestled layers of onions, peppers,

Spanish-flavored potatoes, tomatoes, basil, black olives, and Manchego cheese, all baked together into a perfect pie. I casually watched Elenia and her friends. How had she ended up homeless and possibly penniless?

Gin slid onto the stool next to me.

"Feeling better?" I asked.

"Yes. I had one of my headaches this morning. It went away later in the morning, thank goodness." When Tim's helper came by, Gin ordered a glass of chardonnay and a pizza.

We were surrounded by others busy with drink and talk. At first we didn't discuss the murder. That didn't last long, though. My gaze lit on Officer Kimuri. She sat alone with her back to the wall, nursing what appeared to be a root beer. She wore a lightweight blazer over a turtleneck, with jeans and sneakers.

"Gin, that woman sitting alone there? She's Nikki Kimuri, a Westham police officer. Have you met her?"

Gin glanced over, then back at me. "No, I haven't."

"She's out of uniform, but doesn't she look like she's on duty?"

"You're right. She's not drinking alcohol, and she's got her eye on the room. Especially on Nia, don't you think?"

I looked again. "I do. Think the jacket covers a gun?"

"I wouldn't be surprised."

"She was on duty the morning we found Annette." And not on duty yesterday morning when I'd seen her in Doris's shop—unless maybe she had been. A purchase of expensive cans of cat food while out of uniform could go either way.

Speaking of Doris, she sauntered in, followed immediately by Ogden. From the looks of him, he could have won the Mr. Uncomfortable crown right here and now. If the two were a couple, had there ever been a less likely one? And if they weren't, what was a Quaker—albeit a modern one—doing at a pop-up pub event? I thought members of the Society of Friends didn't drink alcohol, but maybe that was only in the past.

Gin nudged me.

I nodded. "I see them."

Doris, who had looked straight at Elenia, seemed to pretend she hadn't. She tucked her arm through Ogden's, nearly dragging him to the bar a few feet down from where Gin and I sat. Tim greeted them and took their order. We were close enough for me to hear Ogden order a seltzer water.

"Give me a pint glass of red wine, please." Doris winked at Tim. "And fill it up." She tapped long thick nails on the bar, nails with a fresh coat of red polish.

My man gave a single slow nod. I imagined Doris wouldn't be served a second round.

I leaned over. "Hi, Doris and Ogden. I haven't seen you here before."

"It's not my cup of tea." Ogden blew out a breath.

Doris whipped her head our way. "It's a public event, isn't it, Mac?"

"You can ask Tim that question," I said. "Did you find your cat?"

She barked out a laugh. "The silly beast had hidden behind a storage bin. Sorry for the alarm earlier."

"Do you both know Gin Malloy?" I looked at Doris and Ogden. "She owns Salty Taffy's."

Before Doris and Gin could finish exchanging greetings, I looked beyond Gin to see Elenia, who stalked up with fury written on her face. Here came trouble. She pushed past Ogden and grabbed Doris's shoulder, yanking her to face away from the bar. To face her.

"The more I think about it, the more I think you should be in jail for what you did to me," Elenia snarled, and not quietly.

"What are you talking about?" Doris reared back, scowling.

"Dorrie," Ogden ventured. "What's going on?"

The place stilled. Tim, their seltzer and wine in hand, set the drinks on the bar.

"Everybody here should know what this witch did to me." Red-faced, Elenia pointed a trembling finger at Doris. "She's a criminal."

"That's total BS and you know it, Elenia. I acted in complete accordance with the rules. I think it's you who should be locked up," Doris spat out. "For murder."

A collective gasp echoed around the room. Tim gave me an intent look. Gin swore under her breath.

Nikki materialized at Elenia's elbow. Her right hand pushed back the blazer to rest on a gun. "Let's calm down, now, everyone." Her voice, both soft and firm, projected so everyone could hear. "Ms. Sandersen, I'll thank you not to make false accusations."

"It's not false," Doris said. "She had plenty of reason to kill Annette." She held her elbows at her sides, those flaming nails waving as if she wanted to claw something—or somebody.

Nikki glared at Doris. "That's enough. You can take your reasoning to Detective Sergeant Haskins." She turned to Elenia. "Ms. Rodrigues, I need you to sit down."

Elenia's eyes flashed. Then her shoulders sank, and

she shuffled away. Instead of resuming her seat, she went straight out the door.

Doris lifted her chin and turned her back on Gin and me. She grabbed her glass and chugged a considerable dose of wine.

"Thank you, Officer," I murmured to Kimuri.

"All part of an evening's work."

CHAPTER 35

"Can you come by the bakery, Mac?" Tim asked. I'd just put in my contacts and had been getting ready to walk with Gin when he called soon after sunrise. I put the phone on speaker so I could finish tying my shoes.

"I have an emergency," he continued.

"Are you all right?" I heard the worry in my voice even though he didn't sound panicked.

"I am. But come soon." He disconnected.

I stared at the phone.

"I have an emergency." Belle mimicked Tim's deep voice exactly. "I have an emergency."

"No, you don't, Belle. But Tim does."

Belle emitted her wolf whistle. I shook my head and texted Gin.

I need to cancel or at least postpone. Tim needs me for something urgent. You go ahead.

She wrote right back.

No. I'll wait for you til 8. Hope he's okay.

Thx.

I desperately hoped he was okay. I locked the door and hurried down the street to the bakery under a stunning sunrise in a celestial artist's palette of pinks and oranges. Tim had said he was fine. What emergency had occurred? Had his oven broken down? I wouldn't be able to help with that. My little kitchen had a half-size oven I rarely even used. Had he gotten bad news? He better not have found a body in his walk-in.

I slid through the back door on the alley. The kitchen smelled yeasty. I inhaled aromas of cinnamon and sourdough and toasted pecans and all things heavenly. Two trays of what looked like cranberry scones sat cooling, and a tall rack held shelf after shelf of breads in various shapes. I had to force myself not to grab a boule and tear off a hunk to eat.

Tim stood in intense conversation with dyed, tatted, and pierced Isaac, a big dude in his mid-twenties who had a passion for baking. Neither looked hurt. *Good.* I didn't smell smoke, either.

Tim glanced up. "Mac, thank you. One sec, okay?" He and Isaac both focused on a pad of paper. Tim scribbled one more line in his lefty scrawl.

"I think that's it." Tim extended his hand to Isaac, and the two men shook in one of those complicated guy-handshakes ending in a fist bump. "I really appreciate it, man."

"No worries. My little sister is going to love the work." Isaac smiled at me out of a full beard dyed purple, but the top of his shaved head gleamed as shiny as the little gold ring in his eyebrow. "How's it shaking, Mac?"

"Hi, Isaac. I'm fine." I shifted my gaze to my brand-new fiancé. "Tim? What's up?"

Tim took my hand and led me back out to the alley. He enveloped me in one of his bear hugs. He finally stepped back.

"I have to leave, darlin'." He set his hands on my shoulders, peering into my face. "As soon as possible."

Leave? "Why?" I couldn't wrap my brain around what he'd said. Was he enmeshed in a secret? The complicated past I'd been worried about? *No.* I had to trust him enough to let him reveal his emergency in his own way.

"I can catch a two-fifteen flight out of Logan to Seattle if I make it to the eight thirty airport bus out of Falmouth. Will you drive me over to the bus depot? Please?"

Logan was the major Boston airport, about two and a half hours north of here. "You know I will. But back up, sweetheart. It's only seven fifteen. We have time. Why do you need to get to Seattle?" *Oh.* No secrets. This involved his sister. "Is Jamie okay?"

"No." He dropped his hands and glanced away for a moment. "She tried to kill herself."

Poor Tim. "I'm so sorry. How?"

He nodded, his face drawn with pain. "She took a bunch of drugs."

I stroked his arm. "I'm glad she's alive."

"She's in the hospital, but her kids are with a friend for the moment. I need to go take care of them until she gets out and can cope."

"Of course you do." Of course that would be this big-hearted man's first impulse. "Remind me how old the children are?"

"Eight—the boy—and girls six and two. I've never met the baby, and I haven't seen the older ones in a while."

"You're really good with kids," I told him. "They'll be fine. You know the whole diaper thing?"

"I do. I helped her when the older ones were little. But I hate to leave. You're trying to solve this murder, and we have to plan our wedding, and—"

I laid my finger on his lips. "No. There's time for all that. Your sister needs you. Your nephew and nieces need you. Go. We can get married any time."

"But soon, right?"

I delivered my assent via a big kiss, then pulled away. "Do you have a bag here?"

"Yes. I got the call at about three. I looked into flights, packed, and figured out the business stuff. I'd decided to shut down for the duration, but Isaac has agreed to keep the bakery open until I get back. He has a younger sister who's apparently eager to learn the trade."

"Good. Let me run back and get Miss M. Grab me a scone for the ride?"

He kissed me again. "You're the best, Mac."

Five minutes later we were tooling down the highway, my scone wrapped in a napkin. I thought about Tim's poor troubled sister, and I hoped he'd be able to handle three young kids alone. Helping family was way more important than missing town meeting. I also mused on how much Tim resembled Pa. Not in looks, not in build, not in vocation, but where it counted—in generosity of spirit and an enormous warm heart. Maybe women do look for their father in a mate—but in a good way, not a creepy way. We rode in silence for a couple of minutes.

Tim blew out a breath. "Jamie has struggled with clinical depression for years. She'd been doing better, holding down a job, taking care of the kids, and then she got pregnant again with some lowlife who didn't stick around. Giving birth kicked her into postpartum depression that she never really recovered from.

"She didn't get counseling, meds?"

"My sister is not a person who likes to ask for help."

"I hope she'll accept it now." I turned off toward the bus station. "Tim, what did you think of that interaction between Elenia and Doris last night?"

"It was ugly, wasn't it?"

"I'll say." I pictured Elenia's red face, her pointing finger, and Doris with her claws out, nearly spitting at her, channeling one of her angry felines.

"I know Elenia has had a hard life," Tim said. "That's why I let her and her encampment friends come to Breads and Brews. They should be able to relax, eat, and have a drink like the rest of us. But right now? I think Doris should watch her back."

Or Elenia should.

CHAPTER 36

I arrived in Westham in time to walk with Gin at eight, my stomach happy with the scone I'd devoured on the way back. I knew I would need the exercise before sitting in Town Hall all day. By eight ten we were on the access path that led to the Shining Sea Trail. The path ran alongside the Friends meetinghouse I'd stopped into.

"Thanks for waiting for me," I said.

"No prob, my friend."

I gazed up at the now-dark windows of the meeting-house, which had sheltered Quakers for a hundred and seventy years. "I didn't get a chance to tell you what this Quaker guy told me yesterday."

"Not Quaker Ogden, I gather?"

"No. Silas Carter, the one I met here who told me about Ogden's son. Silas brought his very old bike into the shop and hinted at some irregularity with Ogden.

Then a bunch of customers flocked in and he didn't want to tell me in front of them."

"Did you ask him to text you?"

"I did. Except he's pretty much of a Luddite. He said he doesn't have a cell phone, and he doesn't use email."

"How do people get along that way anymore?"

"No idea. I hope I'll see him at town meeting." The humidity pressed down like a heavy—and damp—cloak. The sky had completely clouded over. "Did you see the sunrise this morning?"

"Wicked gorgeous." Gin nodded as we swung onto the old rail bed. "All those colors made me want to paint it."

"'Red sky in morning, sailors take warning.' Even though red wasn't exactly the color, is it supposed to rain later?"

"I haven't heard," Gin said. "So what urgent thing did Tim have?"

"It's really sad. His sister out in Seattle OD'd—on purpose. She survived, but she has three little kids. He's on his way to take care of them and make sure she's okay."

"That must be tough for him. But Tim's a rock. A generous and sweet rock, but a rock, right?"

"He is. You never know, in families. Siblings can be so different, and he and Jamie haven't been close. I'm not sure why." Derrick and I weren't alike in lots of ways, but we were tight, despite—or maybe because of—our differences.

Gin and I continued to stride along the trail toward the marshy area. Before it opened up, I sniffed a sweet jasmine-like scent that emitted from a winding vine crawling up a tree. Tiny white flowers covering the vine gave off the scent, which might have been cloying had it not been wafting in plentiful fresh air.

"What is this, and why have I never noticed it?" I pointed to the vine.

"That's Sweet Autumn, a fall-blooming clematis. Nice, isn't it?"

"I'm not sure I'd want to be trapped in a closed room with it, but it smells lovely out here."

"I was thinking we should take a road trip to New Bedford tomorrow," Gin said. "We could talk to my mom and see what else we can dig up."

"Ooh. I like the way you think. I have my Sunday crew in place at the shop, and Tim's away. Why not? We can take Miss M."

"With the top down? Goody. That'll be fun. I'll call Mom when the meeting's over and make sure they're free."

"Excellent."

We reached the elevated walkway leading over the marshes. I inhaled the smell of salty reeds, marshy mud, and coastal life in all its glory. I loved this section, where I could watch ospreys and herons stalk their prey, one from the air with outstretched talons at the ready, the other tiptoeing with long skinny legs through the shallow water, its equally long sharp beak perfectly designed to grab unsuspecting minnows and tadpoles.

The walkway rose into the gentle arch of a bridge and widened. Its builders had thoughtfully installed a bench here where one could rest, observe, or meditate. A deeper channel ran under this section, in which tidal water flowed in and out. Right now it made its way out to sea.

"Hang on, Gin," I said. "I need to fix my shoelace." I set my right foot on the bench and retied the sneaker. From this vantage point, sunlight glinted off the elongated head of a great blue heron a few yards away at the edge of the channel. The white stripe down the center of its head contrasted with dark gray stripes on either side and the long yellow beak. "Look," I whispered, straightening slowly. I knelt on the bench and pulled my phone out of my pocket, activating the camera. I leaned over the railing to snap the photograph, hopefully without startling the majestic bird. My hands were sweaty from our exercise. I shifted the phone to one hand to wipe off my other one. The phone slipped out of my hand and plopped into the channel below. I gasped and stared down. The heron flapped its huge wings and took off.

Gin swore. "Mac, your phone."

I returned a stronger expletive. "I have to get it." I had one knee raised to climb over the railing when she grabbed my shirt.

"Get back here. You're not going to be able to find it, and you don't know how deep the water is. Or what lives down there." She gave a little shudder. "It's muddy and icky."

I sank onto the bench. "I . . . but . . . it's my phone! It's my internet, my connection with the world, my camera. It's everything."

"Hey, I know." She set her hands on my shoulders and peered into my face. "You go to the phone store and get a replacement. Everybody loses their phone once, at least."

"But the store is an hour away in Hyannis," I wailed. "We have town meeting. Tomorrow's Sunday. This is a disaster." I knew I was whining but I couldn't help myself. Ignoring her pleading gaze, I sank my face into my hands.

"We can order a new one online if you want."

"That involves research. My phone was getting old. I was thinking about upgrading but hadn't done the work to figure out which model." Part of my obsessive nature included the need to check out every detail before making a major purchase.

"Listen, Mac. Until you get one, channel that Luddite. And you know what? We can get you a new phone tomorrow together. The phone store in New Bed is way bigger than the Hyannis one."

"I guess." I still stared at the larcenous channel below.

"Hey, remember, ten years ago? Fifteen? Nobody had a computer in their pocket, or a camera. If you had a cell, it was a telephone. Maybe rudimentary texting. Nothing more."

True. "Yeah, but we had land lines and pay phones." Real cameras, too. And back then I wasn't trying to help a friend by solving a murder or waiting to hear from my fiancé flying from this coast to the opposite one.

I stood in silence. Gulls shrieked. Wind rustled marsh grasses. Two cyclists whirred by at a good clip. The high-pitched whistle of a northern harrier sounded from overhead.

Gin let out a breath. "Mac, I need to get going. I feel terrible you lost your phone, don't get me wrong. But I have to open my shop and get my employee settled before town meeting starts. Come on." She grabbed my hand.

I let her pull me up. I gave one last forlorn glance at the stream taking my lifeline off to wherever Mother Nature planned for it to be buried.

CHAPTER 37

I picked up a printed warrant—the list of articles to be voted on—when I came into the historic Westham Town Hall. I spied my parents already in seats and headed over to let them know about my phone. Mom said she would text Tim for me. As their row was full, I made my way to the other side. By ten thirty I'd been perched on a coveted aisle seat for half an hour. The hall, constructed a century earlier, retained that antique-building smell of old wood, experience, a whisper of mold, and the hint of long-ago cigar smoke.

The meeting had been scheduled to begin at ten—and nothing had happened. Well, nearly nothing. On the stage the three select people conferred in various configurations with each other, the moderator, and Town Clerk Stephen. Their microphones weren't live, probably a good thing. The finance committee table sat to the left and the school committee's to the right. Both tables were missing a few members.

End seats on the hall's floor were coveted by people who wanted to be able to make a speedy getaway, or at least leave the meeting unobtrusively for whatever reason. People like me. I still hadn't decided if I would abandon my civic duty and drive to Hyannis to replace my beloved smart phone. When I'd gotten home from the walk and showered, I'd tried to get a new one on my plan online using my iPad. I'd resolved to throw aside my obsession, but the universe hadn't cooperated. The site wouldn't accept my card and then it timed out.

Mocking my penchant for neatness and order in my life, this situation had become a big, bad, broken garbage bag of a mess. On my way here, I'd stopped by my shop to tell Orlean she wouldn't be able to contact me for a day or two. I also wanted to make sure she had opened without issues. If my business faltered, life's broken garbage bag would be even messier. I might be taking my situation too dramatically, but that was how I felt about it.

Zane slid into the seat to my right. He greeted me and gave me a kiss on the cheek. "Can you even believe we haven't started yet? Stephen texted that they still don't have a quorum. Isn't that why the town switched the meeting to a Saturday, to get all the parents of little children here?"

The town required a certain percentage of registered voters to attend town meeting in order to vote on decisions to allocate sums over a certain amount.

"Maybe it's taking them longer to drop off their kids at the high school childcare than they expected? I don't know." Come to think of it, I hadn't spied Derrick yet. I waved to Gin, who sat near the front and center. She'd volunteered to share the Our Neighbors' Table news during the section devoted to reports from community agencies. My grandmother had changed her Rasta hat for a snazzy red beret and sat with five other senior ladies near the front. All wore red hats.

"You didn't respond to the group text this morning." Zane twisted in his seat to face me but kept his voice low.

"Gah. I tried to take an up close and personal picture of a heron on the marsh this morning—and I dropped my phone in the water. It's gone, Zane. I don't have text, phone, camera. Nothing."

He gaped. "You poor disconnected darling." He shook his head, as if imagining my dire straits. "And you couldn't fish it out?"

"No. It went into the outgoing tide, or the mud. It's worse than when you drop a phone into the toilet. At least then you can try to dry it out."

"Right."

"So?" I waited, but he didn't respond, apparently stunned into muteness by my predicament. "So I'm a communications orphan. Tell me who texted, and what they had to say."

Bang went the moderator's gavel. "The annual meeting of the Town of Westham will come to order." The moderator waited. Conversations ebbed, but she glared at two men standing in the right aisle near where Pa and Mom sat. The dudes kept talking in hushed voices. "Every voting member will be seated. Now." The moderator, a petite white-haired woman, had a booming voice and harbored no nonsense. She waited until the men hurried to sit in the back. "Anyone present not registered to vote in Westham must sit in the front two rows on my left or leave the hall." She gestured to the nonvoting rows, reserved for people like experts who were invited to present about building proposals, for example. Several men and women stood and moved forward to the designated seats.

Dying to know the content of the group news, I raised my eyebrows at Zane as the hall quieted. He flipped open his palms and mouthed, "Tell you later."

The next hour consisted of boring reports, which Zane seemed to follow closely, or maybe he merely watched his beloved on stage doing his job. The woman who sat in front of me accomplished more than a few inches on whatever green yarny thing she knitted. I didn't do crafts, but I admired her multitasking efficiency. And really, what was tidier than the creation of a neatly stitched garment out of pile of spun wool? I had to know someone who could give me lessons.

When her turn came around, Gin walked to the mike at the front of the middle aisle and gave a summary of what the food charity had done with the town's donation. She got a hearty round of applause for the report. She blushed and sat. I knew she was embarrassed to take any credit for a huge and ongoing group effort.

Derrick appeared at my side and slid in front of me to sit on Zane's other side.

"Did I miss anything?" he whispered.

Zane and I both shook our heads.

"We now move to Article One on the warrant," the moderator announced. She called on one of the select people, who read the article into the microphone, even though we all sat there with the stapled booklet of the warrant, complete with the finance committee—otherwise known as the FinCom—recommendations for each article and other explanatory information. With a motion and a second, discussion opened.

It entailed a lot of blah-blah I had no interest in. Derrick apparently didn't either. He examined his phone and whispered again. "Mac, what did you think of what Norland found out?"

I elbowed Zane, who murmured to Derrick about me losing my phone. Derrick winced but handed me his phone. Norland had kept his message terse.

Sandersen has big-time gambling problem.

I raised my eyebrows at the message, then looked up at Zane and Derrick. "Which explains why she—"

The knitter in front of me twisted in her seat to glare at and shush the three of us. I handed the phone back to my brother.

Gambling. That must be why Doris was hard up for money, and maybe why she rented from Ogden, unless they were in a relationship. He'd called her "Dorrie" last night. Even so, she could still be paying him rent. The only addiction I had was neatness and order, but I understood that many had much more harmful obsessions, Derrick included. Was Doris's gambling problem connected in any way to Annette's death? That was the question we needed to ask.

CHAPTER 38

At twelve thirty, Article Eleven was about to be brought before the town. The first ten articles had involved relatively low-budget funding of things like a new sidewalk snowplow, money for energy-efficient LED lights in the town's lamps, and repaving the playground's parking lot. I found the business numbingly boring, but the town need to conduct it. My mind had been more on murder than motions, anyway. By now my not-so-padded rear end already ached from the ridiculously outdated wooden folding chairs we all were obliged to sit on. I'd noticed the knitter in front of me had brought her own seat cushion. Smart move.

Red-bereted Abo Reba stood in line at the center aisle microphone, followed by Silas Carter. What issue would bring these two together? After a select person read the article, I understood. The article outlined a high-budget request to build a new senior center.

After she stated her name and that she lived on Main Street, my grandmother made the case, in a voice surprisingly deep and loud for such a tiny old being, that the town needed to support its elders. That the current home to the senior center, a room in the Our Lady of the Sea parish hall, was drafty, dark, and most important, not handicapped-accessible. That a new center could provide a gathering space for the entire community.

She had a point. This very town hall was bigger and had tall windows that let in sunlight. The side door didn't involve stairs, nor did the restrooms. Still, it had been built over a hundred years earlier. The bathrooms were narrow and antiquated. The paint on the high ceiling flaked. And these chairs were the pits.

Silas stepped up to the mike and identified himself. He touched his snowy head.

"As you all can see, along with our friend Reba I am of the age to benefit from this center. If we are to provide equal access to all and support our increasingly graying population, we must support this article."

Bravo. Leave it to the Quaker to bring up equality.

As Silas turned away from the microphone, his gaze fell on me. He nodded and gave me one of those looks that says, "We need to talk."

I nodded back. Unfortunately, that talk would have to wait for a lunch break, if they ever got to one. I wished the moderator would call for a vote right now. My stomach complained bitterly of hunger, and I was desperate to hear what Silas had to say about Ogden.

The discussion of the pros and cons of a new center

went on forever, or so it seemed. PTO parents argued for a priority of more school funding. The smooth-talking owner of Jimmy's Harborside maintained a repair of the buckling sidewalks needed the funds more. A man well-known for his Not-in-My-Back-Yard opinions said, "What about that ratty town park with all those wretched homeless people? The town should clean that up first." A few murmurs of agreement arose, but they were over-ridden by a chorus of Nos.

A few rows in front of me, a man stood, ready to make his way to the back of the line of folks who waited to argue for their corner of the universe. *Huh.* Phil DiCicero. I'd missed him entirely. Someone next to him tugged his sleeve. I half rose out of my seat to see who. That thin, sand-colored hair could only belong to Ogden Hicks. And Doris sat next to him.

Phil tried to extricate his arm. I watched, still half-standing. Furious whispers took place between him and Ogden. Phil finally broke free from his business partner's grasp and excused himself repeatedly as he passed in front of a half-dozen sets of knees to reach the aisle.

I exchanged a glance with Zane. Derrick frowned at his phone and seemed to have missed the interaction. Zane lifted a shoulder and his eyebrows in a "Who knows?" gesture. I reached for my back pocket but had to drop my hand. That pocket wouldn't hold a phone until I drove somewhere to buy and activate one. I silently cursed my own need to photograph a pretty bird. Why couldn't I have simply appreciated the lovely sight of a wild bird in its native habitat? What drove me to need to take a picture of it? Maybe it would be good for me to take a sabbatical from texting, from the world always at my fingertips, from social media. The objections rose up instantly. I wouldn't be able to communicate with Tim in Washington, and I'd be out of the Cozy Capers loop. Not to mention using it for my business.

Phil now stood at the microphone. "Philip DiCicero, Pebble Lane."

The moderator spoke. "Do you have anything *new* to offer?"

"Yes, Madam Moderator. If this article passes, I pledge to donate a hundred thousand dollars to the construction of a new senior center. My late wife, Annette, adored older people. If the town so wishes, I would appreciate it if you named the center the Annette Andrade DiCicero Center. Thank you." He bowed his head, then turned and walked, not back to his seat but straight out the door at the rear.

The buzz of conversation in the hall matched the buzz of my own thoughts. Phil had that kind of money? Ogden rose and stared at the back. He looked like he wondered the same. And if the vote was going to be close, why hadn't Phil stayed to add his own? Also, had Annette loved seniors? I glanced at Reba's red hat. I'd have to ask her.

Zane elbowed me. "Seriously? Since when does DiCicero have pockets that deep?"

"No clue," I replied. "Derrick?"

He wagged his head.

"We need to find out," I murmured.

Victoria moved up the side aisle past me. I hadn't noticed her before, which didn't mean much. The police and fire officials usually hung around on foot at the back of the hall, the request of the moderator for town residents to sit notwithstanding. Maybe their jobs exempted them. She must be keeping an eye on the gathering to be sure it didn't get out of control.

The moderator rapped her gavel. "Quiet." When the

conversation continued, she banged it twice. "Article Eleven is still before us. Is there any further discussion?"

Within two minutes, a motion to vote had been made and seconded. The article passed with a resounding chorus of ayes far outnumbering the handful of those opposed.

"We will adjourn for a lunch break of no more than thirty minutes," the moderator announced. "To reconvene at one thirty sharp." *Bang* went the gavel.

CHAPTER 39

The line to the ladies' room upstairs stretched out way too long. I trotted down to the basement to use the auxiliary facilities there. Most people didn't know about this restroom. It was never crowded. Back upstairs, I stepped outside and unwrapped the sandwich I'd brought. I wasn't alone in a need for fresh air, but I headed for the edge of the parking lot so I could think. The list of people I'd like to corner and talk to was long as a heron's beak. Phil, about his donation and where the money came from. Ogden, to learn why he had attempted to prevent Phil from a turn at the mike. Doris about her gambling. And more. But I couldn't just come out and ask. "So, I hear you're a gambler," was not an opening Doris would take kindly to.

When Flo hurried up to me, I greeted her. "I didn't realize you were here."

"Why wouldn't I be here? I'm a citizen of Westham, aren't I? And I closed the library for the afternoon. I wanted more people to head over to the meeting, including my employees. But Mac, why haven't you responded to the thread?" Her words rushed out. "Did you see what Norland uncovered?"

"Slow down, Flo. I didn't respond because I dropped my phone in the marsh this morning. It's gone."

She gaped. "So you are incommunicado for a while. Out of commission."

"Not exactly out of commission, but I definitely don't have a phone. Do me a favor and tell everyone?" I would have thought Gin might have. "And yes, Derrick showed me what Norland wrote. We need to get more information about that." I took a big bite of my ham and cheese while I could.

Flo blinked. "Because if Doris is hard up for bucks, she might have, what? Killed Annette? But why?"

"Mmm." I swallowed. "What if Annette had blackmailed Doris about the beauty pageant stuff Elenia accused her of? Maybe Doris had fixed the results, influenced the judges, whatever."

"If she was paying off Annette, it wouldn't have been only gambling that used up her money."

"It's worth investigating, anyway."

"What did you think of Phil's donation to the senior center?" Flo asked, eyes bright. "Who knew he had money?"

"That seems fishy, but I'm not sure why. You know Gin knew Annette in New Bedford. We need to grill her about the family. Maybe Annette's parents were well off." I popped in the last bite of lunch. I'd dug out my old watch before coming over here, and I checked the time. "Fifteen minutes until we start up again."

"I have to run talk to the head of the library's board of directors. We have a funding article coming up."

"See you."

She waved and bustled off. I spied Silas Carter, the very man I wanted to talk to. He stood gazing up into a big maple tree.

"Hello, Silas," I began when I reached him. "What are you looking at?"

He turned. The smile wrinkles around his eyes deepened. "An eastern screech owl lives in this tree. See there?" He pointed. "It's perched about halfway up at three o'clock near the trunk."

"Wow." Not even as big as a robin, an owl with complex gray bands and spots perched on a thick limb. "I never would have seen that. Thank you." The wind had picked up and the little bird swayed on its branch, but it kept its eyes closed.

With another gust, Silas clapped his hand atop his hat. "We have quite a storm coming. Blessedly, our meeting-house has weathered many a gale over the centuries."

I hadn't thought about the tall windows of the old building and the effect gale-force winds could have on them.

He gazed at me. "I should like to continue our conversation from yesterday."

Good. Me too.

"Ogden served on our finance committee recently. He did not serve as Clerk."

"You have a finance clerk?" I pictured an image out of Dickens, a man with garters on his sleeves bent over a paper ledger.

"It would be what you would call the committee chair-person. We Friends use all kinds of archaic terminology, I'm afraid, sometimes to our own detriment. At any rate, the finance committee oversees all monies going in and out of our congregation. We own a historic building, we rent the basement to a Montessori preschool, and some of our members are exceedingly generous with their funds. We have quite a bit of banking to oversee and outlays to manage."

"I hear you."

"The clerk came to several of us elders and expressed her concern that the accounts showed several discrepancies. She feared Ogden had been responsible."

Aha. I glanced around to make sure nobody had an ear cocked. "You told me his son's care is quite costly. Is Ogden unable to fully pay for it on his salary alone?"

"I believe so. Our nominating committee relieved him of his position on the finance committee without telling him why. One of the guiding principles of our faith is integrity, you understand. We did not want to publicly shame our Friend, but we couldn't abide fiduciary mismanagement with an eye toward personal gain."

Stealing, in other words.

He cleared his throat. "I bring this to your attention primarily because I am aware that the murder victim served as accountant for Ogden's and her husband's furniture business. I worry that . . ." His voice trailed off.

"That he did the same with the business accounts, and Annette discovered it." The same thought had occurred to me.

"Yes. I pray this is not the case, that her murder was at the hands of another, perhaps a stranger." He bowed his head and gazed at his still-clasped hands.

Or maybe he wasn't gazing. Had he closed his eyes? Maybe he was actually in prayer.

For Ogden's sake—and his son's—I also hoped Silas's musing wasn't true. "For the record, I do think you should tell Detective Haskins of your church's suspicions about Ogden."

He gazed into my face. "Would he attempt to investigate a past crime?"

"Maybe. And if it leads to a resolution of a current one, you'd want that. Wouldn't you?"

"Yes, I would."

If ever sorrow was written on a person's face, I saw it right here, right now, on this thoughtful Quaker's.

CHAPTER 40

On my way back in, I slid around a few amblers to reach Gin. "Hey. Nice job on the presentation."

"Thanks. I'm glad it's over. The town doesn't contribute much, but I figure every additional person who knows what we do for the community is either a potential donor or knows someone who could benefit from the services we offer."

"Exactly." I glanced around. "We still have a couple minutes before the meeting resumes." I beckoned to a quiet corner in the foyer and kept my voice to a murmur. "Phil's donation."

"Amazing, wasn't it? And then he left."

"I know. Where did that money come from? Is Annette's family wealthy?"

She frowned. "I'll have to ask my mom. I don't think they were particularly well off when I babysat Annette. I mean, the house looked modest. Nice, but no bigger than it needed to be, and not flashy or anything. Solid middle class, you know?"

"Huh. Some rich people live simply, which only makes them richer. We can check tomorrow, right?"

"We're not going to be able to go." She shook her head. "Another storm is coming up the coast. Whether it hits land—that is, Westham—depends on how it tracks."

I stopped. "Silas mentioned that. Is it forecast to become a hurricane?" If we underwent the brunt of a hurricane, I hoped my tiny house would survive. It had done fine in a couple of uber-windy tropical storms but hadn't yet been put to the test of hurricane-strength gales.

"Not yet. Is your place anchored to the ground?" Gin asked.

"I've thought about that. Yes, the guy who built it attached it to several posts that are sunk into the concrete pad it sits on. It can be unbolted if I want to move it, but I'm pretty sure it won't blow away."

"Does Derrick board up the lighthouse windows?"

"I think he told me it has storm shutters. The lighthouse sits out on that point. It must be extra vulnerable. I can't imagine they would have built it back in the day without adding window protection."

"I would expect so."

My brain still dwelled on Phil's apparent generosity. "Back to Phil, I guess the funds for the senior center could be his own money. Do you know anything about his family?"

"Nada."

"I'm sure Flo will get on Phil's finances like white on rice." The river of residents flowed past us back into the hall. "Anything new on the thread?" I hadn't seen Norland at the meeting, but I expected he sat here somewhere among the four hundred of us dedicated to the tradition of governing a small New England town.

Gin pulled out her phone at the same time as the mike went live in the hall, along with the bang of the gavel.

"Take your seats, Westham," the moderator announced. "We have more business before us. This is your two-minute warning."

I turned toward the wide entrance into the hall. I stopped and sniffed, turning back to face the door to the outside. The reek of cigarette smoke grew closer along with Doris. Ogden held her elbow and seemed to be persuading her to return to the meeting. Doris held a takeout bag with the Lobstah Shack logo, a grinning lobster lounging on a picnic table in front of a shack that looked like it belonged on the Maine coast. She always claimed to dislike Tulia and her restaurant. Why would Doris have eaten lunch there?

"It's stupid," she rasped in her deep smoker's voice. Today she wore her hair up in some kind of a messy twist. "It's boring. The seats are crap."

She had that part right.

"Hello, Ogden, Doris," I said.

Seeing Gin and me, Doris blinked. "How do you tolerate these meetings, Mac?"

"It's my civic duty?" I spread my hands. "I was just talking with Gin about the call for new members of the town's finance committee. They're looking for volunteers." I didn't glance at Gin.

Ogden slowed his forward trajectory. To say he froze didn't exactly describe what he did, but it looked like I'd hit a nerve. A sensitive one.

"Is that something you're interested in, Ogden?" Gin played right along.

He faced us. "Serving on it wouldn't be a good fit for me."

The gavel sounded again. "Take your seats, please." The moderator sounded peeved.

"Well, we'd better go on in." I smiled at Doris. "Don't worry, they won't keep us here overnight."

She shook her head, but nudged Ogden. "Hey, you dragged me here. You coming, Oggie?"

He grimaced as if he'd tasted moldy bread. At the nickname? Gin and I hurried in behind them. I hoped I hadn't said too much. Ogden remained on my—and likely Lincoln's—list of suspects.

Zane had saved my seat, and the one next to Derrick had opened up for Gin. Norland appeared and edged in next to Gin. Heck, if Flo joined us, we'd have a Cozy Capers quorum, minus only Tulia. I surveyed the room. The clutch of elderly red-hat ladies seemed to have vanished. I knew Abo Reba had a fondness for her afternoon siesta. Maybe her friends did, too.

The meeting started up again, and I covered my yawn with my hand. Did anyone really care that the town needed to spend money to repaint the hydrants? To freshen up the yellow temporary-parking curbs and the red no-parking ones? I might join my elders in dreamland if a more exciting article didn't pop up soon. I glanced around in an attempt to prop open my eyelids.

Doris and Ogden had taken seats across the aisle and a few rows up. It looked like she was spooning chowder into her mouth. *Funny.* I brought a hand to my mouth. Doris knew Annette well. She would have known of her seafood allergy. If Annette had blackmailed the pet shop owner, Doris could have given former beauty queen the tainted soup. But how? Under what guise?

The current article involved funding the Parks and Recreation department. When it opened for discussion, a trim woman in an aqua sweater and expensive-looking cream-colored slacks showed up first at the microphone. Her streaked hair looked expensive, too, as befit the owner of a high-end jewelry shop in town, the only really pricey store we had.

"I offer an amendment to the motion. Westham needs to assure its parks are welcome to all. When addicts, drunks, and crazy people camp in our public spaces, it scares our children and drives away tourists."

I doubted her private-school-educated children ever played in a public park in their entire childhoods.

"Our town depends heavily on tourism," she went on. "I have had clientele worried about being robbed by that riffraff. And who only knows what illegal substances they sell to our youth."

More comments were offered, both pro and con. Pa made his way to the mike.

"Rather than worry about our financially comfortable visitors, Westham should be more concerned about how we take care of the least in our midst. We need to provide for these troubled souls, not eject them. Perhaps our friend," he gestured to where the original speaker sat, "would like to instead lead an effort to provide counseling, employment, and permanent shelter for the inhabitants of the park." Applause erupted while he returned to his seat. The assemblage voted down the amendment.

Phil appeared in the aisle to my left and made his way

to the only empty seat in the row in front of us. He excused himself, passing in front of awkwardly turned legs to reach the middle. Zane nudged me. I nodded that I'd seen. The way Phil had left earlier, I'd thought maybe he'd been overcome with grief. If so, he'd had a quick recovery.

Derrick reached out a hand and touched Phil's beefy shoulder. Phil twisted toward the back with a sharp move. Derrick gave him a thumbs up.

"Very generous of you, man," Derrick murmured.

Phil looked startled. Or alarmed? He took in the whole row of us, then relaxed. He bobbed his head to Derrick in acknowledgment before turning back to the front.

Why had he seemed alarmed? Maybe Derrick had simply surprised him. If my loved one had been murdered, I'd be jumpy, too.

The business of the town went on. And on. And on. I was mid-yawn at two thirty when a siren came to life outside. The muttered buzz of communications radios overcame the droning from the stage. A dozen men and a handful of women, all in civilian clothes, stood and hurried with purpose toward the back of the hall, Victoria at their heels. A fire in town, perhaps, or a major traffic emergency must have caused this odd civic flash mob.

The select person at the microphone paused her reading of the article. Officer Jenkins hurried down the aisle on the other side toward the row where my parents sat. Now wide awake, I followed the officer's progress. My insides turned to ice when Jenkins got Pa's attention and beckoned to him. Pa murmured to Mom, then stood. Wearing a grave expression, he hurried out after Jenkins.

Was Abo Reba all right? Or had another crisis happened at the church? I whipped my head to look at Derrick, who also looked worried. I learned over Zane to whisper, "Should we go?"

"I don't think so. Mom's still here." He pointed across to where our mother sat bent over her phone. "Maybe they needed a pastor at an accident, and Pa was the first one they saw."

I bobbed my head slowly. "Maybe." What he said made sense. If Reba had had any kind of medical emergency—a stroke, a heart attack, a fall—Mom would have hurried out too. Wouldn't she? And if an issue had arisen at the church, my brother and I would only be in the way. Still, I was antsy not knowing and without a phone to give me updates. "Tell me the second you hear from him?"

Derrick nodded and settled back in his seat. Zane patted my knee. The moderator rapped the gavel. The hall quieted again, returning to the business of the town. My racing mind did not quiet.

CHAPTER 41

When the meeting blessedly ended at three, everybody seemed to want to linger and chat in the town hall. I stood, eager to get out of there.

Derrick looked up from his phone, frowning. "That Cape Alert site says the alarm was for a fire at the church."

"A fire?" My breath rushed in. What was going on in our world? Murder was awful enough. For Pa's church—our church—to have a burst pipe and a fire in one week made me wonder about sabotage.

Derrick gestured across the hall to where our mother stood in intent conversation with a woman on the school committee. "I'm going to check in with Mom."

"Thanks," I said. "I'll head over to the parsonage. I hope it's a small fire."

"Sound like a plan. I haven't heard any more sirens.

That might mean Westham didn't need help from other
towns."

"I hope so. Want to grab dinner tonight?" I asked Gin.
"Sure."

"I'll stop by your place in an hour or two."

She nodded her acknowledgment. I hurried out, weav-
ing my way through clumps of residents while they
talked, ambled, conferred. A steel cable of worry pulled
me along the Main Street sidewalk through the wind toward my father's church, which sat at the end of Westham's main drag.

Several minutes later, my eyes bugged out at the sight
of red fire engines surrounding the UU edifice's calm
white presence. A lot of fire engines. I broke into a run,
swearing. Acrid smoke tainted the air.

Kimuri stood guard. She held up a hand, palm out in a
"Stop" gesture. "Ms. Almeida, you can't—"

Oh, yes, I can. I shook my head and ignored her, slipping around the biggest fire truck. Now I stopped. I stared
at the scene the vehicle had obscured. Covered by a white
blanket, Abo Reba lay strapped onto a wheeled ambulance gurney. Pa stood at her side, with an EMT at the
other.

Elenia huddled at the left edge of the wide granite
church steps nearby, knees up, arms wrapped around
them, gaze downcast. In the back seat of a cruiser sat a
disheveled-looking man. The big front doors to the church
stood open. Water ran out of the foyer and down the middle of the steps. Suited-up firefighters moved here and
there, but I didn't see any flames. Victoria, who conferred
with the fire chief, glanced in my direction, then back at
the chief.

I hurried to my grandmother, whose eyes were open.

She was alive. I covered my noisy exhale of relief with my hand. "What happened?" My words tumbled out mixed with a sob.

"Isn't this silly?" Her voice was weak, but her words were all Reba. "I took a little tumble. That nice girl over there helped me." She shifted her eyes in Elenia's direction, but she didn't move her head, as if it would hurt to do so.

Whew. I bent down and gently kissed her forehead. "I'm so glad you're okay, Abo Ree." I gazed at Pa. "And the fire trucks?"

"A disturbed man attempted to set a fire in the foyer." His tone was lower than usual and somber. "Ms. Rodrigues stopped him and called the authorities. Your grandmother came over to see what was going on and fell on the steps."

My always inquisitive grandma. Her curiosity was unstoppable. "Did you hit your head?" I asked her. "Break anything?"

Another EMT appeared. "She'll have a thorough exam at the hospital. We need to get going, ma'am."

"Can I ride in there with her?" I asked.

"No, ma'am," the taller EMT said. "You'll have to follow us."

"Astra will meet you there, *Mai,*" Pa said. "She'll stay with you. I'll be over as soon as I can."

We watched them bundle her into the ambulance and get her settled. One EMT hopped out, secured the door, and climbed into the driver's seat. The ambulance drove away, lights flashing and siren ablare.

"Shouldn't I go, too?" I faced my father.

"You don't need to. Your mother is on her way to Falmouth now."

"They didn't take Abo Reba to Hyannis?" I asked. "Isn't that hospital bigger?"

"Yes, but they're both part of the same organization. *Mai* will get good care in Falmouth and they have an excellent emergency department."

"It's a lot closer for us to visit, too. But is the church all right?"

"There's some water damage. It's not serious."

I looked at the guy in the cruiser. *Witter?* "He's the disturbed guy? I met him at the free dinner the other night. He seemed odd but harmless."

"Yes, he goes by Witter. I'm afraid he suffers from untreated mental illness. He somehow thought having a campfire in the entryway would be a good idea. He used lighter fluid, and it caught easily."

"Seems like Elenia acted as an angel twice over today." I looked at her. She hadn't budged from her step. Someone must have asked her to stay.

"Indeed, she did."

"It surprised me Mom didn't come with you when the alarm went up. She and Abo Reba are so close."

"The alarm was only about the fire. They told me it wasn't a big one, and I told Astra I didn't think she needed to accompany me. Your grandmother fell while I and the fire department were on our way."

That explained it. Other pastors' wives might have insisted on being at their husband's sides. Mom had always led her own life, and Pa was fine with that. If they'd known my grandma was injured when the alarm went up at town meeting, Mom would have rushed over here with Pa.

Victoria beckoned to Pa to join her and the fire chief.

Firefighters coiled hoses and carried gear back to their vehicles.

I went over to Elenia and sank onto the step next to her. "Thank you for helping my grandma." I didn't know if Elenia had murdered Annette or not. Right now, gratitude for what I did know rose up. "And for calling in the fire."

She raised her head off her forearms, squaring her shoulders. "She's a sweet lady. Who wouldn't help her? You know, she brings us socks and new toothbrushes. Us in the park, I mean."

"I didn't know, and it doesn't surprise me. She's tiny but her heart is huge." I looked at the man in the cruiser, who now banged at the window with his fist. "Is he all right?"

"Maybe. He's part of our community in the park, the one you all think is disgusting and offensive." Her mouth drew down.

I could have objected that I didn't think that, but would she'd believe me?

Elenia continued. "Witter's crazy, but believe it or not, he has a big heart, too. He can't stay on his meds, says they make him feel wrong."

"Why did he want to start a fire in the church?"

She gave me one of those looks that meant, *Isn't it obvious?* "Because he's crazy? I don't know. We often come in during the day and sit in the pews in the back. It's quiet and peaceful."

Plus warm and protected from the elements. The wind element, at least, was picking up. A mini twister of leaves circled in the gutter and a white plastic bag floated crazily near the top of a tree.

"Your father is a lot like his mother." Elenia wrapped her arms around her knees again. "He's generous. He doesn't lock the doors to the sanctuary. He doesn't give us grief about our situation." Her stomach rumbled and she looked away.

I stood. "Do you have to stay here?"

"Lady chief asked me to." She tilted her head toward Victoria. "Why?"

"I want to buy you lunch. To say thank you in a different way."

She frowned, but looked wistful, too.

"Tell you what," I said. "I'll be right back. I know where I can get the best takeout sandwich around."

"I'd appreciate that." Elenia stared at her crazy friend. "I bet he's hungry, too."

I didn't know if the authorities would take Witter to jail or the psych ward, either of which would feed him, but when? A darker thought hit me. I stared at him in the cruiser, where he now talked and gestured to himself behind the window. If Witter was that crazy, could he have been involved with Annette's death? Or have been hired to poison her? I shook it off. For now.

"Lunch for two, then," I said. "Don't go anywhere."

"Like I have somewhere to go."

CHAPTER 42

"I heard the sirens," Tulia said. "And when I went out in the alley, I smelled a little smoke, but nothing popped up on the thread. I ignored it."

We were alone in the Lobstah Shack, so I'd followed her back to the kitchen and filled her in on the facts of the fire and my grandmother's fall. But first I put in an order for two large lobster rolls, which Tulia made on crusty sub rolls, not the airy hot dog rolls many establishments used. I didn't care what the lunch cost. Elenia and her friend deserved a healthy, protein-rich meal, even if the friend had come close to seriously damaging Pa's church building. I knew Pa wouldn't blame the man for his illness.

"As you can imagine, I'm glad the fire wasn't more serious." I watched her work. "And I hope my grandmother's injuries aren't, too."

"I hope they aren't, too," Tulia said.

Not having a phone was going to kill me, but Pa might have an update by the time I got back to the church. "Tulia, has Lincoln been back around? I mean, I wonder if you're still a person of interest in the case."

"Nobody has told me I'm not, but I also haven't been questioned in a day or two, thank goodness."

"Good." I frowned. "Come to think of it, Lincoln didn't attend town meeting."

"You know he lives in Mashpee, right?"

"Yes. He would have had to be there in the role of an observer. Maybe he's out tracking down alibis or poisons. I wish I knew the autopsy findings. If it's been done, what they found, the works."

"My cousin works in the morgue." Tulia laid two sheets of waxy paper on her counter. "I'll ask her what she knows."

"Seriously?"

"Yeah. She's a forensic pathologist and had a job out in Worcester. But she wanted to come back home and got the gig with the state over in Barnstable." She rubbed her nose with her forearm. "How did town meeting go, anyway?"

"Mostly boring. But at the break I got some goods on Ogden Hicks."

Tulia paused her knife. "Remind me who he is?"

"Phil DiCicero's business partner. A guy who goes to the same church said they had to fire Ogden from their finance committee. They thought he'd skimmed money from their accounts."

"I remember. He's the Quaker fellow."

"Yes. And then Phil, wow. He said he would donate

a hundred thousand bucks to the proposed new senior center."

Tulia gaped.

"Exactly my feelings." I nodded. "And he said he 'would appreciate' it being named for Annette."

"Hmm." She spread butter on the cut sides of both rolls, then laid shredded lettuce on one half. "Sounds kind of like hush money to me."

"I hadn't thought of that. I can't believe he would think it would work."

"Same here. And Norland's message about Doris and gambling stunned me." Tulia spread a thick layer of her lobster salad mix on both rolls, patting it into place with the spreader.

"I know. And you heard about my poor phone, right?"

"Yeah, bummer."

Even though I'd eaten lunch, my own stomach complained audibly at the sight of the rich mayonnaisey lobster mix. Only one scoop of it remained in the container. "Hey, make me a small on a hot dog roll? I think I might die if I don't eat a sandwich right this minute. And you can skip the lettuce."

"Sounds good to me."

I went on. "Gin and I had planned to take a road trip to New Bedford tomorrow to see what her parents know about Annette's family—and about Doris back in the day. But now we can't."

"Because of the storm?" She sliced both sandwiches crosswise before wrapping them in foil, then handed me the small in a paper boat.

"Right." It seemed like we'd been talking for too long considering I was doing this so Elenia and Witter could eat, but Tulia had been working the whole time. "Maybe it won't be a bad one."

"Did you hear they've named the storm Vicky?"

I snorted. "I wonder how Victoria feels about that."

"Wouldn't you say she's too restrained to be any kind of a storm?" Tulia slid the sandwiches into one of her branded paper bags.

"Restrained, disciplined, tightly wound? All of the above."

"Anyway, it's supposed to hit sometime tonight. I hope it's not too bad. I haven't boarded up my windows or anything."

"I hope it isn't bad, too." In the face of lobster salad, I couldn't help my own weakness. I stood there and devoured the whole packed small roll while she rang up the lunch. The storm had canceled our research tomorrow. Gin and I would figure out another way to uncover facts from the past, but it wouldn't be via my phone now interred in its watery graveyard.

CHAPTER 43

On my way back to the church, a gust of wind nearly knocked the bag out of my hand. By the time I arrived, only one fire vehicle remained—a red SUV—and one cruiser. Elenia paced at the base of the steps. The police car with arsonist Witter in the back seat had left. *Shoot.* I'd missed giving him his lobster roll. I shouldn't have schmoozed with Tulia for as long as I did. I'd also barely thought about my grandmother, now in the ER, while I talked in the Lobstah Shack. What was wrong with me?

Elenia hurried toward me.

I extended the bag. "I'm sorry I didn't get back here sooner."

"They wouldn't tell me where they took Witter." Her lovely face was drawn with worry. "He's really sick. How can I be sure they take care of him?"

"I'm sure they will." Again I wondered how Elenia arrived at the circumstances she lived in. She didn't seem a bit sick and I'd never seen jitters or signs of addiction, nor smelled alcohol on her breath. Pa might know. But would he tell me? Probably not. "I can ask my father to keep track of him, if that would help."

"Thanks."

"Is Witter his nickname or his last name?" I asked.

"I don't know. That's the only name he's ever told me."

Victoria stepped out of the cruiser. "Everything all right, ladies?" she called from the curb.

"Please take your lunch," I said to Elenia. "I'll go ask her where your friend is."

She accepted the bag at last and sank down on the second step to unwrap one of the rolls. I made my way to Victoria.

"All's well," I said. "I brought Elenia a lobster roll."

"And where's mine?" Victoria set her hands on her waist and gave me a mock frown.

"Very funny." Could Victoria actually be loosening up? I'd never heard her joke about anything. "I got a sandwich for her friend Witter, too. Elenia's worried about where they—you—took him. Can you tell me?"

She raised an eyebrow so blond it almost disappeared. "Your father chose not to press a charge of arson, with the condition that the gentleman agreed to seek help. We took him to the psych department at the hospital in Hyannis. I didn't agree about the charges, but the decision was the reverend's, not mine."

More proof of Pa's big heart. As long as mentally ill Witter didn't set more fires once they released him. "Is my father still here?"

"Inside with the fire inspector."

"Thanks." I looked at Elenia as she plowed her way through the lobster roll. "You won't harass her, right?"

"Mac, what do you take me for? We're here to serve." Victoria slid back into the vehicle and closed the door.

"Gotcha." I returned to Elenia. "She said Pa didn't press charges as long as your friend agreed to get mental health help."

"So he's back in the loony ward."

"The psych department at the Hyannis hospital, yes. Listen, I have to go talk to my father. Do you guys have a place to stay if this storm gets worse tonight?" *Vicky.* I checked the police chief's vehicle. Had she heard of her namesake? She had to have.

Elenia wrinkled her nose. "Town opens the high school gym as an emergency shelter. Some folks choose not to go, but I will. And the storm will probably achieve that rich lady's dream to clear us out. Our ragtag tents are worthless against high winds."

I plopped down next to her. "Can I ask you a question?"

"Okay," she mumbled around a mouthful.

"Did you know about Annette's allergies?"

She swallowed. "Of course. Who didn't? That girl wouldn't go near shellfish like this." She gestured at the end of the lobster roll in her hand.

Elenia hadn't reacted as if she'd suspected anything about my question. She'd been open with me just now. Maybe she would talk more about her predicament.

"How did you get here?" I asked. "I mean, homeless and in Westham?"

She wiped her mouth with the back of her hand and crumpled the foil into a ball before she spoke. "Home-less? It's a long sad story. Westham? I wanted to talk with

Annette. I felt like she owed me. We were friends when we were younger. Competitors, but friends, too. I heard she lived here, but I never got up the nerve to talk with her." She tucked the foil into the bag and pushed up to her feet. "That detective thinks otherwise."

"Does he?" I stood, too.

She cocked her head. "I think you know he does. Hey, thanks for the food, Ms. Almeida."

I opened my mouth to ask her to call me Mac, but she walked away, head held high.

CHAPTER 44

Inside the church I found Pa in conversation with the fire inspector. "We're almost done, Mac."

I nodded and gazed around the damaged foyer and the dark spot on the marble tile. Yellow police tape blocked access to it. At least the foyer didn't have a wooden floor, unlike the rest of the church. The notices pinned to the bulletin board on the wall behind it were sodden, and the odor of wet smoke residue smelled worse than the actual smoke had outside.

"I'm heading over to the hospital in a minute," Pa said after the inspector left. "*Mai* is still in the ER and they've run all kinds of tests, but your mother says they will admit her for the night at some point. Just for observation."

"Should I go, too?"

He laid his large, smooth hand on my cheek, a gesture

he'd done since before I could remember. "She knows you love her. From what Astra told me when she called, your *abo* is tired and bruised. Let's let her rest. Depending on the weather, you can sit with her tomorrow once she's settled in a room. I'll be here holding services— storm and the good Lord permitting—and I'm sure your mother will appreciate being spelled."

I covered his hand with mine and peered at his face. "Abo Ree will be all right, won't she? She didn't break anything or get a concussion?"

"Neither, by some miracle. God willing, she'll make a complete recovery from her fall."

My throat thickened. "I'm not ready to let her go."

"None of us is, *querida*. And you know as well as I how strong her will is. You don't think she'll let herself slip away before seeing you marry your love, do you?" He dropped his hand, but his gaze stayed full of love.

"I don't." I swiped at full eyes. "Give her my love and a kiss. Tell her I'll be there tomorrow even if I have to hitch a ride with a storm chaser."

"Thanks for the reminder." He frowned. "I need to make sure Rose is on board with taking free food over to the gymnasium."

"For the shelter? Elenia told me about that."

"Yes. Thank you for buying lunch for her. She let me know where you'd gone."

"Do you know why she's homeless? Why she doesn't have a job?"

He gazed at me. "I do, but now is not story hour. I need to go. I heard you lost your phone. I'll call Derrick with an update on your grandmother when I have one. Be sure you check in with him." He embraced me and hurried toward the side door that led to his office.

I slipped into the sanctuary and sank onto a pew half-way to the front. The already strong winds rattled the high antique windows. Pa had no way of covering them. I closed my eyes, letting the stillness inside wash over me. Folding my hands in my lap, I fingered the ring on my left hand like a talisman. "Let Abo Ree be well," I whispered, holding my grandmother's image in my mind. "Let Tim come back safely." I pictured his face on which every emotion showed. "Let Lincoln solve Annette's death. Let there be no further violence. And let the windows stay intact."

Someone cleared their throat behind me. I jumped in my seat. My heart sped up. I whirled.

Phil loomed in the aisle to my left. His arms hung at his sides, and his face looked grim.

CHAPTER 45

"You surprised me, Phil." I patted my still-racing heart.

"Door's open." He gestured backward with his head. "Anybody can come in."

He still didn't smile. He faced me, effectively blocking my exit from the pew. Should I run out the other end?

I stood, which gave me a couple of inches of height on him, and took one step back. "That's how the minister likes it."

"Your father."

"Yes." I mustered a helpful look. "Shall I get him for you? He's in his office."

"No, he's not." Phil sounded as grim as his expression. "He just drove away."

I swore silently. His presence menaced. How did he find me here? Had he followed me? I couldn't believe he'd shown up by accident, that this Catholic Italian had happened to stop into the UU church exactly when I had. Maybe he'd driven by while I was outside talking with Elenia and decided to stop. Time for me to get out of here. I turned away.

He grabbed my arm with a hand surprisingly large for such a short man. A strong hand, too. My own hands turned clammy. My skin tingled with goose bumps despite my cotton sweater.

"Hey! Let me go." I pulled away but he kept his grip.

"I want to know what that group of yours is up to." His dark eyes bore into my face. "I saw you all sitting behind me in town hall. I know you've been snooping around, cozying up to the detective, asking questions of my partner."

"We're not up to anything." I tried to twist out of his grasp. "Let go of my arm." I tried to peel his thick fingers off with my other hand. I failed.

"Even Derrick, who has tried to get all bro-like with me, is getting nosy. He's asking too much, too." Phil kept hold of me. If anything, he squeezed harder. "I did not kill my wife, do you understand me?"

"Seriously, Phil, let me go or I'll call the police." I reached my right hand toward my back pocket, pretending I still had a phone in there.

He glared at me, then dropped his hand. My arm throbbed. I took another couple of steps back, in case. I knew every door in the building. I could outrun Phil if I had to.

"I think that Indian fish lady did it," he said.

Tulia? He had to be kidding. "Why would she commit murder?"

"Because she wanted to rob my heritage of its one holiday. Change Columbus Day to Native People's Day or whatever ridiculous thing they have in mind."

Whoa. Racist much? "What about honoring the Wampanoag heritage?" I asked. "They were here long before Columbus." I didn't add that the explorer had never reached New England at all.

"So you're on their side. I should have expected as much."

I edged another step toward the side aisle.

"Don't worry," he scoffed in disgust. "The fuzz are keeping a close eye on my whereabouts. I know they're following me. Some cop is probably out there right now, making sure I don't 'murder' someone else." He used finger quotes, but his scathing tone would have gotten the message across without them. "Why would I kill Annette? If I was convicted, it would leave my daughter an orphan." His voice caught and he glanced away.

So he had a heart, after all. Or he had acting chops.

"Then you don't have anything to worry about, do you?" I asked.

"If that Indian detective knew his job better, he'd have the real killer behind bars. Instead I get harassed from every corner." Phil leaned toward me, his angry tone back in full force. "Including yours." He strode toward the back and out the door.

I sank my newly wobbly self back down onto the pew. I was so done with going places in public alone, at least until Lincoln closed this case.

CHAPTER 46

I hurried to my shop at five, but the Open flag wasn't flying and the lights were off inside. Just as well that Orlean had closed up early. I missed my phone more than ever. Maybe I could get Gin to text her and the other weekend employee to tell them not to bother coming in tomorrow. I wished I'd put a storm plan in place earlier. Finding someone now to block the windows with plywood would be impossible.

I blew out a breath. I only wanted to go home and collapse, but I'd told Gin I would stop by.

As I passed the parking lot to the right of Mac's Bikes, which led to the path to my house, Derrick's small car pulled in.

He lowered the window. "Hey, Mac."

"Hi." I peered in the back to see Cokey and Kendall

poring over a book in the back seat. "Hey, girls." I waggled my fingers at them.

They returned the greeting, then bent their heads to point at the picture book again.

"I'm dropping Kendall off at home, then Cokester and I thought we'd stop by your place for a few. She said she misses Belle."

"I do," Cokey piped up. "Kendall wants to meet her, too. And we're having a sleepover in the lighthouse."

Derrick looked at Cokey in the mirror. "We'll see, honey. It depends on what Kendall's daddy says." He shifted his gaze to me. "Is it all right if we drop by? "

"You know it is. Would you do me a favor and text Gin to ask her to come over later? We agreed to eat dinner together, but I'm beat, and I don't want to walk all the way to her shop to make arrangements. I want to get home."

"You bet."

"You contacted Tim for me, right? About my phone?"

"I did, sis."

"Did you hear back?"

He shook his head.

"He might still be in transit." I glanced at Kendall. "Does somebody's father know you're bringing her home?"

"Yeah." Derrick frowned. "Why?"

"I'll tell you when you come back." I held a finger to my lips.

"Whatever." He put the car in gear and drove off.

I trudged down the path, wondering what kind of reception Phil would give my brother, based on what he'd said to me.

This weather event was definitely on its way. If I'd been wearing a hat, it would have been long gone with

the wind. My patio furniture and trash barrel were still secured from earlier in the week. They were as set for a
storm as they could be. I'd read that one was supposed to
take everything inside before a big storm, but my tiny
house didn't have room for a barrel, not to mention another table and more chairs.

I had basic food and drink in the deckhouse and planned
to ride out Vicky with my parrot pal. And my iPad, which
connected me to the outside world—as long as we had
power. Sure, I'd be alone with a murderer at large, but I
had good locks and tight double-paned windows. I'd be
safe. I hoped.

Inside, I found half a bottle of white wine in the fridge
and poured myself a glass. Belle went nuts with excite-
ment that I was back. After I gave her dinner, I sank onto
my little couch to consider all that had happened today.
Tim's sister's plight and his quick departure. The tragedy
of losing my phone.

I missed Tim already. I grabbed my iPad and sent him
an email to that effect. Even though Derrick had said he
texted Tim, I outlined the accident with my phone and
asked about his sister. I told him I hoped he would send
messages through my brother or Gin.

I sent it and returned to my thoughts. Norland's news
about Doris's gambling. Phil's surprising pledge. The
suspicions Silas shared about Ogden. The fire and Abo
Reba's fall. Phil's accosting me. The advent of Vicky. If I
had any energy, I'd write it all down. With a storm on its
way, I figured I'd have plenty of time for that tomorrow.

Mid-musing, stroking Belle as I thought, Derrick and
Cokey arrived. Sure enough, Kendall was in tow, too. But
my brother wore a frown.

I welcomed them all in. "Girls, a juice box and some goldfish crackers?"

"Yes, please," Cokey lisped.

Kendall nodded. She gazed at Belle, her eyes wide.

"Come sit down to have your snacks." I set them up at the table.

Belle hopped over. "Snacks?"

"Titi Mac, can we give her goldfish?" Cokey asked.

"A couple. Let me get you her frozen snacks. She'll be happier with them." I handed the girls a bowl with frozen grapes and carrot chunks. "She'll eat out of your hand if you want."

"Like this, Kendall." Cokey giggled when Belle gobbled up the grape out of her little palm.

Kendall smiled shyly but shook her head at the idea of feeding a big-beaked bird.

"Girls, a juice box?" Belle imitated me. "Yes, please." She nailed Cokey's lisp, which brought a gale of squeals from said girls.

"A ginger ale, Derr?" I offered.

"Sure, thanks." He plopped down in the armchair next to the sofa. I joined him a minute later, handing him his drink.

"Why the frown?" I murmured.

"Phil was borderline rude to me." He kept his voice low. "He agreed to let Kendall sleep over, but he clearly wanted to get rid of us, and fast. He's been friendlier previously."

I nodded and told Derrick what had happened in the sanctuary earlier. I left out the part where he accused Derrick of being too buddy-buddy.

"That's bad behavior." He pressed his lips into a line.

"But is it bad because he's guilty, or bad because he feels wrongly accused?"

"Good question. Did you tell . . . oh, you can't tell Haskins. Here, use my phone. I even saved his number."

I tapped out a text to Lincoln. I identified myself and told him what Phil had done and said. I knew Lincoln would agree with Phil that the Cozy Capers should not be nosing around.

I wrinkled my nose and extended the phone to Derrick before I hit Send. "This will only justify Lincoln's objections to our sleuthing. Should I send it?"

"Hmm. I see what you mean. What if you write that you were alone in the church and Phil grabbed your arm and threatened you?"

"That's better." I fixed the text. I added one more line.

He let go only when I said I would call the police. He seemed to think you were tailing him. I'm using Derrick's phone because mine drowned. I don't have a replacement yet.

A firm tap on Send, and I'd completed my civic duty.

"Phil also told me he wants to plan his wife's funeral." Derrick kept his voice low. "He thought to have it tomorrow, but the church told him they don't do funeral masses on Sundays. Plus the storm. He's shooting for Monday."

"Does he have her, um, remains back?"

"I guess so."

I glanced at the little girls. At Phil's innocent daughter, who'd finally overcome her fear and had let Belle eat frozen carrot bits out of her palm. If her father was guilty of murder, her life would change even more. For her sake, I hoped someone else did it.

CHAPTER 47

G in surprised me by bringing pizza and red wine at six thirty instead of stopping by to talk about where we wanted to eat. Derrick and the girls had taken off twenty minutes earlier to pick up a kid-friendly dinner—frozen chicken fingers, tater tots, and applesauce—and other supplies at the market, so they could hunker down in the lighthouse.

"I thought this would be more fun than eating out." Gin poured the wine into the squat stemless glasses I'd set out.

"Definitely." I took a bite of the pizza and savored caramelized onions, Kalamata olives, goat cheese, and fresh basil.

"Meat-free is okay, right? I'm trying to cut back."

"Uh-huh," I mumbled, holding my hand in front of my full mouth.

"Meat-free is okay," Belle mimicked Gin's voice, then repeated it four more times.

I rarely gave Belle meat, since she already ate a high-protein diet, but the occasional bite of chicken or a small meatball didn't hurt her.

"Belle, you're amazing." Gin shook her head.

"Shh, don't tell her," I whispered. Too late.

"Belle's amazing. Belle's a good girl. Snacks, Mac? Snacks, girls?"

I tore off a piece of crust and set it on the floor for her. I enjoyed three good-sized pieces of pizza before sitting back, and Gin munched on her third. I sipped the wine, a smooth California blend.

Gin had set her phone on the table, and it vibrated as it dinged. She wiped her hands before picking it up.

Her eyebrows rose. "It's Flo. She wants to talk with you in person."

"Tell her to come over. I'm not going to have any more." I gestured at the remaining pie. "There's plenty of pizza, and I have a bottle of Cabernet Sauvignon in reserve if we need it."

"Done." After a few taps and another ding, Gin said, "She'll be here in a flash."

"It's too bad our excursion tomorrow to your hometown is off."

"Because of Vicky. The office of naming storms clearly doesn't know our chief of police. She'd never be that wild."

"I don't know. Victoria actually made kind of a joke today. And have you noticed her new hair style? Maybe she's loosening up."

"Mayyybeee." Gin stretched out the word like she didn't believe me.

"Since our road trip is off, could you call your mom and sound her out about Annette's family, instead?" I asked.

"Good idea." She pointed at me. "Why didn't I think of that? She and Dad are almost always home Saturday nights."

"I have a bit to tell you about Phil, but let's wait until Flo gets here." I sipped my wine and gazed at her phone. "I should probably text Lincoln what Silas Carter told me today."

"About Ogden?"

"Yes. Or maybe he already talked to Silas." I could have added it to my text about Phil, but I hadn't thought of it at the time.

"Wait a minute." Gin pointed at my iPad. "Don't you have texting on that?"

I shook my head. "I don't have cell service on it, and I don't have a phone to relay messages to it. But as long as I have Wi-Fi, I can email and browse the internet."

She unlocked the screen of her phone and pulled up the message app. "Have at it."

I tapped away.

Silas Carter, member of Wsthm Quaker church, told me O Hicks on their Finance comm. Others found discrepancies and fired him.

Was that enough? I thought so. Lincoln could pick up the investigation from there. I made sure I identified myself by name, and that I wasn't Gin. I sent the message.

"I guess churchgoers of any stripe can do bad things," I said.

"Yeah." Gin cocked her head. "Do you think he's getting anywhere? Haskins, I mean?"

"I don't know. I haven't seen him as much this week as in the previous cases." When a branch tapped against the side of the house, I plugged in a power strip and put it on the table. "We should keep your phone charged up."

"In case we lose power?"

"Exactly." I grabbed my iPad and almost plugged it in. But if I lost power, I'd lose Wi-Fi, too. Not much point in keeping the thing charged.

Flo's face at the window next to the door appeared at the same time as her knock. Out of an abundance of caution, I'd locked the door after Gin arrived. Home and awake, I normally didn't lock myself in. Not this week. Gin and I welcomed Flo, and I got her settled with a plate and a glass of wine. The silver-haired librarian bit into a piece of pizza and took a glug of wine to wash it down.

"Charge up if you want." I pointed to the power strip.

"Good idea." Flo found her charger and plugged in her phone. "This storm is now being called a bomb cyclone."

"It is?" Gin asked, wide-eyed.

"Yeah. When the barometric pressure drops precipitously."

"Cyclone sounds bad. Like a Kansas cyclone?" I asked.

"Yes and no. On the coast it's different, but the high winds are the same. Probably not a twister, though."

"But not a hurricane," I said.

"No," Flo responded. "So I checked out Seaview nursing home today."

"By checked out do you mean researched it online or drove up to Bourne?" Gin took a sip of wine.

"I decided to just go there. It's not that far. The receptionist happened to be new and didn't quite get the HIPAA regulations."

I narrowed my eyes. "You mean she told you confidential health information? She can get busted for that."

Flo batted away the idea. "Not health stuff. But get this. She said Ogden is behind on his payments. Medicaid doesn't cover the entire amount of his son's room, board, and ongoing therapy."

"The poor guy," I said. "The son, I mean."

Gin nodded in sympathy. "The father, too, really."

"We already knew Ogden supported him." Gin tapped her glass.

"Why wouldn't he be able to make the payments?" I asked them. "Is the place exorbitant?"

Gin's phone vibrated. Flo's dinged at the same time with what had to be a group text.

"Tulia," Gin said.

She and Flo read the message.

Flo whistled. "Her cousin sent her the results of Annette's autopsy."

Another message dinged its arrival.

After she read it, Gin extended her phone to me.

Death from paralytic shellfish poisoning. Saxitoxin found in A's system. Stabbing was postmortem.

I handed it back.

"So we were right," Gin said. "Whether he took her to Tulia's walk-in or not, it was Phil who killed his own wife by giving her soup with shellfish in it. Bad shellfish, at that."

"But we don't know that for sure," I said.

"Bad shellfish, Mac?" Belle cocked her head.

"Yes, Belle." I got up and poured a handful of the parrot treat I'd bought at Doris's into a bowl for her. Maybe that would keep her quiet for a while. I could put her to bed soon. *Good.* I loved my bird, but she could get a little annoying.

"But Annette wouldn't have touched any kind of seafood soup," I protested—quietly—to my friends.

"Wait a sec." Flo bent over her phone, madly tapping. "Not entirely."

"Not entirely what?" I asked.

"Saxitoxin is produced by *Alexandrium fundyense,* a byproduct of red tide."

Gin frowned. "But red tide is . . . in the ocean. In the sea. What does it matter if someone gave her tainted seafood or any seafood? And when's the last time we had red tide?"

"She would die either way if she didn't get help," I added. "Seriously, girls. She would not have gone anywhere near that kind of soup. Would she? How did it get into her system?"

"We need to know what kind of soup he made," Flo said.

"I told Lincoln what Kendall said to Cokey." I stared out at the windy dark. "I hope he went straight to the Di-Cicero house to confiscate the bowl or the pot or whatever, if he hadn't already."

"Aren't there all kinds of ways someone could have gotten seafood into her?" Gin asked. "Like fish oil, maybe."

"Or somebody could have injected Annette with the toxin." I swallowed as my house shuddered from the wind. The tight windows didn't rattle, and the structure was well-secured. I hoped. We did not want to end up flying through the air like Dorothy on her way from Kansas to Oz.

"Didn't we read a cozy where the villain injected a poison in the fold under a woman's buttock to hide the injection mark?" Flo asked.

"We did." I thought, then snapped my fingers. "Yes. One of the Country Store Mysteries, the Christmas one. *Candy Cane Murder*, maybe?"

Flo looked up from her phone. "*Candy Slain Murder*. You were almost right, Mac."

"So maybe the soup has nothing to do with Annette's death," I said.

"But hang on. If that's how they killed her, the autopsy should have found a puncture mark. Gin, ask Tulia if the report includes one."

Gin tapped out the question.

I held out my hand. "Can I use your phone again?" After she handed it to me, I texted Derrick.

Mac here. Kendall told Cokey her daddy made soup the day before Annette died, and that they left a bowl for her mommy and took the rest to her grandmother. Please gently ask her what kind of soup made, if you can.

I sent it. I gazed at my friends and told them what I'd written. "What if Phil made soup and by mistake used a stock with shellfish in it?"

"If he didn't kill her on purpose," Gin began, "who deposited her in the walk-in and tried to make it look like the stabbing killed her?"

"That's a question that needs an answer no matter who killed her first." I saw Annette's body again, the lobster pick in her neck, Tulia's shock and fear. It happened six days ago, an eon in homicide investigations, as I'd come to learn. I itched to know what Lincoln and team had discovered. I resolved to find some way to get him to tell me. With the howling gale out there, conversation with the tall detective would have to wait until tomorrow.

CHAPTER 48

I asked if my friends didn't want to start home because of the storm.

"Another hour of hanging out won't make any difference, right, Gin?" Flo asked.

"Right," Gin confirmed. "I'm good."

"So, Mac, what went down with the fire engines at the UU today?" Flo asked.

I twisted out the cork from my reserve bottle of red and poured for all three of us. I dug my last box of girl scout Thin Mint cookies out of the freezer, arranged the contents of one sleeve of cookies on a plate, and brought it to the table.

"A guy off his meds named Witter thought it would be a good idea to have a campfire inside the church," I said. "Luckily Elenia Rodrigues was with him and called the fire department. They put it out in time."

"I know Witter," Flo offered. "He comes into the library nearly every day. He's homeless—and a big reader."

"He has a temporary home in the psych department at the hospital for now." I nibbled on a cookie.

"Witter has always been well behaved at the library," Flo said. "I think he used to be a professor."

"He wasn't that well behaved today—or more so was being delusional." I frowned. "And then my grandma went over to check out the scene and fell on the church steps."

Gin's breath rushed in. "Reba? Is she all right?"

Flo looked worried, too.

"Abo Reba." Belle cocked her head. "Abo Reba."

"Yes, Belle, Abo Reba," I said. "And yes. She'll be fine. I think. She apparently didn't break anything or get a concussion, thank goodness, but she's bruised and shaken."

"What a blessing," Flo chimed in.

"You can say that again." I pressed my eyes closed for a moment. I pictured my tiny pale grandmother strapped into that stretcher. "My parents are at the hospital. The doctors wanted to observe her for the night. I'll go over in the morning if I can."

"She's in good hands." Gin patted my arm. "Speaking of family, I'm going to make that call to Mom." She shifted to sit on the couch for the conversation.

"Back to Witter," I said to Flo. "It's sad somebody with mental illness isn't getting good care. And it's sad for any of them to have to live in tents."

"Especially with whozit trying to get them cleared out entirely," Flo added.

"Whozit being the jewelry store owner who spoke at town meeting?"

"That one."

"Whozit." Belle always muttered when she tried out new words or phrases. "Whozit. Whozit. Cheese it, the cops." She hopped up to the back of my chair.

"Quiet, Belle." I reached around and stroked her back.

"I really admired your father for what he said in defense of the people camped out." Flo selected her second cookie. "He's a good man with his heart totally in the right place."

"Thank you. I agree."

"Whozit?" Belle asked.

Gin giggled. She sat at the table again, her call concluded.

"Sorry." I spread my hands. "She comes with the territory."

"I love Belle," Gin said. "Right, bird?"

"Right." Belle fixed one eye on Gin.

"Flo, are they asking this area to evacuate?" I asked. Clearing out with a bird in tow would be nearly impossible.

She worked her phone. "No, but definitely shelter in place."

I glanced at the clock. If this bomb cyclone got crazier later, Belle had better get her beauty sleep now. Seven thirty wasn't too early at all, and she was way too manic for this time of night. Guests tended to elicit her talkative side. My reward for loving a social bird. The storm wasn't helping, either.

"Time for bed, favorite parrot." I picked her up, kissed the top of her silky head, and deposited her in her cage.

"Sweet dreams, Belle," Gin said.

"Sweet dreams are made of this." Belle began the Eurythmics song, bobbing her head in time, her voice a

drop-dead imitation of Annie Lennox. "Who am I to dis-
agree?"

Gin erupted in laughter. I latched the door and pulled
the cover over to the diminishing strains of Belle's second favorite song after Pharrell Williams's "Happy."

"Mac, don't you want to order a new phone online?"
Flo asked. "It's easy. You can use my phone to do it."

"Thanks, but I can't do it on the fly like that." I hated
not having everything lined up and clear. "I have to do all
my research. You know me."

"I suggested she order online this morning, but she
turned me down," Gin said.

"I actually tried on my iPad, but the order didn't go
through. It's okay."

"Whatever." Flo focused on her phone.

Flo looked up with a frown. "Tulia replied on the
thread. Said she didn't see the whole autopsy report but
has asked her cousin to send it to her."

"Good." I washed my hands and returned to the table.
Belle stopped singing. My iPad made the incoming mail
sound. I brightened to see Tim's name.

**At SeaTac waiting for shuttle to rental car. Will send
news later. Love you.**

I glanced at my friends. "Tim arrived safely. He's at
the airport and is on his way to his sister."

"Glad to hear it." Gin patted my hand. "I'm sure his
sister will pull through, Mac, and you'll get him back
home soon."

I wasn't sure where her confidence came from, but the
thought comforted me. "Gin, what did your mom say?"

Gin nibbled on a cookie and gazed forlornly at her
empty wine glass. "I'm walking home, you know."

I laughed and poured more Cab for her. "Better?" I asked.

"Yes, thanks."

"I can give you a lift, Gin," Flo offered.

"Thanks. Anyway, Mom said she knew Doris pretty well back in the day. And what she knows is kind of troubling."

Flo's attention remained at high alert. She covered her glass with her hand when I extended the bottle. "Unlike you both, I have to drive home. So . . ." She rolled her hand in the universal "continue" gesture. "Troubling like how?"

"Mac." Gin looked at me. "Didn't you say Elenia claimed Doris had manipulated the beauty contest results?"

I nodded. "She said Doris had promised she would win, but she didn't. Annette got the crown, not Elenia."

"Apparently Doris had some kind of influence over one of the male judges," Gin said. "Mom didn't know what kind, but she implied Doris might have uncovered dirt on his financial machinations. The dude's job was bank president."

"Did she know his name?" I asked.

"She didn't remember."

"I'll see if I can find who the judges were." Flo's fingers flew on her phone.

"What year would that have been?" I asked.

"It was sixteen years ago," Flo said.

Thinking about Doris, my brain moved on to Ogden. "If Ogden had been up to financial fishy stuff, maybe Doris discovered it. If she has some kind of hold on him, do you think she coerced him into killing Annette?"

"But why?" Flo asked.

"Maybe Annette knew of Doris trying to fix the contest," I said slowly, thinking out loud. "Annette might have threatened to go public with the information. But I don't understand her reason for doing it now rather than at some earlier time."

"I don't know. She felt secure in her life?" Flo shook her head. "We might never know."

"Mom also said Elenia wasn't totally without blame," Gin said. "Sure, she came from a poor family. Her father had been unemployed. Her mom had a drinking problem, and Elenia had five younger siblings. But she went right along with Doris in the scheme."

"How does your mother know all this?" I asked.

"She owned the dress shop where lots of the girls bought their gowns and had them altered. Mom heard all the gossip, all the accusations. All the dirt."

"Wow." I shook my head. "Did no one ever bring Doris to task? I mean, did the pageant officials understand the situation? Did they know?"

Flo pointed at her phone. "Found a news article. It says the contest officials were the most corrupt of all. That—"

Crack! The lights went out. The soft Mozart I'd had playing in the background silenced. The illumination filtering in from the streetlight went dark. All the never-noticed background noises of household appliances and electronics disappeared into stillness. The only light came from the two phones.

"I guess Vicky's here," I said. The storm now sounded like a rushing train.

Gin laughed. "Ya think?"

CHAPTER 49

My sleep was fitful. I must have seen every hour on the little battery-operated analog travel clock I kept by my bed. The storm battered my tiny house and made it shudder more than once. So far, the sturdy new construction held fast. Before going to bed, I'd donned a long-sleeved Cape Symphony tee and PJ pants decorated with Scotty dogs in case I had to make a quick exit in the night.

The noise made my thoughts go every which way, too. Derrick hadn't gotten back to me via Gin's phone about what Kendall's reply was. And had I told Gin and Flo about Phil in the church? I didn't think so. I lay tossing and turning, scrambling my bedclothes. I pictured my grandmother in the hospital. I had to think she wasn't sleeping too soundly, either. Surely nurses would wake her up to take vital signs and make sure she remained stable. She had to be all right. She was my Abo Ree. I knew I would lose her at some point in the next decade or two, but right now I wasn't ready to. No way.

When I startled awake at three twenty, new noises had mixed with Vicky's roar. They were smaller, closer. Had Belle awoken? Usually nothing roused the parrot from her deep bird-slumber. I jammed on my glasses and crept down the steps from the sleeping loft.

Belle stayed quiet under her cover. It hadn't been her. What had I heard? I sat on the bottom step and listened with all my senses alert. A *snick* came from the door. Was somebody trying to break in? *Yikes.* My pulse picked up. I gazed frantically around the dark room. Did I have any heavy furniture to wedge under the door? Anything that wouldn't make noise dragging it over? Not really. Or maybe I should make noise to scare the intruder away.

I knew I had an excellent dead bolt. And my windows were locked. Still, not having a phone made me uneasy. No, I was terrified. I crept to the kitchen and grabbed my biggest knife, the one with the eight-inch chopping blade. I stood, knife in hand, and waited.

Who wanted to get in? Since I'd closed the blind on the window next to the door, I knew they couldn't see me. All the other windows were too high for anyone short of seven feet—or standing on a ladder—to see in. Plus zero light shone. The place was really dark.

I perched on the bottom loft step again and thought. A pulse beat in my neck. Was this Annette's killer, because I'd been asking questions? Phil? Doris? Ogden? Surely not Elenia. Definitely not Witter—he'd been committed.

A bump sounded. *Gah!* Did they have a battering ram? A voice shouted an obscenity worthy of a sailor. Male voice? Female? The storm masked the shouter's identity.

I kept listening. I strained my ears but heard no more shouting. No more bumps. The small sounds of a break-in progress ceased. I waited until I thought twenty minutes had passed. I sat on the couch, knife in hand, until I found myself nodding with sleep. I brought the knife back up to bed with me.

Once I was horizontal, sleep didn't return for a long time. My brain roiled with questions. Had it been two people out there? Maybe one tried to break the door down but hit the other by mistake. Had a limb broken off the big tree behind my shop and crashed into my attacker? Had someone come to my rescue? I kept trying to calm my mind. I wasn't successful until glimmers of cloud-filtered dawn played at the window.

CHAPTER 50

Thanks to pre-ground coffee—always in reserve in my pantry—plus a single-cup drip cone with filter, and a gas stove, I blessedly had coffee to savor not long after I woke up at eight thirty. I needed the caffeine after last night. The power remained out, but the sun was up. Not shining, exactly, but illuminating the world. And the wind and rain had vanished with the darkness.

After I got Belle up and fed, I washed my face, put in my contacts, threw on a sweater and jeans, and slipped on sneakers. Gin and I never walked on Sundays, because I saved weekend mornings for Tim. Today? I flew solo. I hoped Tim had both seen Jamie and taken charge of the children without incident. I wouldn't be able to get actual information until Derrick or somebody else had heard from him. I unlocked the door to the outside and pulled it open.

Whoa. The term "storm damage" barely described the reality. Thirty yards away, a pale gash marred the trunk of the swamp oak behind my shop where a major limb had broken off. Detritus lay on the ground all around my house. My efforts to secure my trash barrel had failed. It sat upended, caught by the hedge of rosa rugosa that ran along the path to the Shining Sea Trail. The sturdy spiny beach rose bushes themselves were bowed sideways from the battering they had taken.

Leaning against the landing right here in front of me must have been the cause of the bump from last night. A branch as long and as thick as my leg lay on the ground near the bottom of the two steps coming up to the door. I turned around and closed the door so I could examine it. Sure enough, scratch marks marred the heavy wood around the lock. The jamb had been dented, too, as if my would-be attacker had used a pry bar.

I swore. If I had my phone, I could snap some pictures. Instead I dashed back in, grabbed my iPad, and used that to document the damage. Carrying the device down the steps with me, I squatted to examine the limb of at least five inches in diameter. I had no idea if wood carried fingerprints, but I pulled down my sleeve to cover my hand before I picked up the end. Might as well play it safe, especially since it hadn't been cold enough last night to warrant someone wearing gloves. Someone innocent, that is. Whoever made those marks on my door was the definition of Not Innocent.

A shaft of silver sunlight split the clouds and shone nearly horizontally in my direction from the east. I turned the branch this way and that. Then froze. A coin-sized dark blotch marred the bark at the thickest point. Blood? I couldn't tell. Something had gone bump in the night. Something had made that "bam" sound. Maybe the limb struck the person on the head, and their head hit my door.

Turning the limb with the dark blotch facing up, I set it on the landing and took several more pictures, then laid it back on the ground. I supposed Lincoln would chastise me that I'd moved it at all. Too late now. What if the person had dropped an object that could identify them? Jessica Fletcher would look for clues. Julia Snowden would, too, along with all the other amateur sleuths in the cozy mysteries our group read. I could mount a search as well as they could.

I started on the landing. I squatted and examined every square inch. I spied the corner of a piece of cardboard or paper sticking up from between the boards. I coaxed it out only to see the stub of the ticket for a Baroque concert I'd attended three weeks ago and must have dropped. I kept up my search. For hair, scraps of fabric, whatever could lead me to the person bold enough to think they could roust me from my home mid-cyclone and presumably do me harm. Except I came up empty.

Wait. It had rained all night. I had a driveway of sorts, covered with crushed shells. I didn't park there, though. I left Miss M in the paved Mac's Bikes parking lot and the only people who used the driveway were visitors who drove here, like Flo last evening. I hadn't heard the crunch of a vehicle on the shells in the night, but the storm could have masked it. Maybe there were footprints I could find. It seemed like the police were always taking impressions

of footprints and comparing them to the sole of a suspect's shoe.

But I'd already stepped on the ground when I pho-
tographed the branch. Had I ruined the chances of the experts finding an intruder's print? Directly around the
landing lay an area of mulch. Right now it looked squishy
and like it wouldn't keep a shoe impression for long. The
mulch extended on a pathway to the driveway so my feet
didn't get muddy when I left the house. On either side of
the path I had a small lawn, or what passed for one in our
sandy soil. I wasn't into gardening or using chemicals,
and the grass looked ratty all summer. The lawn showed
off its greenest self right now with the cooler tempera-
tures, despite being overdue for a mowing.

I squatted on the bottom step and scanned the ground.
I ran my gaze in a tight arc around the step, then in increasingly larger ones. Nothing. *Oh well.* The police could
look for themselves. I stepped onto the path. Had I missed
anything? Once again I squatted, this time checking under
the steps. They were treads only, without risers or side
pieces to close them in.

The gap in the eastern clouds widened. Sunlight glinted
on metal under the second step. I pulled my sleeve down
again to protect my hand and reached way under to grab
the item. I stood and peered at it. The thing, about five
inches long, had a flat textured handle made of sturdy
black plastic or rubber that reminded me of a nail file's,
except longer. The metal part was a two-inch narrow
spike of metal that curved slightly at its tip. I'd never
seen anything like it. The end reminded me of one of the
tools of torture the dental hygienist employed, or the
electric tooth flossing device my mom used, that Water-

pik thing so heavily overadvertised on television. I stared at it. *Pik.* Could this be a lock pick?

I trotted inside with it and laid it on a clean dish towel on the table. "Time for this sleuth to eat and go find the cops."

"Go find the cops, Mac," Belle said. "Go find the cops!"

CHAPTER 51

After breakfast, I first made a beeline to my shop to check it out. Last night I'd had Gin text my weekend mechanic to stay home, thinking the storm would last longer. I'd lettered a notice about being closed on a piece of paper before I left the house. Now, tape in hand, I fixed it to the front door. I shivered, glad I'd thrown on a light jacket over my sweater. The mercury had dropped back to a more seasonable—if chilly—fall temperature.

I strolled around the building. Blessedly I didn't see any damage to my business. Windows were intact, and the flowers in the window boxes weren't too drowned by the rain. Clearly the big branch from the swamp oak had blown in the opposite direction. I sucked in a breath. What if it had landed on Miss M? I hurried around the side where I parked her and let my breath out. It had been close, but the limb had fallen a few feet away.

I needed to spell my mom with Abo Reba. Instead of walking, I decided to drive to the station to turn in the pick. I could head to the hospital after that.

Church bells in town chimed once for the half hour, which meant nine thirty had already rolled around. Pa would start his service at ten. He was like that postal carrier creed: "Nor fire nor power outage nor broken water pipe shall keep him from his appointed sermon." I clicked the key fob for Miss M, dishtowel-wrapped tool in hand.

At the police station, I leaned toward a speaking disk set into heavy tinted glass. "Is Detective Haskins in?" Lights were on in the foyer and behind the glass. Having an emergency generator would be a requirement for them, I should think.

The voice of the person who sat behind the glass came out tinny. "No, ma'am. What is it in regard to?"

"Someone attempted to break into my house last night. Can I talk to Officer Kimuri instead, or Chief Laitinen?"

He swiveled in his chair and called out behind him, "Kimuri? Someone to see you."

She approached the window. "Ms. Almeida?"

"I need to talk to you about an attempted break-in at my house last night. I found an object Lincoln might be interested in." I held up the dishtowel. Which looked silly. Now I wished I'd dropped the pick into a clean envelope.

She peered at the dishtowel and at my face. "All right. Meet me at the side door." She pointed to her right.

A moment later the door to my left opened. She held it for me and ushered me into an interview room in the middle of the station.

"Is Lincoln here?" I asked.

"No."

Kimuri sat across the table from me and tapped into a digital device in front of her. She identified herself and the date. "Mac, please say your name and address."

"You're recording this?" I'd thought I'd come simply to tell her what I knew.

"We record all interviews, although the video is on the fritz right now."

"All right. My name is Mackenzie Almeida." I added the address, then folded my hands. I didn't want to fiddle with them and look nervous.

"Did I hear you say someone tried to break into your house?" Kimuri asked.

"Yes, during the storm in the middle of the night. Around three thirty. I don't have a phone right now or I would have called it in." I described the scratching sounds, the noise of something heavy hitting, and the person's obscenity. "I couldn't tell if the voice sounded male or female."

"And you're sure the scratching wasn't from a branch in the wind? We did have a super storm, after all."

As if I didn't know that. I knew she had to ask, and I tried to stay patient. "A branch was involved, but I found scratch marks around my lock this morning that weren't there yesterday. They'd dented the jamb, like they'd used a pry bar."

"Do we have your permission to check out the area?"

"Please do." I unfolded the towel. "This had been left under my steps."

She pulled the towel toward her but didn't pick up the object. "A Peterson hook. They make one of the best lock pick sets around."

"How do you know the brand?"

Kimuri stared at me. "Because it says so?" She pointed to the haft.

"Oh." *Duh.* PETERSON was pressed into the thick plastic. I must have covered that when I picked it up or looked only at the other side. "I thought maybe it was a lock pick. I also found a pretty big branch at the foot of the steps and there's a blotch on it. Here, I'll show you." I pulled the iPad out of my bag and found the pictures.

"Interesting. Thanks for taking pictures. Can you send them to me?"

"No. I don't have cell service on it. Do you want to connect me with the station Wi-Fi?"

"No, but I can extract them after we're done."

"Okay. I think maybe the limb blew off the big tree behind my shop and hit the person on the head as they worked on my lock. The blotch could be blood, right?"

"It's possible."

"I know the scratching noises stopped after that *bam* I heard." I tapped the iPad. "Can you convey all this to Lincoln? He should see if any of the murder suspects has an injury on their head."

"Yes. Is there anything else you've learned that you'd like to share?"

My reputation must have preceded me. I thought at high speed. I didn't want to go into the whole beauty pageant controversy. Doris's history with it, and Elenia's. Should I mention Phil's borderline threat? I'd already told Lincoln. I didn't need to go into with Kimuri.

"No, I don't think so."

She picked up the iPad and stood. "Do I have your permission to extract the photographs?"

"Yes, of course. You'll see. It'll be the last, I don't know, eight or so. I'm not sure when I used it to take pictures before this morning, but they were probably of my parrot." Normally I shot photos with my phone, not the iPad.

"I'll be right back."

I drummed my fingers on the table in her absence. I admired my new ring, but my thoughts were on a different man. Where in heck was Lincoln? How I wished I knew more about his investigation. I'd have to figure out some way to track him down today. Or maybe I should pay visits to the persons of interest and see how their heads looked. But that was way too dangerous.

CHAPTER 52

On my way to the hospital, I slowed, driving past the Westham park with the homeless encampment. My heart broke for Elenia and her friends. The storm had destroyed most of the ragtag shelters. Tarps, chairs, and plastic bags of possessions were scattered everywhere. Mother Nature had made their owners' lives even harder than before. I hoped Elenia and her friends had stayed safe in the shelter last night.

I continued to drive toward Falmouth and spied storm damage everywhere. To the side of an antique house, the door of a shed hung by one hinge at a crazy angle. Lawn furniture and trash barrels had roamed far from their homes. Other people must have homes or apartments too small for storing such items indoors, too. Tree branches and leaves littered the streets. Two men hoisted a piece of plywood to cover a broken picture window.

Litter cluttered my brain, too. I tried to put it to rest. My priority right now was to hang with my grandma. Lincoln was good at his job, and I had to trust that he would be successful at it. And soon.

I turned off the busy road onto the street that ultimately led to the hospital. *Uh-oh*. Flashing police lights greeted me. The road had been blocked off a little ways after a side street. Car after car turned left onto the smaller road instead of going straight. When I reached the officer who directed traffic, I lowered the window.

"I need to get to the hospital."

He shook his head. "A massive tree fell and blocked the road. Are you an employee?"

"No, but my grandmother was admitted last night. Isn't there another way—"

He held up a hand. "Sorry. The second access is reserved for emergency vehicles and medical personnel only."

"There's no way to get in?" My voice rose. I had to see Abo Reba.

"You can get back to town that way." He made a two-armed traffic-directing gesture toward the left, the kind of crisp signal every officer seemed to be expert at.

I swore under my breath and added a curse about my lack of a phone. I should have let Flo convince me to order one online last night. I needed to call my mom and tell her I wouldn't be there—and I couldn't.

"And there's no parking on these streets, either," he added.

Shoot. How did he know I'd thought about parking and walking in? The car behind me beeped. I glanced in my mirror to see a long line of vehicles. Soon they would all be as disappointed as I was. I made the turn.

Sure enough, the narrow street was plastered with orange Temporary Parking Ban signs, and the one after that was, too. How far away would I have to go to find a place to leave Miss M? I didn't know anybody in Falmouth whose driveway I could borrow.

I pointed my ride back to Westham, but I pounded the steering wheel. I pictured Abo Reba in her hospital bed. I thought of Mom, who surely needed a break by now. I imagined whoever had tried to break into my house last night returning to do more damage. I wondered if Pa knew about the road closure. Maybe not. My dash clock read ten forty-five. He'd be winding up his service pretty soon.

My driving seemed to be on autopilot, because I found myself in front of Salty Taffy's after I arrived back in town. Gin didn't open on Sundays until noon. I parked in her driveway and trotted up the outside stairs to her apartment above the shop. She didn't answer the door. I pressed my nose to the glass in door and called, "Gin? Are you there?" with no success.

I slapped the side of my head. She was probably downstairs in the kitchen making candy. I should have looked there first. Down I went, trying to shake off a memory. Earlier in the year Gin and I had had a scary encounter with a murderer in the candy kitchen. A spooky premonition washed over me. Could I be about to find my friend in trouble again? I told myself not to be ridiculous.

The side door opened at my touch. I sensed too much quiet.

"Gin?" No answer. I crept through the hall to the clean and dark kitchen. She wasn't here. I slapped my head again, but mentally this time. Naturally she couldn't make candy if the town didn't have power. Was she even here? But . . . if she wasn't, I knew she wouldn't have left the door unlocked.

Was that a noise from the shop proper in front? The door to it swung both ways. Nervous, I tiptoed over and pushed the door open a couple of inches. *Whew*. Rag in hand, Gin polished a glass-fronted candy case. I knocked on the door, not wanting to startle her. A cool wave of relief washed away my worries.

She paused and glanced over. "Hey, Mac. Some storm, huh? We're lucky it moved through quickly."

"I'll say." I thought of everything else I could say, like, *I'm glad you're okay*, and *Someone tried to break in last night*. Instead, I asked, "Can I borrow your phone again?"

"Sure. I thought you planned to spend the morning at the hospital."

"I tried. The main road is blocked, and they've reserved the other one for hospital people and ambulances." I took the phone she offered, found the number of the hospital, and asked the operator who answered to put me through to Reba Almeida.

My jaw dropped. By the time I mustered a question, the woman had disconnected. I swore, this time out loud. Gin didn't care.

"What is it?" She stilled her swiping hand.

"They said she's not there. They hung up before I could ask for details. Gin, what if she got worse and has been transferred up to Boston?" A sob threatened to interrupt my question.

"Hey, now." Gin set down her rag and spray bottle. She laid her hands on my shoulders and gazed into my face. "I know you love her, but why have you jumped to the worst possible outcome?"

I shrugged, barely in control.

"Consider this. She's well enough to be discharged. Your mom brought her home, either to her apartment or to the parsonage. Reba Almeida is a tough old broad. Why don't you call Astra and ask her?"

I stared back. "Why didn't I think of that?" Maybe because I'd barely slept last night.

"Phone. You. Astra." She resumed cleaning.

I poked the number with a shaky finger.

"Hello, Gin," Mom's voice said.

"Mom, it's me. Is Abo Ree all right?"

"You bet she is. She got sprung a couple of hours ago. We're here at the parsonage having tea and apple muffins. Come by whenever you can."

"Give her my love."

"Honey, you can do it yourself. In person." She disconnected. I pressed my eyes closed for a moment.

"Was I right, or what?" Gin asked.

All I could do was nod.

CHAPTER 53

Before I left Gin's, I used her phone once more to text Lincoln. I asked for a meeting with him and said I would be around the parsonage for the next hour, or otherwise probably at home. I tried to word it as if I had information to share. I wasn't sure I did, other than the business with the lock pick, which I had every confidence Kimuri had already told him about. Mostly I wanted to see if I could pluck any information from him.

Five minutes later I'd parked Miss M back at Mac's Bikes, hurried to the parsonage, and wrapped my little grandma in a huge—and delicate—embrace. She sat ensconced in the upholstered rocking chair in the den, tucked into a fleece blanket. She looked tinier than usual. Tucker snoozed on the floor next to her.

"Now I don't want you to worry about me, Mackenzie." Her voice came out stronger than her appearance would suggest. "I'll be fine. Why, the doctor wouldn't have let me leave if she didn't think so. Isn't that right, Astra?"

Mom bustled in with a tray holding three cups of tea, a stack of Thanksgiving cocktail napkins, and a plate of muffins, freshly baked by the delicious smell of the house. "That's right."

Abo Reba accepted a mug and a muffin on a napkin. "It's ridiculous and dangerous to stay in the hospital when you don't need to be there. People get sick all the time from germs they pick up solely by virtue of breathing the air in there. By having nurses and whoever touch a sick person and then touch their next patient." She shook her head. "No, indeed, I demanded to be discharged."

Mom beamed at her. "I expressed my full support. I told them we would take excellent care of her." She handed me my tea.

"All I have is a few bruises," Abo Reba said. "Nothing that won't heal."

"I, for one, am glad you're here," I said. "The main road must already have been blocked."

"Indeed, it was." My *abo* nibbled at her muffin.

"We slid out the back way," Mom said. "Goodness, what a headache for the police."

"They wouldn't let me through, and I lost my phone yesterday." I took a bite of muffin and savored the cinnamon flavoring the tiny chunks of apples scattered throughout. "Mom, this muffin is fabulous."

"Thanks."

"Sent your phone for a salty swim, I heard," my grandma said.

"Or a muddy one." I nodded. "It seemed like the better plan to come back to Westham and track you down."

"What's up with the murder investigation?" Reba asked, eyes twinkling. "Has your group solved it yet?"

"No, unfortunately." Should I tell them about the break-in attempt? My grandmother seemed strong, and I knew she would hate not knowing. "During the storm last night, somebody tried to break into my house."

"And you were there alone because your man had to travel," Abo Reba said.

"Yes."

My mom frowned. "Did you find any clues as to the person's identity?"

"Maybe. They dropped—and left—a lock pick. I took it over to the station earlier this morning. Officer Kimuri said they would check out the scene."

"What has Lincoln uncovered about Annette's murder?" Mom asked.

I scrunched up my nose. "I haven't talked to him in a couple of days. I don't know if he's made progress or not. Have you heard of an arrest?"

"No."

"I expect he's busy behind the scenes," Abo Reba said.

"Hey, the power's back on." I shook my head at my own lack of observation. Mac Almeida, the Clueless Detective. "I just realized you have lights on. Cool."

"Yes, it popped back into life about, what, half an hour ago?" Reba asked my mom.

"Yes." Mom sipped her tea.

"It must have been right after I left Gin's." I took another bite of muffin. Breakfast seemed like it had been days ago.

The outer door creaked. Derrick and Cokey blew in

with a gust of fresh air. Tucker raised his head and yipped a greeting. My niece ran to her great-grandmother.

"I was worried about you, Bithabo," Cokey said, using her version of the word for great-grandmother. "Daddy said you hurted yourself." She buried her face in Reba's lap and hugged her.

Abo Reba stroked her angel hair. "I'm fine, Cokinha. We'll be back on the trail together before you know it." She and my mom sometimes took Cokey, on her pink bike with training wheels, for a short ride on the Shining Sea Trail when they went out on their adult trikes.

"Goody." Cokey straightened and spied the muffins. "Abo Astra," she lisped. "May I have one, please?"

"Surely, sweetie. Sit on the floor there and make sure the crumbs fall onto the napkin." After Cokey folded her legs under her—which made my knees hurt to even think of doing the same—Mom handed her a muffin on a napkin.

"What about this sweetie?" Derrick smiled.

"You, too, my boy," Mom said to him. "Help yourself."

He demolished his in quick order. "Cokey, tell Titi Mac what Kendall said about the soup."

Right. I'd asked him to ask Kendall what kind of soup Phil had made. As I remained phone free, the answer hadn't come straight to me. Or maybe my brother hadn't gotten a chance to relay it yet.

"She said her Granny Dee made soup, and her daddy made soup from it." She returned to plucking pieces off her muffin to eat.

"Yeah," Derrick said. "I found what she said a little confusing. But we asked her."

Soup from soup. What did that mean?

Reba piped up. "Would that grandma be Annette's mother?"

"No, Phil's," Derrick said.

Dee for DiCicero.

"We know Rose DiCicero," Mom chimed in. "Don't we, Reba?"

"Yes." Abo Reba set down her mug on the end table next to her. "Mac, your mother and I know her from the Buzzard's Bay Garden Club. But Rose also occasionally attends Joseph's church, and she volunteers regularly for Our Neighbors' Table."

Rose? The Rose I'd met who volunteered at the free market? It could be. I hadn't learned her last name. And she was petite with dark hair, possibly dyed that color. She could easily be Phil's mother.

"Wait," I said. I glanced at the clock on the mantel, one Mom's father had inherited. I'd never met that grandfather, but I'd loved the reassuring tick of the clock and the smooth bell shape of the top. The timepiece had always sat there, never interfering, just regular and organized and, well, there. It now read eleven thirty. "Do you mean she might be at the church now?"

"Who might be at the church now?" My father ambled in from the kitchen.

I stood and gave him a hug. "Rose DiCicero."

He regarded me somberly for a moment. He'd always known my thoughts. He beckoned me back into the kitchen with him.

"Is this about the investigation?" he asked in a quiet voice.

"It might be. I learned that the Rose I volunteered with earlier this week is Phil's mother."

He nodded. "In fact, I believe she went down into the free market a few minutes ago to do some stocking. I told her that was not necessary on the Lord's day. She asked me, 'What better to do on exactly this day?' to which I had to agree. But go lightly, Mac, will you?"

I studied him. "I will, but why?"

"She has lost a daughter-in-law. Her son is under suspicion for murder. She's feeling a bit fragile at the moment."

"Deal." I hugged him again. "Tell Abo Reba I'll be back in a flash."

"I'll make no false promises." He chuckled. "I'll tell her you'll be back as soon as you can be." His expression turned to serious. "If you think you can learn important information, you should. But please be careful."

"Girl Scout's honor."

CHAPTER 54

I knew all the back stairways. I pulled open a seldom-used door into the free food market. Sure enough, Rose consolidated cans of tomatoes to make room for those in the box at her feet. I knocked on the wall to let her know I was there.

"Hi, Rose," I called.

She whipped her face toward me with wide eyes and flared nostrils. The look faded when she saw me.

"Mac? You surprised me."

"Sorry, I didn't mean to startle you. Keep on with your work. I'll help." I went to her side, extracted cans from the box, and handed them to her so she could arrange them how she liked. How I'd never seen her resemblance to Phil, I wasn't sure. The short stature, the dark hair, the square face, all of it. I must have missed their similarity because I hadn't been looking for it.

After a few minutes, she murmured, "Somehow I don't think you're here only to stock." She finished the row and faced me, dusting off her hands.

"Well, no. I was just in the parsonage with my mom and grandmother. They said Kendall's grandmother volunteers here and also sometimes attends my father's services. And Pa said you were down here."

"All true." She folded her arms and cocked a hip.

Uh-oh. Had I gotten her back up? I'd promised my father not to upset her. "We were on the same shift the other day, but I didn't learn your last name. I'm pretty irregular in my attendance at the UU services, too. I hadn't realized you were Phil's mother."

"And?"

I tried a different tack. "I thought your family was Catholic."

"What my late husband believed and my son's current religious practices are, frankly, none of your . . . business."

It sounded like she'd stopped herself from uttering an expletive in that pause. How had I gotten off to such a bad start with her?

"You're right. I'm sorry." I set the last can on the shelf, since her arms were still across her chest. *Protecting*. "Here's the thing. Kendall told my niece that you had made soup and then her father made soup from it."

She glanced away. As if she didn't want to hear it? I waited. Pa had said she was feeling fragile, but right now she seemed bullish, not delicate. Maybe Phil got his swagger from her. Or maybe this formed part of her self-protection. People put up all kinds of defenses when they felt vulnerable. Built walls when their world felt threatened.

"That detective has pestered me about the soup stock, too." She dropped her arms but set her fists on her hips. "What can I say? I gave my son some fish stock. It's all 'soup' to Kendall. Annette wasn't allergic to regular fish, only shellfish. Phillip made soup from it." She glared at me. "So what?"

Behind her, I caught movement outside the casement window, which sat right above ground level. From the khaki-clad knees down—all I could see—I was pretty sure that amble belonged to Lincoln Haskins. When he squatted to peer in the window, he confirmed the ID.

"I'll let you get back to your shelving, Rose. Thanks for talking with me."

Rose headed for the storeroom. As she went, she muttered, "Like I had a choice."

I made my way out the side door and up the steps, kicking broken branches out of my way.

"Interviewing a person of interest, are we?" Lincoln leaned against the trunk of a big spruce tree.

"Thanks for finding me, but I didn't interview her." I glanced back at the window. Rose had come back into the market. She stood under a light and jabbed at her phone. She held it to her ear. Had she called Phil? Told him I had been asking about the soup? If I could see her, she could see me with Lincoln. "Rose is a person of interest?"

"Possibly."

"Maybe we should move out of sight of the window."

He nodded, leading the way to a long wooden bench in the garden behind the church. "You wanted to speak with me?"

"Yes." I perched beside him and twisted to face the somber detective. "You heard about the attempted break-in?"

"I did. Good find on the lock pick, and you did an excellent job to protect the evidence. However, next time please leave it *in situ*. It's much more useful to us that way."

"I took a picture of it there. And I couldn't call." My voice rose. "What if I left the pick in place under my step and the person came back to retrieve it while I was out at the station relaying the information?"

He made a tamping-down gesture. "Under the circumstances, it's fine. At any rate, we've added that investigation to our long list." He sounded tired.

"Just so you know, Phil's daughter Kendall slept over with my niece at my brother's last night."

His dark eyebrows rose. "Is that so?"

"Yes. Phil was probably alone last night. He could have been the one trying to get into my house." I glimpsed a female cardinal, who hopped about in the dwarf maple tree across the garden. The turning leaves nearly camouflaged her feathers of the same color. "I told you Phil accosted me in the church yesterday afternoon."

"You did."

"It felt threatening."

"Which could mean he felt threatened by you. Why would that be, do you think?"

Darn. I shouldn't have brought up Phil. "He said you'd been tailing him. That you suspect him."

Lincoln stared up at the back of the tall, white, nineteenth-century building. "And maybe you'd followed him, too?" He kept his tone mild.

"No way." I pointed to the basement. "Just now, Rose DiCicero admitted she made a fish stock and gave it to Phil. But you know that, right?"

"We have had discussions with her, yes. An empty

container in the victim's kitchen had been clearly labeled
with Mrs. Rose DiCicero's name. Or, that is, the label
read, 'Granny D.'"

Granny Dee.

"Remains of the soup are at the lab for analysis," he
added.

"Good." I wasn't sure I should let on that I knew about
saxitoxin. "What did the autopsy show?" I tried mightily
to keep my tone innocent.

He gave me one of his "are you kidding?" looks. Apparently, I'd failed. I couldn't admit that Tulia's cousin
had revealed confidential police information or she'd get
sacked.

"Okay, I know. You can't tell me." I snapped my fingers. "Have you gotten anywhere looking into Ogden
Hicks? Or Doris Sandersen? I told you I heard she has a
gambling problem, right?"

He folded his hands in his lap and gazed down at them
in silence. Deciding how much to tell me, or whether to
share anything? The square black face of his watch
dinged. He tapped it, then stood.

"I have to be somewhere. Thank you for sharing what
you know. I appreciate your interest in the case. As always, I need to caution you to stay out of it. And be very
careful where you tread."

I rose. "I will. I promise."

He bent over to gaze intently at my face. "Please, Mac.
I'm serious. We have a murderer at large. You have en-
dangered yourself before. Stay. Out."

CHAPTER 55

By the time I got back to my parents' living room, my grandma slept in the rocker, and Derrick and Cokey had gone home to give a tour of the lighthouse. Pa, making full use of his recliner, snored away with his feet up, the Sunday paper half off his lap. Tucker was napping again, too.

Mom beckoned me into the kitchen and closed the door to the den.

"Mom, it smells awesome in here." Onions frying in the middle of the day lured me in every time. It evoked the smells of Thailand, Mexico, and other places I'd traveled where everybody cooked at home, often in the morning or at midday. And what was a good meal without onions? "I feel like I'm in another country."

She laughed. "Mac, honey, you are right here where you were born."

It was true. Mom had bucked the trends and given birth to me at home with a midwife. Right upstairs in this very parsonage.

"But listen, why don't you take my flip phone for the day?" She sliced mushrooms on a board.

"Really?"

"Why not?" She turned to the Dutch oven on the stove. "I don't need it until tomorrow. I've trained my clients to contact me via email rather than text or phone, and my computer is right there." She gestured toward the messy desk at the end of the kitchen, which served as her second office. Such disarray would drive me nuts, but this was her desk, not mine. "The phone is over there somewhere."

"Thank you. That's a huge gift, and I accept. I'll get up to Hyannis tomorrow to get a new one." Or maybe submit to the modern age and order one online right here at Mom's laptop. I peeked over her shoulder at diced onions shimmering golden as they sautéed. "What are you making?"

"Beef bourguignon. It's Sunday, isn't it?"

I squeezed her shoulder. "It is." Mom always made a big meal for Sunday afternoon dinner, usually meat or chicken, always served at five o'clock, with anyone around welcome to join her and Pa at the table. In the summer it might be barbecued burgers in the backyard, but the open invitation never varied.

"You'll join us, I hope." She swiped chopped garlic off a board into the pan and stirred.

"I'll do my best. Right now I need to go." I needed to find Doris and talk to her. Call Tim. Or maybe go hang with my bird.

Mom threw in a mess of sliced mushrooms. More stirring.

"I hope you come. Don't forget the phone. The charger is there, too." She gestured with her head. "And so you know, I have a special 9-1-1 button on the home screen. You know, in case."

"I definitely don't plan to need that, but thanks." I fetched both devices and pocketed them. I'd be able to call Tim. I could ask the Cozy Capers to copy Mom's number on any investigative thread. Texting, while possible, was rudimentary on a flip. Today? Possible worked for me. And I'd have access to the police. I hoped I wouldn't need it, but I had previously, and one never knew. I couldn't believe the relief a connection with the world brought. I tiptoed into the den, grabbed my bag, and returned to the kitchen. After Mom added half a can of tomato paste and a cup of red wine to the pot, she filled a teacup with the wine and took a sip. I smiled and kissed her cheek.

"Sweetie, take the rest of the muffins home," she said. "I made two dozen."

"I'd love to, thanks." I grabbed the paper bag she pointed to. "See you in a few hours, Mom. Thanks again."

"Be safe, darling. Your—"

I held up a hand to stop the inevitable astrological prediction. "I'll be careful." I slipped out the back door.

Once I reached the sidewalk in front of the church, activity in the park across Main Street caught my attention. The encampers were back and hurrying to restore their flimsy and sodden homes, from all appearances. Elenia's watch cap popped up among the bustlers. I wished I'd asked Pa earlier for an update on Witter, even though he might not have had one. I doubted Elenia would have any

information on his status. Still, I'd like to know if she
knew of Doris's gambling issue. I glanced down at the
paper bag in my hand. The muffins might give me an entree into the conversation.

My gaze on Elenia's cap so I didn't lose her, I waited
to cross the road until a light-colored Prius passed slowly
by. I hurried across but slowed my step. This band of people knew each other. They worked to find tent poles, to
rehang pieces of blue tarp. A woman roamed the park and
collected various species of lightweight chairs that had
blown to every corner. A guy hung wet bedding from a
tree with lots of low branches. I was an outsider with
nothing to offer but muffins. Maybe I should go home.

Elenia caught sight of me and hurried over to where I
stood on the sidewalk. "Did you hear any news about
Witter?"

"No, I'm sorry. My father didn't mention anything, either."

Her face dropped.

"Can I ask you a question?" I blinked out a speck of
dust that blew into my contact lens.

"Witter would say you just did." Her smile was sad.
"What do you want to know?"

"When you knew Doris on the pageant circuit, did she
gamble a lot?"

She gazed at me. "You think trying to throw pageant
results isn't gambling?"

"I suppose. I mean like in going to casinos or whatever."

"I worked hard for the prize I deserved. Doris? She
likes to cut corners wherever she can. If she thinks a
scratch ticket or a slot machine will get her a fast buck,

she goes for it," she scoffed. "Hasn't gotten her too far, though, has it?"

"El," a man called from the tent area. "Need a hand here."

She looked at me. "If you hear anything about my buddy, you'll tell me, right?"

"I promise." I remembered the muffins. "Here. My mom baked them a couple hours ago."

"Thanks." She accepted the bag. "I'll share them with the gang. And Mac? You probably oughta watch your back. Doris can be ruthless."

I watched her shuffle back to her community. *Ruthless.* Yes, Elenia, you can be sure I'll watch my back.

CHAPTER 56

As I walked home along Westham's main drag, I barely saw where my feet landed. Doris had a confirmed gambling problem, which could have made her desperate. Ogden was hard up for funds, too. Phil's mom had been defensive. And as much as I hoped for her innocence, Elenia hadn't been cleared in the least. I only prayed Lincoln had made way more progress on a resolution to this case than I had. I stopped abruptly, making a woman behind me exclaim.

"Excuse me?" She slid past and gave me a strange look.

Oops. I guess I wasn't watching my back at all. "Sorry." I stopped because I'd forgotten I had Mom's phone. A bench in front of the toy store presented itself. I sank onto the seat and dug out the flip. I opened a text message, planning to ask the Cozy Capers to include Mom's num-

ber on the thread until I got a new phone. And swore. I'd
relied on my contacts list for numbers instead of my
memory. Curse modern technology. I squeezed my eyes
shut. I'd known Derrick's number by heart for years—he
was my brother, after all—and that kind of memory belonged in the knowing-how-to-ride-a-bike category. It
didn't go away.

I poked the number into the To box, then laboriously
composed a text. I kept it as short and telegraphic as I
could.

**Mac here. Have Mom's phone. Pls add num to group
thread. Thx.**

Once sent, I considered a call to Tim right now, but decided to wait until I'd returned home to a quiet environ-
ment. The West Coast time zone was three hours earlier,
and it would be nine thirty there. Little kids in the house?
He would have been up for a while, that is, if he'd already
reclaimed them from Jamie's friend. I'd barely thought of
Tim's sister. Some fiancée I was. I hastily sent out heal-
ing energies to her.

I thought back to my interaction with Rose a little
while ago. She'd been prickly when I asked about the
soup. Because she thought I'd accused her son of murdering his wife? Or . . .

"Oh," I said aloud, drawing it into two syllables. A
man with a leashed dog glanced toward me. I gave him a
sheepish smile. What if Rose had her back up because she
poisoned the soup stock on purpose? She might have
been in cahoots, as they said, with Phil. Or she might
have flown solo, thinking Annette was bad for her son,
that he deserved someone better. Rose herself deserved a
much closer scrutiny, a possibility our group of wannabe
sleuths hadn't even considered.

The phone dinged with a text from Tulia. I opened it to see Derrick had already added Mom's number to the thread.

News, Mac? Progress?

I thought for a moment. Did I have news since last night? I texted back. Again I kept the message as tele-graphic as I could. Hitting a number repeatedly to pro-gress from R to S, for example, was the poster child for frustrating, and involved way too many backward dele-tions and corrections.

Failed break-in my house overnight. Found lock pick, took to stn. Perp might have head injury from flying branch.

And on the topic of head injuries, I knew I shouldn't rule out Elenia because I liked her. She could still be a murderer, and she could have made her way mid-storm to my house with a break-in tool. And with her ever-present watch cap pulled low on her forehead, I hadn't spied a trace of contusion.

I thought. What else should I convey to the group?

El confirms D long-time gambler.

I hit Send.

Tulia responded:

Reba all right?

Derrick beat me to the answer.

Yes.

I thought about how to convey my thoughts about Rose.

Shd take closer look at Phil's mom. Poisoned stock on purpose? Alone or in combo with son?

Tulia wrote back first.

Stock?

Ugh. I didn't want to have to type all that out on a flip. Maybe Derrick would. I called his number.

"Hey, bro, do me a favor?" I told him what I'd learned from Rose. "I also ran into Lincoln. He told me they know she gave Phil soup stock, and they're analyzing the container labeled Granny D. Can you text the group, please? Mom's flip makes it a real pain in the you-know-where."

He said he would. "While I have you on the phone, what did you mean by the person who tried to break in might have a head injury?" he asked.

"I heard the scratches of the lock pick during the storm," I began. "Then I heard a thud and the person swore. This morning I found a big branch that had blown over, probably from the swamp oak behind my shop."

"And you think it might have hit him in the head?"

"Him or her, yes. I didn't get a chance to tell you over at the parsonage." *Wait.* "You saw Phil earlier. Did you notice a contusion on his head?"

"Because he was alone last night?"

"Exactly."

He didn't speak for a moment. "He wore a hat. I didn't get a look at his head or even his forehead."

Shoot. "Thanks."

We disconnected the call, and the next group text in came from Derrick, with an explanation of the soup situation.

Norland chimed in, saying he had a contact in Pocasset who might know Rose.

I responded.

Thx.

CHAPTER 57

I continued on my way home. I couldn't wait to relax with Belle, a book, and a beer. A talk with my best guy. Ruminations on what we knew and what we still were missing.

My pace slowed when I spied more than minimal lights on inside Paws and Claws, even though the sign on the door read Closed. I tried the front door, but it was locked. Instead I backtracked around to the alley and found the back door ajar. I'd nearly pushed it open when I snatched my hand back. I glanced around. There wasn't a single car here. A terrible flashback of seeing Annette's dead body next door at Tulia's slammed me, just as it had at Gin's. Had Doris been attacked? Would I find her dead on the floor if I pushed open the door and went in?

Eyes wide, I stepped back a pace, one clammy hand to my mouth. My other hand dug frantically in my bag for the phone. No, I'd slipped in the pocket of my jeans. I might need Mom's preprogrammed emergency number sooner than I'd expected.

The door swung all the way open. Doris appeared in the doorway with a pendulous plastic bag in her hand. She wore yellow cleaning gloves and a store apron printed with the store's logo. I remembered she'd said she walked everywhere, thus no vehicle.

She cocked her head. "Mac, what are you doing here?"

I abandoned my search for the phone and let out a weak laugh. "I, uh, was walking home and saw your lights on in front, but the door was locked. When I came around here, I saw the door ajar and I was worried about you." I barely kept myself from ending the statement in a nervous question upswing. No need to tip her off about my blessedly false premonition.

"Okay." She tilted her head. Maybe she didn't believe me. She glanced behind her. "Oh, no, you don't." She darted back in. After an interior door clunked closed, Doris reappeared. "She's a sneaky one, that cat. Always trying to make a break for it." She glanced at the bag. "I'm on litter duty."

I thought fast. "Those treats I picked up here? Belle loved them, and I wanted to get some more for her." Those very expensive treats. "Are you open for business?" I tried to peer at her forehead for signs of an injury from a flying branch, but her long thick bangs covered it, as usual. If she'd been my intruder last night, the limb could have hit the back of her head.

"No, but come on in. I'm always happy to make a sale." She tilted her head. "And, actually, I wanted to talk to you. You know, about Annette's murder."

She did? This I wanted to hear. But alone in the store

with a murder suspect? That was not a portrait of being "very careful," as I'd promised Lincoln, Elenia, and anyone else who'd thought to caution me. I'd better stay out here. I had my emergency button close at hand. And I might be able to pick up new information on the case.

"One second. I was about to send a text to my mom about, um, dinner." I pulled out the flip phone. "And can we talk out here? I'm allergic to cats."

"Whatever." She dropped the bag in the barrel and secured the lid.

I stared at the back of her head. If she had a contusion under all that black hair, I'd never be able to see it.

She turned back and caught me at my examination. "What are you looking at?" She gave me a glare.

Uh-oh. I shouldn't get her suspicions up. "You have such thick hair. You're lucky."

Her expression switched to preening. "Thank you. It's always been one of my assets." She set one hand on her hip and patted her hair with the other.

"Excuse me a second." I tapped out a heads-up text to the group.

Outside Pws Clws w/D. Rscue me if no text in 30 min.

I sent it and crossed my mental fingers. "Okay."

"You said you wanted parrot treats, and I carry five kinds. Which one did Belle like?"

"I don't remember."

"You'd better come in and look. I'm not hauling them all out here."

I could tell her I'd come back another time, but I'd miss a chance now to talk to her. "Okay, but I should make it quick.

"After you." I followed her in, careful to shut the inside door behind me quickly. I didn't want to let her cat escape. I'd have rather left it open, but we did what we had to do in the name of justice. Or so I told myself.

I'd never been in the back of Paws and Claws before. Unlike Tulia's or Gin's extra-clean kitchens, this back room was a mess. My skin crawled at the disorganization, and my hands itched to make it orderly. Open cardboard boxes threatened to tumble off big plastic bins with cracked lids. One corner of the floor held a nest of discarded bubble wrap. An ashtray overflowing with cigarette butts sat on a desk littered with papers and a dusty laptop. To top it off, the air smelled of stale smoke with overtones of used cat litter. I sneezed. And here came the cat, gray tail held high in the air. It trotted straight for me in that unvarying instinct felines had for allergy sufferers like me. I sneezed again.

"Bless you." Doris gestured toward the front. "Let's go through. The store itself shouldn't bother you as much."

That would be safer, too. The lights were on in the retail area and it had big windows on the street, just in case. Doris's messy desk was next to the door to the front. She had pinned two dozen lottery tickets to a bulletin board.

"You have a lot of lottery tickets there." I pointed to the board.

"There's some big money to be had in the mega drawings, you know."

She must be lured to any kind of gambling, even when the odds were wildly against her. Were all the tickets current? I didn't ask as she led me to the bird section of the store. I pointed to the ones I had bought before.

"Those are the ones Belle liked."

Doris selected a bag and took it to the cash register.

"Did you say you had some information on Annette's

murder?" I handed her my credit card. The clock was ticking, and I didn't want my friends to race here and save me without cause.

She set down the card and faced me, crossing her arms on her chest.

"Yes." She swallowed again. "You might know that I rent a room from Ogden Hicks."

I waited. The anticipation made me want to shake the information out of her.

"And, uh, we've kind of hooked up a few times, as the kids say."

"Friends with benefits?" I asked, keeping my tone light.

"Right, sort of. You're young. It may seem gross to you."

I shook my head. "Not at all." She wasn't that old, anyway.

"I like the guy, and he helped me out of a tight spot. But . . ." Her voice trailed off.

"But?"

She swallowed again. "I have an alley cam. You know, one of those security cameras. The night of Annette's murder? Ogden's car drove in the alley."

Aha. I waited for her to go on.

"He didn't stop here."

"Does he have a key to your shop?" I asked.

"He does. Anyway, he slowed when he approached the Lobstah Shack."

"Then what?"

She bit her lip. "Then he went out of range of the camera."

I cursed, but silently. "What time was that footage taken?"

"The time stamp read nine ten."

Perfect timing for Ogden to bring Annette—dead or alive—to Tulia's cooler. "Did you tell the detective?"

She shook her head slowly. "No. I was afraid."

"Afraid of what?"

"Ogden's a Quaker and all that, but the man has a temper." Doris hugged herself. "You really don't want to mess with him."

Ogden with a temper? He and Phil were quite the pair. "Why are you telling me this?"

"I keep thinking about poor Annette. She should be alive, taking care of little Kendall. Her husband shouldn't have to plan her funeral."

"You have to tell Detective Haskins, you know, and hand over the file from the camera. I hoped you saved it."

She bobbed her head.

"Haskins hadn't already asked you for the footage?" I asked.

"I lied to him. I was afraid of Ogden."

Aha. "If you're worried about Ogden, tell him the detective made you hand it over."

Her face relaxed at my suggestion.

"What kind of car does Ogden drive?" I asked.

"A light-colored car."

"Do you know the make or anything?"

"I don't know anything about cars, Mac. It has four doors, if that helps?"

CHAPTER 58

I barely made it out of Paws and Claws under the half hour limit I'd set myself. I didn't exit through the back, either, instead telling Doris I needed to use the front door.

I pointed myself toward the closest beach, a small stretch of sand a quarter mile away. A solo breath of salt air would do wonders for my mental health and clarity, although I'd rather have shared the walk and the sand with Tim. Instead, I'd call him once I was out there.

Once I was clear of Main Street, I laboriously composed a flip-phone text to the group.

AOK at shop. Wlkng to Short Beach.

I resumed walking at a brisk clip, the parrot treats stashed in my bag.

No. I needed to call Lincoln. I slowed again and

pressed the Westham police department's nonurgent number. I didn't have Lincoln's cell memorized.

After I identified myself, I said, "I need to speak with Lincoln Haskins. It's urgent."

The woman who answered gave me the runaround but finally connected me with his voice mail.

"Lincoln, Doris Sandersen has camera footage from her alley. She lied to you the first time. She said Ogden Hicks drove by there at nine P.M. and slowed at the Lobstah Shack before he went off camera. He drives a light-colored four-door car. She knows she should have given you the footage and is willing to now." Should I tell him where I was? No, I'd told the group. Besides, who knew when he'd listen to this? I might be home by then. I ended the call and slid the phone into the patch pocket of my jacket.

As I walked, I mused about the cream-colored Prius I'd spied cruising by the church this morning. And the Prius parked in front of Phil's furniture shop. I tried to remember if I'd seen it elsewhere, but I wasn't sure. All models of Prius definitely had four doors. I'd be happy to be proven wrong, and yet I fully expected a light-colored Prius was parked in Ogden's driveway. For a moment I considering heading over there to check. But that would make me too stupid to live, the plight of a few of the protagonists the Cozy Capers read about. And that was fiction. This was real life, with an actual detective who could follow up on the video of Ogden's car.

Breathless, I slowed when I spied the glittering water a dozen yards ahead. Narrow Short Beach Road, not in the so-called better part of town, dead-ended at the sand and had only a few houses on it. The last one was a squat bun-

galow, whose clapboards had been painted red way too
long ago. A shutter listed crookedly behind overgrown
lilacs, their leaves now burnished an ominous red. The lawn
was scraggly. Across from the cottage was an equally
scraggly wildflower meadow. Tall grass seed heads waved
amid late blooms, an autumn bouquet of yellows, reds,
and oranges but fading with the fall and now half-broken
by the storm.

I walked on until I stood on the edge of the sand. An
upright blue Schwinn recreational bike was chained to
the post of a town sign, which warned, "No Lifeguard on
Duty. Swim at Your Own Risk." A pair of red women's
sneakers sat in the bike's front basket. A weather-beaten
shed with silvered clapboards stood to my left, its walls
festooned with faded lobster buoys. A former clammer's
shack, maybe. Now the structure probably stored oars
and paddles for the rowboat and the two canoes pulled up
above the tide line and tied to a cleat in a big rock between the shed and the sand.

I slipped off my shoes and socks. A barefoot walk
along the water would soothe my soul.

A low voice spoke behind me. A point pressed into my
back. "Why are you snooping into my life?" Ogden
growled.

CHAPTER 59

I twisted to look at him, but Ogden squeezed my shoulder, hard. "Face the water." Staying behind me, he forced me to turn away from him.

"That hurts!" I struggled to get loose.

He only gripped harder. He must have come from behind the shed. How had he tailed me without my noticing? Or . . . was that ramshackle bungalow his house, and he saw me walk by? Either way, this was bad. Why hadn't I taken that self-defense class Gin and I had talked about?

My heart pounded in my chest. "Let go, Ogden."

"Not going to happen. You're coming with me." He tugged at me, forcing me to take a step backward.

I resisted. "What are you doing?" I struggled to look at him, but he only pressed harder. Was that a gun poking into my back? What happened to peaceable Quakers? "I wasn't snooping. I was only out for a walk on the beach.'

"You've absolutely been snooping." He tugged me back again, pulling me behind the shed. The pressure of the point didn't lessen. He must want to keep the weapon hidden in case someone walked by.

"Help," I yelled as loud as I could. I hadn't seen anyone around, but I had to try. "Help!" I screamed.

"Shut up, Mac." He pressed harder.

Pretty soon we'd be out of sight of the road, not that it went anywhere except the beach. I touched Mom's phone with fingers nearly numb from fear. Did I have any way to open it and find the emergency call button? No. I didn't have a snowflake's chance in the Atlantic. I hoped I'd be alive to see another snowflake.

"I want to see both hands out of those pockets," he snarled. He pulled me back, fast. I stumbled.

I swore to myself. And pulled out my hands.

The point moved up to my neck. "Don't try to pull anything, Almeida. I know exactly where to insert this awl."

An awl. Another sharp lethal object like the lobster pick. The point nearly piercing my neck stung my skin. Could I possibly stall him from killing me?

"Why did you kill Annette?" The pulse in my neck beat so fast I could barely talk.

"What?" The pressure lessened only slightly. "I didn't kill her!"

"Then why are you attacking me?"

He let seconds tick by. A sharp-shinned hawk alit on a scrubby cedar tree and regarded me with a beady yellow eye. "You know why."

"No, I don't," I protested.

"I didn't kill Annette, but I let her die." He spoke in a harsh whisper.

Was there any difference?

"I picked her up at home that evening. We were going to go over the books at the shop. She'd told me she'd found discrepancies and wanted to give me a chance to explain." His voice lowered. "I'd planned to kill her at the shop. But in the car, she said she couldn't breathe. She clutched her throat and looked awful."

"And you didn't call 9-1-1? You didn't drive her to the nearest emergency room?"

"No, I, I . . . She'd found me out."

Did I hear an engine? Please, let it be the police. Let someone have seen us and called in the assault.

He continued. "She planned to ruin me, and that would have killed my—" He broke off at the crack of a branch.

His grip on my shoulder eased. The pressure on my neck lessened. I grabbed my only chance and jammed my hand into my pocket. Flip phone sticking out of the front of my left fist, I brought it up and over my shoulder into his face with all my strength. Eye, nose, I didn't care what I hit. I lifted my knee and jammed my foot down onto where I hope his instep was. I whacked my head back into his face for good measure.

He cried out and fell away behind me. An object hit the boulder with a clink.

I whirled and stepped back. Ogden lay writhing on the ground. His nose was covered with blood, and he clutched his face. The awl lay next to the rock. I edged near the lethally sharp wood-handled tool, careful to skirt his feet, and kicked the weapon a few yards away. I still gripped the flip phone, now bloodied, and dashed into the road. The slippery phone slid out of my clammy hand onto the pavement.

"Mac, are you all right?" Rose DiCicero rushed toward me from the beach. "When I saw that man attacking you, I called 9-1-1." Her feet were bare and dusted with sand below her Capri pants.

I stared at her, my rescuing angel. "I'm okay. Where did you come from?"

"I rode my bike down here on the trail and needed a walk on the beach to clear my head." She pointed at the blue cycle.

A state police SUV raced around the bend toward me. I waved my arms. I pulled Rose back with me and pointed toward Ogden. The vehicle crunched over my mom's phone on its way to a screeching halt. Three WPD cars followed. Two officers hurried out of the SUV, weapons drawn, and ran at Ogden. Kimuri, clad in SWAT vest and helmet, slid out of the first WPD cruiser.

"You okay, Mac?" She looked me up and down as if checking for injuries.

"Yes. Barely." My legs and hands shook.

"And you, ma'am?" she asked Rose.

"I'm good, thank you."

"I got this, Kimuri." Lincoln materialized, also wearing a thick vest. She stepped away. He peered into my face. "You are all right, then."

I nodded. "Thanks for getting here."

"Ms. DiCicero alerted us that Ogden had a weapon and a hostage."

"She told me. I can't thank you enough, Rose. I'd just managed to subdue Ogden when you guys showed up.

Lincoln, I think it was the . . ." I let my voice trail off as I glanced at Rose. "Excuse us for a minute."

"Of course," she said, wrapping her arms around herself.

I gestured for Lincoln to follow me across the road. I couldn't tell him my idea in front of her. I went on in a low voice. "I think the soup killed Annette. Did you know that?"

"We recently got the results back from the lab. The soup contained *Alexandrium fundyense* toxins."

"Phil made the soup from stock his mom gave him. Do you know how that happened?"

He let out a deep sigh. "He apparently went fishing at the start of an algal bloom. She made the stock from a whole fish he brought home. Neither knew red tide had tainted it."

"So why didn't the rest of the family get sick?" I asked.

"Our friend there explained." His gaze drifted to Rose.

She'd unlocked her bike and was seated on the rock. She dusted the sand off her left foot and slid on her sneaker.

"She'd already made dinner that evening. They didn't eat the soup." Lincoln continued. "We found the full container still in her refrigerator a couple of days ago and took it as evidence."

That explained why no one else was poisoned. "Ogden told me he'd planned to kill Annette at the shop. But he let the anaphylactic shock do it for him."

CHAPTER 60

Ogden didn't resist arrest. He seemed to deflate once the police arrived. A broken nose didn't help. After Lincoln told me I could go, Kimuri said she'd give me a ride home.

"Can I use your cell?" I asked her from the passenger seat in her cruiser. "Mine got crushed out there." Mom's, more precisely.

"Sure." She activated her cell and handed it to me.

I sent Derrick a quick text.

This is Mac. Am fine. Heading home. Ogden attacked me near Short Beach, but police have him now. Pls tell group and parents. Will go to parsonage four-ish.

I sent it and returned the phone. "Thanks.

At home, I spent a couple of hours alone processing what had happened. I put a load of laundry into my compact stacked washing machine. I emailed Tim saying I hoped Jamie was better and that he was having fun with the kiddos. And that I missed him. Telling him about my brush with danger could wait for a phone conversation. I made a cheese sandwich, opened a beer, and hung out with Belle as I ate.

"That was a close one, Belle." I stroked her feathers and fed her halves of frozen grapes.

"Close one," she muttered. "Close one."

I'd seen—and felt—the awl's sharp tip. I shuddered as I pictured it piercing my carotid artery. Or my brain stem. It had been the definition of close.

How troubled Ogden must be to act with such desperation. At least he hadn't had a knife, or worse, a gun. The awl was lethal, but he could have pulled a trigger a lot sooner. He must use the awl for wood or maybe leather at the shop.

An email came in from Gin saying the group was going to gather for dinner at Tulia's restaurant at six. I replied that I'd be there.

At four thirty I walked to my parents' house, where Derrick and Cokey had showed up for dinner. Reba and Derrick sat in chairs at the kitchen table. I sat, too. Mom cut biscuits out of flattened dough and Pa tore lettuce leaves into a salad bowl. The French beef stew made the house smell like heaven.

"Abo Ree, how are you feeling?" I asked after we all exchanged greetings.

"I'm fine and dandy, honey."

"You look much better than this morning." I covered her hand with mine.

"We tried to call you, Mac," Pa said. "You didn't pick up. Then Derrick told us you were fine. For which we are blessed and thank the good Lord."

"I am fine." I gazed at my niece and back at my father. I couldn't talk about what had happened while Cokey was listening. "I'll tell you all about it in a minute."

The little girl wrestled with the dog. She bounced a tennis ball that he leapt to catch, but he knocked down a kitchen chair in the process.

"Cokey, no balls in the house," Pa said in his firm grandfather's tone.

"Honey, take Tucker and the ball outside." Derrick pulled open the sliding glass door.

"Okay. Come on, Tucker. Ball!" She held up the tennis ball.

Girl and dog headed out. *Good.* A fence surrounded the yard, and we could see them through the glass.

Abo Reba nodded her approval. "Children and dogs need regular exercise. As my mother used to say, they need to go out and get the stink blown off."

I suppressed a giggle. She'd said that to Derrick and me when we were kids, too. Now, while the next generation of girl played, I filled in my family on the details of what had happened with Ogden.

Abo Reba's eyes went wide. "Good heavens, Mackenzie. I'm glad you're all right. But that Ogden Hicks, I always wondered about him."

"You did?" I asked. "Why?"

"We were never quite sure what happened to his wife." My grandma rapped the table with a knobby finger. "I mean, how she died."

"Really?" I'd hadn't heard a word about suspicious circumstances regarding the late Mrs. Hicks.

"That's right," Mom said. "I believe he had taken out quite the insurance policy on her."

"But the authorities didn't charge him in her death, remember," Pa admonished.

"No." Abo Reba sounded almost disappointed.

"Mom, I'm sorry about your phone," I said.

"Don't worry about it. We can go together tomorrow to get new ones. Won't that be fun?"

"You might want to upgrade, Mom." Derrick rolled his eyes. "Just saying."

"We'll see." She slid her pan of biscuits into the oven and set a timer. "You're staying for dinner, Mac, right?"

"I can't, after all. The book group is going to have a debriefing dinner, but thank you." I gazed at my lovely new ring. "I'm going to use the land line here to call Tim, if that's okay."

"Our phone is your phone," Pa said. "Please give him our fond regards."

I planned to do that, and much more.

CHAPTER 61

"Here's to happy endings." Tulia lifted a plastic cup of bubbly.

Most of the Cozy Capers sat around a table at six o'clock in the Lobstah Shack. I'd filled them in on what had gone down this afternoon. Now I lifted my cup in response to Tulia, as did Gin, Zane, and Flo.

"Happy for all but Annette and Ogden," I said before I took a sip. And happier for Tim's sister, at least for now. He'd told me she would be all right and had agreed to commit herself for treatment for a couple of weeks. His father had already hit the road to travel north from California to take over the childcare. I'd have my man back by next weekend. We could return to our wedding planning—and the rest of our lives.

The remains of our takeout supper littered the table. Tulia had offered to cook, but instead Zane had picked up sub sandwiches for everyone from Subanza, the hip subs and pizza shop in town. My caprese on toasted sourdough had been perfection, while others had enjoyed the range of the menu, including Gin's classic Italian, stuffed with cured meats, provolone, and peppers, and dripping with oil. We'd asked the whole book group, but Norland had his grandkids for the evening, and Derrick wanted to put Cokey to bed on time, even though tomorrow was Columbus Day and she didn't have school.

"So maybe not that happy for Phil's mom?" Zane asked.

Tulia nodded. "Rose killed her own daughter-in-law inadvertently."

"Today at midday Rose got really defensive to me about the soup stock," I said. "Lincoln told me Rose didn't know the fish Phil had caught at the start of the alga bloom was tainted with the *Alexandrium fundyense* toxins. And Phil used it to make more soup. He had a hand in it, too. And my grandma raised a curious point about Ogden's late wife before I came over here. Or more exactly, about her death. Do any of you remember suspicions about him related to that?" I'd missed so much in the ten years I'd been gone from town.

"People talked, as they do," Gin said. "You know, big insurance policy on wife who dies. But nothing came of it. Snoopy gossips were responsible for spreading suspicion. Apparently gossip was all it was."

Flo nodded, then pointed at a turkey and cheese sub still in its paper wrapper on a plate in front of the only empty chair. "I thought you said Lincoln would join us to fill in the gaps."

"He said he would," I said.

At a knock on the front door, Tulia hurried to peer

through the glass. She'd turned the sign to Closed and locked the entrance, so the public didn't think the restaurant was open. Now she unlocked it to admit Lincoln, then secured it after him.

"This sandwich has your name on it, Lincoln." Gin pointed at the empty chair across from me. "We were just talking about you."

He lumbered over and sank onto the seat as if he hadn't sat in a week. He smelled of fresh air and exhaustion. The detective gazed around at us, ending with his focus on me.

"Are you off duty, Lincoln?" Tulia held up the bottle.

"As a matter of fact, I am, at long last."

She handed him a full cup, then poured around for the rest of us except herself. The bottle ran out before she got to me. "Be right back."

Flo got busy on her phone.

"Eat, Detective," Gin urged.

Zane had arrived with three cold bottles of various sparkling wines: Spanish, Californian, and Italian vintages. After a pop sounded in the back, Tulia returned in a minute with a second bottle and filled my cup.

"No seconds for you?" I asked her.

"You know me." She shook her head. "I'm a light-weight."

Right. She'd told me once that, because of her ethnic heritage, she lacked an enzyme to digest alcohol, and if she drank, it hit her hard. She didn't totally avoid the stuff but restricted her imbibing to slow sips.

Flo glanced up from her phone. "Red tide happened from September first to the ninth. Remember? People were furious they couldn't swim in the ocean over Labor Day."

Zane nodded. "I had extra good sales over that holiday

weekend. Tourists couldn't frolic in the sea. Instead, they drank more."

"I don't get why Phil went fishing during a red tide bloom," Gin said.

"He says he didn't know the alga was blooming," Lincoln mumbled around a mouthful, then swallowed. "It's not as obvious at the start."

"Phil mentioned he'd gone out on a boat around that time. He came in all proud he'd caught something," Zane said.

Lincoln held up the cup of bubbly, which he hadn't touched yet. "Here's to a closed case. And none of you much the worse for it."

We matched his gesture.

"But how did Ogden get in here to leave Annette in my cooler?" Tulia asked. "And why did he stab her?"

"We asked him," Lincoln said. "He confessed he'd planned to leave her in the pet store, since Doris had given him a key, but he didn't want the cat to bother the body. Then he thought of the cooler next door. As you're aware, Tulia, your lock isn't worth the packaging it came in." Lincoln took a bite of his turkey sub.

"I know," Tulia said. "I had new locks installed on Thursday."

"Did Ogden want to blame the death on Tulia? He stabbed Annette with the lobster pick to make it look like Tulia must have killed her?" I asked Lincoln.

"Exactly. But he clearly doesn't know much about corpses."

"The man had a lot of nerve." Tulia folded her arms as her face reddened. "What did I ever do to Ogden Hicks? I didn't even know him."

"I'm aware of that." Lincoln continued. "He said he

grabbed rubber gloves from under the sink. We found them in his car, and we're testing them for his DNA."

"I wondered where those gloves went," Tulia said. "I had to break open a new package. Guess I should have told you they were missing."

Lincoln nodded.

"Just to be sure, Detective, Tulia isn't under suspicion, correct?" Zane.

"She is not." Lincoln shook his head slowly.

Whew.

"Is Phil in the clear?" Gin asked Lincoln.

He nodded again. "We have no reason to suspect him in his wife's homicide."

"Or Doris or Elenia, right?" I asked.

"That would be correct." He cleared his throat. "I will say, if Ms. Sandersen had come forward with her security footage sooner, it would have been most helpful. But we won't charge her with obstruction. And we had been closely tracking Hicks's movements."

"Lincoln," I said, "what can Ogden be charged with? Is it murder if someone is dying, and you don't get them help?"

"For his attack on you, he faces assault with a dangerous weapon, definitely. Plus burglary for unlawfully entering the premises of the Lobstah Shack. As for Ms. DiCicero's demise, he could have claimed she died suddenly in his vehicle. Instead, he gave us a signed confession, stating what he told you. That he intended to kill her in his shop." Lincoln ticked off the statements on his fingers. "That he witnessed her distress when he drove her. That he did not try to obtain medical assistance for her, not even by telephone. That he abandoned her body in Tulia's cooler and defaced the corpse."

"Is not getting help for her a charge of manslaughter?" Flo asked, her gaze intent.

Lincoln nodded, but stared at me. "By virtue of Hicks coming clean to you, his will to defend himself appears to have vanished."

"Maybe it's his Quaker values finally coming out," Zane offered. "I've always admired those people for their peace work and their honesty."

"His fellow congregant, Mr. Carter, has been quite forthcoming, I'm happy to say." Lincoln took another small sip of champagne. "Apparently Hicks's financial worries about his son's care have taken precedence over his ethical values for quite some time."

"Annette had discovered he'd been cheating the business and called him on it," I said. "How did he do it?"

"He skimmed funds in several ways," Lincoln replied. "He would offer a client a so-called discount if they paid cash, which wasn't a discount at all, and Hicks would pocket the extra cash. The company also had a company credit card for business expenses. Hicks opened a personal card with the same bank, but he paid it out of the corporate account. Nobody noticed for a while."

Zane whistled. "Tricky stuff."

"Annette had smarts," Gin said. "I bet she figured it out without too much trouble."

"Ogden became desperate because of his son's expenses," Flo said.

"If only he had asked for help." Tulia looked sad. "From the community, from his church."

"What will happen to the son now, I wonder," I said.

"Mr. Carter volunteered that the church will make sure the young man is taken care of," Lincoln said.

Wow. "Good."

"Too bad they didn't offer that assistance earlier," Gin said.

"Maybe he never asked for help." Tulia looked around at us. "Some people find it hard to."

Just like she hadn't asked for help cleaning out her walk-in. I looked around at my fellow sleuths, amateurs that we were. "That's all the loose bits on the case, right?"

Gin and Zane nodded.

"I got nothing else," Tulia said. "I won't ever forget finding Annette in there with the shrimp and the peppers. But I'm glad the mystery is solved. And we have a whole 'nother year to change the name of the dang holiday."

"I'm glad, too," I agreed.

"What a tragedy for the DiCicero family. Phil and Kendall, and Rose, too," Flo said.

I knew how much Kendall would miss her mother as time went on. "It's going to be hard for all of them to overcome."

Lincoln let out a heavy sigh. He drained his cup and stood. "Thank you for inviting me. I'm grateful you all stayed safe. Frankly, right now I need some rest."

I rose and walked him to the door. I held out my hand. "Thanks for not getting on our case about wanting to solve this." Not too much.

He took my hand in both of his. "You're a civilian, Mac. You and the rest have no idea how dangerous this work is, and I worry about you." He smiled even as he rolled his eyes. "With any luck, there won't be a next time." He called out a good night to the group and let himself out.

I gazed through the glass. He ambled, hands in pockets, under a streetlight before disappearing into the darkness. In the reflection behind me were my book group members—and friends—talking and laughing. None of us had been hurt in our pursuit of the truth. Tim was on his way home soon. I had a wedding to anticipate and a life, however messy, with the man I loved.

No more homicides in Westham sounded like an excellent plan. If the only unnatural deaths I heard about from now on were fictional ones, that would be fine with me.

RECIPES

Apple Cidertini

Tim prepares this refreshing fall cocktail for Mac before dinner at his house.

For one serving:
½ cup apple cider
2 ounces vodka
1 ounce apple brandy
Cinnamon stick to stir
Apple slice for garnish

Shake over ice, then strain into a glass. Add apple slice and cinnamon stick.

Lobster Quiche

Tim treats Mac to a homemade lobster quiche.

Ingredients:
4 eggs
2 cups milk
¼ cup minced fresh dill
Kosher salt and freshly ground black pepper
2 tablespoons olive oil
2 shallots, minced
12 ounces mushrooms, sliced
1 cup cooked, diced lobster meat
1 pastry crust, store bought or homemade from the
    recipe of your choice

Directions
Preheat oven to 415°F.
Beat the eggs with milk, dill, salt, and pepper, and set aside.
Heat the oil over medium heat in a cast-iron skillet. Sauté the shallots and mushrooms until limp. Remove from heat.
Lay lobster meat on unbaked pie shell. Cover with mushroom mixture. Pour egg mixture over top.
Set a baking sheet on the oven's middle shelf. Slide the pie pan onto the sheet.
After 15 minutes, turn the temperature down to 350°F. Bake until the quiche feels set to the touch in the center and a knife comes out clean, 45–55 additional minutes. It should be golden-brown and slightly puffed and should not slosh when you jiggle it.
Let it set up for 10 minutes before serving hot. Can also serve at room temperature.

Soba Seafood Salad

This Asian-flavored salad is one of Tulia's specialties at the Lobstah Shack. You can vary the seafood according to your tastes and what is available.

Ingredients:
1 package soba (buckwheat) noodles
1 tablespoon peanut oil
½ pound scallops
½ pound shrimp, shelled
2 tablespoons toasted sesame oil
4 tablespoons unflavored rice vinegar
1 tablespoon soy sauce
2 teaspoons sugar
1 carrot, peeled and cut into 1-inch slivers
½ red pepper, seeded and cut into 1-inch slivers
1 celery stalk, trimmed and cut into 1-inch slivers

Directions:
Bring a pot of water to a boil and cook the soba to al dente stage, as per the directions on the package, about 5–8 minutes. Drain and set aside.

Heat peanut oil over medium high heat. Sauté scallops until lightly browned on one side. Turn and cook for 2–3 more minutes. Remove to a plate and add shrimp. Stir fry until they just turn pink. Remove to the plate with the scallops.

Whisk sesame oil, vinegar, soy sauce, and sugar in a large bowl. Add vegetables and noodles and toss.

Cut cooled scallops into quarters and shrimp in half. Add to bowl and toss.

Serve immediately, or chill for serving later.

Tomato Torta

Tim prepares this Spanish-flavored mini pie for his Friday night pop-up bar, Breads and Brews. This recipe is for one standard-sized pie.

Ingredients:
2 medium potatoes, scrubbed
1 medium tomato
1 onion, minced
½ green pepper, seeded and minced
1 pastry crust, store bought or homemade from the
    recipe of your choice
1 teaspoon dry basil or one tablespoon fresh, minced
¼ cup pitted Kalamata olives, chopped
¼ cup Manchego cheese, grated

Directions:
Preheat oven to 425°F.

Slice the potatoes and steam in microwave until almost tender. Set aside.

Slice the tomato and set in a colander to drain.

Sauté the onion until tender. Add green pepper and sauté another 3 minutes until tender. Remove from heat.

Layer the onion-pepper mix, tomatoes, and potatoes in the crust in that order. Sprinkle on the basil, olives, and cheese.

Bake for 15 minutes at 425°F. Turn oven down to 350° and bake 20 more minutes or until pie crust is lightly browned.

Enjoy warm with a salad and a glass of a full-bodied Spanish red wine, or serve at room temperature as an appetizer.

Cranberry Scones

Tim offers these yummy treats at his bakery, Greta's Grains, featuring Cape Cod's own native cranberries.

Ingredients:
1 cup all-purpose flour
¼ cup sugar, plus more for sprinkling
1½ teaspoons baking powder
⅛ teaspoon nutmeg
⅛ teaspoon salt
¼ cup cold butter, cut in ½-inch cubes
3 tablespoons sour cream
1 egg, beaten
¼ cup dried cranberries

Directions:
Preheat oven to 425°F. Line a baking sheet with parchment paper.

In a food processor, combine the flour, sugar, baking powder, nutmeg, and salt. Add butter and pulse until mixture resembles coarse crumbs.

In a small bowl, combine sour cream, 2 tablespoons beaten egg, and cranberries. Pulse into crumb mixture just barely moistened.

Turn onto a floured surface; knead gently 6–8 times. Pat into a 6-inch circle. Flour a sharp knife and cut into 6 wedges. Separate wedges and place on a baking sheet. Brush with remaining egg; sprinkle with sugar.

Bake for 15 minutes or until golden brown. Serve warm.

Apple Spice Muffins

Astra bakes these easy fall muffins as a Sunday morning treat.

Makes 12.

Ingredients:
2 eggs
½ cup brown sugar
½ cup milk
2 cups chopped apples (about 3 small apples)
1 teaspoon vanilla
2 cups whole wheat flour
1 tablespoon baking powder
½ teaspoon baking soda
½ teaspoon salt
1 teaspoon ground cinnamon
½ teaspoon nutmeg
½ cup finely chopped walnuts (optional)

Directions:
Preheat oven to 375°F and grease a standard muffin pan.

Combine eggs, sugar, milk, apples, and vanilla and mix well.

Separately combine flour, baking powder, baking soda, salt, spices, and walnuts (omit nuts if allergies are an issue).

Stir dry ingredients into wet with a fork until just mixed. Spoon into a muffin pan. Bake 20–25 minutes or until brown on top. Run a knife around each muffin and cool in the pan on a rack.

Serve warm or at room temperature with butter, peanut butter, or cream cheese.

Connect with U

Visit us online at
KensingtonBooks.com
to read more from your favorite authors, see books
by series, view reading group guides, and more.

Join us on social media

for sneak peeks, chances to win books and prize packs,
and to share your thoughts with other readers.

facebook.com/kensingtonpublishing
twitter.com/kensingtonbooks

Tell us what you think!

To share your thoughts, submit a review,
or sign up for our eNewsletters, please visit:
KensingtonBooks.com/TellUs.